HERE, THERE & EVERYWHERE

BUTLER, VERMONT SERIES, BOOK 8

MARIE FORCE

Here, There & Everywhere
Butler, Vermont Series, Book 8
By: Marie Force

Published by HTJB, Inc.
Copyright 2022. HTJB, Inc.
Cover Design by Kristina Brinton
E-book Layout: E-book Formatting Fairies
ISBN: 978-1952793578

The Green Mountain and
Butler, Vermont Series

The Green Mountain Series

The Butler, Vermont Series
(Continuation of Green Mountain)

More new books are always in the works. For the most up-to-date list of what's available from the Butler, Vermont Series as well as series extras, go to *marieforce.com/vermont*

CHAPTER ONE

Bitterness is like cancer. It eats upon the host. But anger is like fire. It burns it all clean. —Maya Angelou

*W*hat the hell was Cabot Lodge doing in her kitchen? Izzy Coleman was still asking herself that question two days after coming home from the hospital with Cabot as her primary caregiver. This was the same man she'd spent time with before, who'd subsequently dropped off the face of the earth.

Until he heard she'd been badly injured in a car accident.

He'd shown up in her hospital room almost two weeks ago, the day after the accident, and had been by her side ever since, even insisting to her mom and siblings that he be the one to care for her once she came home, sparing her a trip to rehab by being willing to provide around-the-clock care.

Again, she wanted to ask him *why* he was putting his frantically busy work schedule on hold to nurse her back to health. His silence after their two previous meetings had sent a pretty clear message about his interest in her—or lack thereof. Yet there he was, washing her dishes and wiping her countertops like it was the most normal thing in the world for him to be staying in her house and taking care of her.

Why, why, why?

Izzy wasn't known for being reticent, but Cabot had grabbed her attention at her cousin's wedding last summer, which had also been his daughter's wedding, and then hurt her feelings when he'd gone silent after that event and then again following a subsequent dinner in the fall. While the question burned at the tip of her tongue, she couldn't bring herself to ask him, and that wasn't like her at all.

"Your mom sent brownies with Henry," he said. "You want one?"

"A small one. I need to be able to fit through the doorways after I eat all this food my family is sending over."

"You can afford a few brownies before we have to worry about the doorways," Cabot said with the sweet smile that made his brown eyes sparkle.

His hair had turned silvery gray early, but that only made him more handsome to her. From the first time she'd met him at Wade and Mia's wedding, she'd been intrigued by him. The story of how his long-lost daughter had come back into his life twenty-five years after her mother had taken off with her had touched Izzy—and everyone else, for that matter—deeply.

Cabot had been an emotional basket case the day of his daughter's wedding in Boston, which had only endeared him more to Izzy. They'd had a marvelous day dancing and celebrating the marriage of two people who truly deserved the best of everything.

And then... Nothing.

If she was being honest—and what was the point of lying to yourself?—Izzy would say she was surprised she hadn't heard from Cabot after the wedding. She wasn't used to men showing interest in her and then ghosting her, especially a man like Cabot, who didn't seem the type to lead someone on and then disappear.

Not that he'd led her on, per se, but they'd spent an entire day dancing and talking and connecting. At thirty-five, Izzy had been around the block enough times to know that truly connecting with another human being didn't happen every day, and when it did, it usually led to something special.

Except, in this case, all it had led to was confusion that persisted even as he bustled around her home like he lived there, which he apparently did for the time being. And why was that, exactly?

Her thoughts were officially spinning in circles as she shifted her broken left arm on the pillow it was propped on, looking for a more comfortable position. The movement caused the incision in her abdomen to pull, making her wince. Being injured like this sucked so bad, it wasn't even funny.

Cabot brought a plate of brownies and a steaming mug of the lemon tea she loved when he came to sit with her on the sofa, moving carefully so as not to jar her.

"Thank you."

"You're welcome."

"Did you have a nice visit with Henry?"

"I did."

"The two of you were very cute when I came out of the office, and his head was resting on your leg as you ran your fingers through his hair."

"He's my baby brother and needed advice about a woman named Sierra who he might be in love with, except she doesn't want him to be in love with her. Not yet, anyway."

"Ah, a conundrum to be certain. What's he going to do?"

"He was heading back to Boston to try to figure that out. I've never seen him so forlorn over a girl before. Or I should say a woman. It's hard to believe he's all grown up."

"It's sweet the way they all come to you for advice."

"They always have." Sarah, the youngest of the eight Colemans, had been by to see her in the hospital before she headed back to school at Northeastern, where she was in the fourth year of a five-year nursing program and wasn't sure she still wanted to be a nurse. That was a situation Izzy planned to keep tabs on in the weeks to come.

"My mom had a lot on her plate taking care of all of us after my dad left. I sort of stepped into the role of counselor-in-chief to the younger ones, and it's a title I've retained as they became adults."

Ally was working way too much and had no life otherwise. Vanessa was at loose ends after leaving her job. Jackson continued to play the field while bartending and wasn't in any apparent rush to grow up. And Henry had no idea what he wanted to do with his life. Despite the three-hour drive between her and her siblings in Boston, Izzy stayed in close touch with them and wasn't at all surprised that they'd come running home when they heard about her accident.

"They're lucky to have you."

"I love them very much." Izzy eyed him over the mug of tea. "What're you doing here?" The question popped out of her mouth before she took even so much as a second to ponder whether she should come right out and ask it.

His brows lifted in surprise. "Uh, I believe I'm helping to keep you out of rehab."

"I have a mother, seven siblings, ten first cousins, an aunt and uncle and a grandfather—all of whom would've moved in to stay with me."

"Oh, well, if you'd rather have one of them, I'd certainly understand. I can go—"

"Cabot! I'd rather have *you*, but what I don't understand is why you're doing all this when you didn't call me after the wedding or after we had dinner in Boston. I really thought you'd call me both times, and when you didn't... I was very disappointed." She'd waited *days*, during which family members had often been around, to have the chance to say those words.

"I'm sorry. I wanted to call you. Both times." He released a huff of laughter. "You have no idea how much I wanted to call you."

"Why didn't you?"

He looked down at his mug full of the black coffee he drank throughout the day. That was something she'd learned about him since they'd come home from the hospital. "You see, the thing is... I'm not relationship material, and you... You deserve to be with someone who can give you all the things you deserve. That's not me."

If possible, Izzy was more confused now than she was before.

Pre-accident Izzy might've let it go and chalked it up to two people who were on different wavelengths. Post-accident Izzy, who was giving thanks for having survived an accident that probably should've killed her, wasn't willing to let it go that easily. "I don't know what that means."

He was quiet for so long that she began to wonder if he was going to say anything else. "I, uh… The last relationship I was in was with my wife."

Izzy did some fast math in her head. Mia was twenty-seven and had been missing for twenty-five years… "*Seriously?*"

"Yep. She did a real number on me, as you can imagine."

"So there hasn't been anyone since then?"

He shook his head.

"At all?"

"Here and there, you know… Encounters. One-night stands. Surface stuff, which was how I wanted it."

"Oh." She had no idea what to say to that. He hadn't been serious with *anyone*… "How old are you?" She'd never gotten around to asking him that question before now, but knew he was at least a decade older than her.

"Forty-eight. I had Mia when I was twenty-one, probably too young to be having kids, but I loved her mother and thought we were happy together. When she left me and took Mia with her… There is no way for me to properly articulate the horror of that. She *took* my *child*. I was a young father, but I was very hands-on with her. I got up with her every morning, changed her and fed her and played with her. I took her on long walks in the woods and built snowmen for her. I adored her with all my heart, but the marriage wasn't working out. My wife was very unhappy. We fought all the time, until she finally said she wanted a divorce."

Izzy had heard bits and pieces of the story from Wade and Mia, but hearing Cabot's side of it was like hearing it for the first time.

"I was young and stupid and went directly to the law firm that had handled my family's legal business for decades. They played hardball with her, which was a mistake. I see that now, but at the time, I just wanted out of the marriage and to gain custody of my daughter. She couldn't afford a lawyer, so I'm sure it seemed to her that I was steamrolling her. Which was why she ran. She took off with Mia, and I never saw either of them again until I got the call that Mia wanted to see me."

"I can't imagine what that was like for you when it first happened."

"I've never felt that kind of desperation, before or since. At first, I assumed they'd come back. That Deb would come to her senses and do the right thing, but she never did. They disappeared off the face of the earth. I spent a small fortune trying to find them, but we never had so much as a single lead that panned out."

"I'm so sorry that was done to you, Cabot."

"Thanks, but with hindsight, I can see how I played it all wrong by engaging hardball lawyers. But that didn't give her the right to do what she did."

"It certainly doesn't."

"You want to know the best part?"

Izzy nodded.

"In order to see my daughter, I had to agree to drop the kidnapping charges against her mother."

"Oh God, I don't know if I could've done that."

"If you wanted to see your child as badly as I wanted to see mine, you would've done *anything*." He cleared his throat and seemed to be battling intense emotion. "The last time I saw Mia, she was two, and the next time I saw her, she was a grown woman with a new husband. It was surreal."

"It's so very, very unfair."

"That, too," he said with a small smile. "What Deb did to me... She broke me on the inside, Izzy. That's why there hasn't been anyone else. Because I'm broken. I have issues trusting people who aren't my immediate family. I'm constantly anticipating disaster. I'd never want to have more children over the fear of something like this happening again. What woman in her right mind would want to hitch her horse to my wagon?"

"I would." Again, the words were said before she took so

much as a second to consider them. She placed her hand on top of his. "I would hitch my horse to your wagon any day, Cabot Lodge."

He turned his hand up to clasp hers. "You're a beautiful, sweet, sexy, smart, talented woman, Izzy. You could have anyone you wanted. A broken-down wreck of a man is the last thing you need, and that's why I didn't call you after two magical days with you."

Magical. That's how she would've described both encounters as well. She could work with that.

"You're not a broken-down wreck of a man, Cabot."

"I am."

"You're not. Want to know what I see when I look at you?"

He shrugged.

"I see a man who had a terrible thing happen to him, but who still has a great capacity to love. I saw that the day of your daughter's wedding when you were in tears for most of it because you were so damned happy. I really, *really* liked that guy, and I want to spend more time with him."

"He made a one-day appearance for the wedding. Most of the time, he's angry and bitter and plots ways to get revenge on the ex-wife who wronged him so terribly. On the outside, he projects light and love and forgiveness, but on the inside, his thoughts are dark and spiteful."

"Those things make him human," Izzy said. "Anyone would feel that way after what was done to you."

"I just don't think it would be fair to bring you or anyone else into my life, knowing what I'm really like. I don't have anything to give you."

"And yet, here you are, waiting on me hand and foot."

"That's no big deal."

"It is to me. You've put your busy life on hold to take care of me, and again, I have to ask *why*. Why are you here, Cabot, if you don't have anything to give me?"

"I'm here because after I heard you were hurt, I couldn't stay away."

"What does that mean?"

"I have no idea."

"You know what I think?" Izzy asked, smiling.

"What's that?"

"I think you might be ready to try again with someone else, or you wouldn't be sitting on my sofa, walking me to the bathroom, helping me with that impossible jigsaw puzzle or tucking me into bed every night."

"We're friends. That's what friends do for each other."

Izzy shook her head. "I have a lot of friends—good, close friends. I have more siblings and cousins than I know what to do with. But you're the only one who *insisted* on caring for me at home."

"I wasn't ready to leave you yet."

"What does that mean?"

"Just what I said. I was so happy to see you after hearing you'd been badly hurt that I didn't want to leave yet."

"You were in New Jersey on business when you heard I was hurt."

"Yes."

"I assume it was important business."

"It's a deal we've been working on for two years."

"And yet, when you heard I was hurt, you dropped what you were doing there, rented a car and drove to Vermont to be with me. Is that right?"

"Yes," he said, looking away. "That's how it happened."

"Did you take two seconds to ask yourself why it was so urgent that you get to me in the hospital?"

"I didn't. I just needed to get there."

"Which goes back to my original question. *Why*, Cabot?"

"I don't know. I just needed to get to you."

Izzy gave him a satisfied smile. "Well, now we're getting somewhere."

CHAPTER TWO

"Adversity is the first path to truth." —Lord Byron

*C*abot knew what she wanted him to say—he'd come to her because he had feelings for her, but that wasn't it. He didn't have feelings for women anymore. His heart didn't work that way after what his wife had done to him. But something had compelled him to walk out of critical meetings in New Jersey so he could get to Vermont as quickly as possible.

That didn't mean he had *feelings* for her. It meant he had *concern* for her. Two totally different things.

Except that didn't take into account the fact that he had thought of her constantly since he'd first met her in June or how happy he'd been when she called to invite him to dinner last October. It didn't account for how frantic he'd been after hearing she'd been badly hurt or how urgent it had felt to get to her.

It'd been so long since he'd felt anything other than bitterness and rage toward a woman that he'd all but forgotten it was possible to feel other things.

"I want you to understand," he said to Izzy, "that I do care about you."

"I know, or why else would you be here?"

He had so little experience dealing with women, after having kept his distance from them for most of his adult life, that her directness knocked him off-balance. "It's just that I'm not capable of more than that."

"Bullshit."

"Excuse me?"

"Don't tell me you aren't capable when I've *seen* your capabilities. You love Mia with all your heart. You love your sister, your brothers, your nieces and nephews. I've seen that with my own eyes."

"That's different. They're my family. Of course I love them."

"If you have the capacity to love them, you can love anyone you choose to."

"That's not true. I *trust* them, and that's how it's possible for me to love them. I honestly don't trust anyone I'm not related to."

"Even the people you do business with?"

"Especially them. I'm always preparing for them to screw me over in one way or another. I expect the worst of people so they can never disappoint me."

"That's no way to live."

"Tell me about it, which is why I'd never want to inflict my way of living on anyone else, especially someone as wonderful as you are."

Izzy seemed to be thinking that over, as she was quiet for a long moment. "Trust is a hard thing to build in any relationship. It takes time and care and effort on both parts. I know what it's like to have my trust broken by a partner. I know how painful that betrayal is, even if it was nothing like what happened to you."

"I'm sorry you went through that."

"It was rough and shocking and all the things that go along with betrayal. But after the initial shock had passed, it became very important to me that I not allow him to change how I lived going forward. If I allowed him to change me, then he won, you know?"

"I do know, and Deb definitely won. My entire life changed after she left with Mia, and it was never the same afterward."

"You were so young, Cabot."

"She broke me. I've never denied that. Rather, I've acknowledged it and lived accordingly. How in the world would it be fair to bring someone else into my life knowing how messed up I am on the inside?"

"I understand."

"I'm sorry that it has to be this way."

"Me, too."

He gave the hand he was still holding a gentle squeeze. "But I'm also glad we had the chance to spend more time together, even if I hate that you had to get hurt for it to happen."

"I appreciate you being here. It's way above and beyond the bounds of friendship."

"I'm happy to do it. I was wondering if it would be okay to ask Mia and Wade to come for dinner tomorrow."

"Of course. My home is your home."

"Thank you. It's nice to wake up knowing she's nearby."

"I'm sure it must be."

"Do you want to watch a movie or work on the stupid puzzle?" They had grown to hate the nearly all-white puzzle made from one of her most iconic photos, featuring a barn in the background and a red cardinal in a tree providing one of the only splashes of color in an otherwise snowy-white landscape.

"A movie sounds good."

As he got busy finding something to watch, Cabot breathed a sigh of relief. It seemed as if he'd survived the "what are we doing here?" conversation with their friendship intact, which was all that mattered to him. He wasn't capable of a relationship with a woman, but if there was any woman he might be tempted to break his rules for, it would be Isabella Coleman.

It was a relief that she understood now why that couldn't happen.

Izzy's heart sank when she saw the relief in his expression. He'd successfully defused her effort to define their relationship and was now scrolling through the TV guide like he had not a care in the world beyond finding a movie for them to watch.

"How about *Ghost?*"

Oh jeez, only the most romantic movie ever made. She didn't think she could handle that after being let down easy by the first man in years who'd truly attracted her. "Maybe something less maudlin."

"*Notting Hill?*"

Cripes, was the universe conspiring against her? After all, she was just a girl, sitting next to a boy, asking him to give her a chance and being gently told no. "How about something with guns and shooting?"

He glanced at her, eyebrow raised.

"What? I'm just in the mood for some action." Izzy cringed at her choice of words. "On the TV, that is."

His lips quivered with the beginnings of laughter. "Got it."

Not that she was in any condition to be thinking about anything other than getting through the day. The house phone rang, and Cabot jumped up to grab it. "Hey, Hannah. Yes, she's doing well. Let me get her for you." He brought the portable phone to her. "Your mom."

"Thanks." Izzy shifted to find a more comfortable position, wincing when even that small move sent pain through her entire body. "Hi, Mom."

"Hi there. Just checking in to see how you're doing."

"All is well." Or mostly well, except for the exasperating man who'd appointed himself her caretaker. "We had the stew you sent over for dinner. It was delicious."

"Glad you enjoyed it. How are things with Cabot?"

Izzy wasn't sure what her mother was asking. "Fine."

"Everyone is buzzing about him insisting on taking care of you."

"No need for that." What could she say with him sitting two feet from her?

"No need at all?"

"Nope."

"Huh, well, that's sort of disappointing."

"Uh-huh."

"I'll come by tomorrow. We'll talk more then."

"I'll see you then."

"Love you, honey. I know I don't say that as often as I should, but your accident was a reminder that we need to say the words."

Hearing her strong, fearless mother sound tearful touched Izzy. "Love you, too, Mom. Sleep well."

"You, too."

Izzy wondered if she'd sleep at all after the strange conversation with Cabot. If all he wanted was to be friends, why would he have put his very busy life on hold to care for her? She kept coming back to that central question. Wouldn't anyone see that as a declaration that the other person wanted more than just friendship?

She wished there was cell service in Butler so she could text her savvy sisters and ask for their input on this situation, but in order to do that, she'd have to get up and go to her computer or find her iPad to hit them up via Wi-Fi. That would take way more energy than she had after another long day of coping with painful injuries.

They'd probably come by tomorrow, and hopefully she'd get a chance to air it out with them. More than anything, she wanted someone else to tell her she wasn't crazy for thinking that Cabot caring for her meant something, regardless of what he'd said.

It'd been a long time—years—since she'd been confused about a man. Overall, she found them rather easy to understand. Her college boyfriend, Jed, had broken her heart when he cheated on her with a close friend. The betrayal of two people she'd counted among her best friends had cut her deeply, but hadn't changed who she was as a person. It had made her more wary, certainly, but it hadn't completely shattered her ability to trust.

What'd happened to Cabot was so much bigger than what she'd gone through at the hands of her boyfriend and friend. As much as she tried to fully appreciate the nightmare he'd endured, she couldn't possibly know what it had been like for him. She'd once lost a treasured cat for more than a week in the heart of winter. The not knowing where he was had been brutal, until he returned home after seven long days looking no worse for wear and wondering what all the fuss was about.

She'd been frantic over a cat.

The horror of not knowing where your child was or if she was safe *for twenty-five years* was unfathomable.

Perhaps it was true that after damage of that kind was done to a person, there was no coming back from it. She should do them both a favor and accept that and move on. Izzy would've done that if she hadn't ever heard from him again after their dinner last October. But knowing he'd left important business meetings in New Jersey, rented a car and rushed to Vermont after hearing she was hurt and then wanting to care for her at home made it impossible to accept there wasn't something more happening between them than mere friendship.

He'd cleared his schedule for the next two weeks to be there for her. That gave her two weeks to show him what might be possible if only he could allow himself to trust her. It was a daunting mission, especially given that she could barely move, and a mission that could ultimately fail, leaving her far more disappointed than she was now.

But Izzy had a feeling that if she could convince him to give them a chance, they could have something very special. Until another thought occurred to her. Maybe she should've kept it to herself, but how could she when she needed to know?

"Are you here because of Mia?"

"Hmmm?" He looked away from the TV. "What do you mean?"

"So you can be closer to her than you usually are. Is that why you offered to stay with me?"

"*What?* No, that's not why I'm here."

"Oh. Okay." She was almost sorry she'd asked, but not entirely. "I think I'm ready for bed." She had a sudden burning need to be alone with her disturbing thoughts.

When she tried to get up on her own, Cabot jumped up to help. "Go slow."

Pain radiated from numerous injuries with every step she took. "As if I have any choice about that."

When she was finally settled in bed, Cabot brought pain meds and a glass of ice water. She hoped she wouldn't need the meds for much longer, but not taking them wasn't an option yet.

"Can I get you anything else?"

"No, thank you."

"Give me a yell if you need anything during the night."

"I will. Thanks again for being here."

He leaned over to kiss her forehead. "My pleasure. Sleep well."

The scent of his woodsy aftershave stayed with Izzy long after he walked away, leaving her wanting much more than a kiss on the forehead.

Could he be any more platonic?

Izzy reached for the phone on her bedside table and called her brother Noah's house, where most of their siblings were staying since they'd come to town after her accident.

Vanessa answered. "Hey, Iz. How you doing?"

"Pretty good, all things considered. What's going on over there?"

"Jackson, Noah and Henry are playing poker, with smelly cigars, while Ally, Brianna and I try to watch a movie. Gray, Emma and Simone were here for dinner, but they just left. Other than that, not much."

"Sounds like fun. I wish I was there."

"I'll come get you and bring you over if you want."

"Nah, that's okay. I'm in bed, and getting here took the last of my energy for the day."

"You're feeling better, though, right?"

Because it was what her sister needed to hear, Izzy said, "Much better every day."

"I'm so glad to hear that. You gave us such a scare."

"Sorry about that."

"We've decided to forgive you."

"Don't make me laugh."

"Whoops. Are you really okay? You sound a little low tonight."

"Can you talk for a minute?"

"Sure."

"Where no one else can hear you?"

"Let me take the phone upstairs."

Izzy heard her telling the others to keep watching the movie, and she'd catch up when she came back down.

"What's going on?" Ness asked.

"Absolutely nothing."

"Uh, what does that mean?"

"Cabot."

"Okay…"

"I came right out and asked him what he's doing here."

"And?"

Izzy kept her voice down so he wouldn't hear her over the TV that was still on in the living room. "He said he's helping his friend through a rough time."

"His *friend*…"

"Yep."

"Ouch."

"Right? I'm so confused, Ness. He came rushing up here, leaving an important meeting in New Jersey, to be there for me in the hospital. He barely left the room the whole time I was in there and insisted on being the one to care for me at home. But when I come right out and ask him why he did all that, he seems perplexed that I would even ask. I'd seen him *twice* before he showed up at the hospital."

"At Wade's wedding and when else?"

"I invited him to dinner when I was in Boston last October."

"Ohhhh. Really? You never told me that."

"I told you I was meeting a friend because I didn't want to make a thing of it if it wasn't going to be a thing."

"I actually followed that."

"I guess it's not going to be a thing, despite recent evidence to the contrary."

"What did he say when you came right out and asked him?"

"That he's messed up because of what his ex-wife put him through."

"How could he not be?"

"I know, but I sort of hoped he might have decided to take a chance on someone new. Namely me."

"Aw, Iz."

"He said he's not sure how he could ever again trust anyone he's not related to."

"You're sort of related to him by marriage now."

"I don't think that's what he meant."

"I'm sorry you're sad about it."

"I really like him. More than I've liked anyone in a very long time. We had an almost magical connection at the wedding, which is how he also described it, and it was the same when I saw him in October. I was so sure I'd hear from him after both those times, but I never did. I couldn't believe it when he showed up at the hospital or when he insisted on taking care of me at home, and I've been in this weird state of confusion about him ever since."

"How long does he plan to stay?"

"He cleared his schedule in Boston for two weeks, starting the day I came home from the hospital. He's going to take some critical meetings from here."

"So that means you have almost two weeks to show him that not only can he trust you with his heart, but that he needs you in his life."

"How do I do that when I look like hell and can barely move?"

"One hour and one day at a time. You show him what life with you would be like."

"What about the pesky fact that he lives and works in Boston, and I live and work in Vermont?"

"Logistics that can be worked out if it comes to that. Don't worry about that now. Focus on the little things. Talk to him. Listen to him. Share things with him. You know how to do this. It hasn't been that long since you've done it."

"Five years."

"Does that mean you've forgotten how?"

"I might've."

"Nah, it's like riding a bike. You got this."

"What if I make this big effort to turn this into *something*, but it just isn't going to happen?"

"You'll know if it's not going to happen."

"He basically already told me it's not going to."

"And yet, he's still there, right?"

"Yeah."

"I agree that the signals are mixed."

"Could they *be* any more mixed?"

Ness laughed. "I feel sorry for the guy. What he went through for all that time not knowing where his daughter was…"

"It ruined him."

"Did it, though? He still runs a successful business. He's a member of the Boston City Council. He has a loving relationship with his daughter and son-in-law as well as his siblings, nieces and nephews. From the outside looking in, I don't see a life that was entirely ruined. I see one that was altered by a horrible situation, but if you ask me, he's a man with so much left to give."

"He says he wouldn't inflict himself on anyone, especially someone as great as me."

"Maybe he just needs to be shown that you think he's pretty great, too. And it probably wouldn't hurt to make Mia your ally in this."

"How do you mean?"

"I assume she'd love to see her dad happy and moving on from the trauma of the years when she was missing. I bet she'd be thrilled to see you two together."

"That's an interesting idea."

"I'm full of interesting ideas that are available to you any time you need them."

Izzy laughed, even though it caused her pain. "Thanks for listening to me whine about my confusing situation."

"You're not whining. The situation is definitely confusing,

but he's living in your house for the next little while. This is your chance to show him what's possible, Iz."

"I hear you."

"I'll come by tomorrow to see you."

"How long are you staying in town?"

"Not sure yet. I'm looking for a new job, so it's day to day."

"What happened to the old job?"

"That's a story for another day. Get some rest and try not to worry. I have a good feeling about you two."

"I'm glad you do. I'll see you tomorrow."

"Night."

Talking to Vanessa had helped. It made Izzy feel better to know she wasn't crazy for wondering what the hell was happening under her own roof.

In the living room, she heard Cabot laugh.

He could laugh, he could cry with joy at his daughter's wedding, he could come running to a friend he'd met only twice in her time of need.

In her mind, that man wasn't as broken as he thought he was.

She had twelve days to find out if that was true.

CHAPTER THREE

"I don't think you can ever be bitter about anything, because if you don't allow your heart to stay open, then all you have is a filled heart of hate and bitterness, and you're never able to love or like anybody."
—Debbie Reynolds

The next morning began with a visit from Izzy's aunt Molly and uncle Lincoln Abbott, who brought breakfast sandwiches, Butch's famous home fries and freshly baked blueberry muffins from the diner.

"At this rate, I'm going to weigh nine hundred pounds by the time I'm recovered," Izzy said between bites of the tasty breakfast.

"Your body needs energy to heal," Molly said.

"She's seen tons of kids through a lot of injuries," Linc said. "So listen to your aunt."

"I'm listening—and I'm eating."

Cabot stood to refresh their coffee.

Izzy looked up at him and smiled. "Thank you."

"No problem."

He looked sexy in a red-and-blue-plaid flannel shirt with a navy fleece vest and well-worn jeans.

"How long are you here, Cabot?" Linc asked.

Izzy gave her uncle the side-eye. He and her grandfather

were known for their matchmaking efforts on behalf of the Abbotts and Colemans. She hoped they hadn't set their sights on her. Or did she? Hmmm...

"I'm here until the end of next week. Possibly longer if I can swing it."

That was news to her.

"Are you able to work remotely?" Molly asked.

"Thankfully, yes. I have a great team supporting me in the office, and as long as I'm checking in every day, they have things under control. My only quandary is my city council responsibilities, but so far I've only missed one meeting. I may have to go back next week for a vote on a big project that's pending before the council."

"Tell me again what it is exactly that your business does?" Molly asked.

Izzy wanted to thank her, because she and Cabot had talked about it in only broad terms with no specifics.

"I invest in start-up companies and then contract with them for consulting services. So if we invest in a new restaurant chain, for example, I make my team of accounting, marketing, social media, event planning and real estate professionals available to them. One of the most difficult parts of starting a business is figuring out things like payroll and advertising. We try to take the guesswork out of it for them."

"It's a really cool business model," Linc says.

Uncle Linc was CEO of the family's Green Mountain Country Store, started by Izzy's great-grandparents, and he was a graduate of Yale Business School.

"How'd you get into that?" Molly asked.

"It sort of grew out of the investment side. Time after time, businesses we invested in would ask who we recommended for this or that, and after a while, it occurred to me that providing those services on a contractor basis would be another profitable line of business."

"Is it?"

"Very much so. By hiring us on a contract basis, companies

save the cost of bringing on full-time employees for the roles we fulfill for them, and we profit from the fees."

"That's very interesting, Cabot," Molly said.

"It's been fun to grow the business and to see it become successful beyond anything I dared to dream at the beginning. A little investing here and there has turned into so much more. We've reached the point where we provide consulting services even for companies that we aren't investing in."

Izzy enjoyed listening to him talk about his work and seeing the obvious pleasure he took in it. His passion for it was further proof that he wasn't totally broken. She ought to start making a list of all the ways he wasn't broken so she could eventually make her case to him.

Before she could fully explore that thought, her landline rang with a number she didn't recognize. "I'd better take this. I'm dealing with insurance companies for both the medical stuff and the Jeep, which was totaled."

"Go ahead, honey."

"Hello?"

"Uh, Isabella?"

She'd know that voice anywhere. Part of her wanted to hang up. The other part was too curious to do that. "Hello, Dad."

Molly grimaced while Izzy rolled her eyes in response.

"How are you?" her father asked.

"Better than I was."

"I'm glad to hear that. I'm sorry I didn't make it to the hospital to see you. My doctor advised against me going there due to being immunocompromised."

"It's okay."

"I was wondering if I could see you at home."

"Um, sure. That would be fine."

"Are you home today?"

"I'm here all day."

"All right, then. I'll come by around two if that works?"

"Okay. Do you know where I live?"

"I do. I'll see you then."

"Sounds good. Bye."

"Bye, honey."

Her dad had called her *honey*, the same way he always had before he lost his mind and left their family when she was fourteen. She'd seen him only sporadically since then, which was why a call from him, along with a request to visit, was so unsettling.

"So I guess my dad is coming to visit at two," Izzy said to the others.

"You don't have to see him if you don't want to," Molly said with an unusually harsh edge to her voice that Izzy could certainly understand.

Mike Coleman had left Molly's sister, Hannah, with eight children to finish raising on her own. There was no love lost for him in the extended family.

"It's fine," Izzy said, even though she wasn't at all sure that was true. Seeing her dad always messed her up for days afterward, and with all her energy needed for her recovery and Project Cabot (that was the official name), she didn't have the time to be sidelined by emotional crap from her childhood.

"You should give your mom a heads-up so she doesn't come by at that time," Molly said.

"I will. He said he didn't come to the hospital because his doctor told him not to." For Cabot's sake, she added, "He had a bone marrow transplant a year ago thanks to my brother Grayson. None of us had heard from him in years when he suddenly resurfaced with leukemia and in need of a donor."

"Wow, that must've been pretty intense," he said.

"Just a little."

"If you ask me, it takes some nerve to make a request like that of eight children you walked away from decades ago," Molly said.

Linc reached over to put his hand on top of hers, which seemed to calm her ever so slightly.

Izzy watched them the way she always did—with a combination of awe and envy. They were the perfect couple, in her opinion. She wanted what they had, the innate understanding of each other that was so obvious to anyone who knew them well. They were the epitome of love, affection, marriage and overall couple goals.

She had no memory of her parents being happy together, so having Linc and Molly around to show her and her siblings the way it was supposed to be had been invaluable. "You guys are too cute, as always."

"We are?" Molly asked, seeming perplexed.

"Super cute."

"We're very cute, my love," Lincoln said as he put his arms around his wife.

Molly scowled. "Old fools like us aren't cute."

"Yes, you are," Izzy said. "You have no idea how many younger people look up to you two as the gold standard for a happy marriage."

"We are rather happy," Linc said with a goofy grin.

"That's what I want," Izzy said, sighing. She'd almost forgotten Cabot was in the room, but hey, he might as well hear what her life goals included. A relationship like the one her aunt and uncle shared was close to the top of her list. She wanted to find someone she could love the way Molly loved Linc and to be loved back the way he loved her. She wanted a family and a life partner who supported her photography career while she supported his endeavors.

For a long time, she hadn't wanted any of those things—well, except for the career she'd pursued with relentless focus for the last ten years. But after recently turning thirty-five and then nearly dying in a serious car crash, she felt her priorities shifting in the direction of happily ever after. She even had a man in mind to play the starring role, if she could convince him he had what it took to hold up his end of the bargain.

She glanced at him as he leaned against the counter, drinking his coffee.

He met her gaze and didn't blink for the longest time.

Izzy wasn't sure what passed between them in those charged seconds, but it wasn't nothing. That was for sure.

Her heart gave a little jolt of awareness that sent a prickle down her spine. If she was being entirely honest with herself, she'd admit that her thinking on the matter of happily ever after and forever had changed after meeting Cabot at Wade and Mia's wedding. Before she knew him, she hadn't met anyone she could imagine spending the rest of her life with. Way back in college, when she'd thought she'd found her one, maybe she'd entertained the idea of forever with him even as she hoped he'd eventually grow up and behave like an actual adult. Then he'd cheated on her—with her friend—and showed her who he really was. Since then, she'd had hit-and-run relationships with men, including one in New York she saw whenever she was in town, another in Boston, and one in Stowe.

But none of them was particularly exciting or interesting beyond an occasional night here or there.

Cabot had been different. She'd been captivated by his sweetness on Mia's wedding day, his emotional reaction to giving away the daughter he'd missed for a quarter century, how he'd worn his heart on his sleeve that entire day, even as he celebrated and enjoyed the occasion. Who wouldn't be attracted to a handsome, successful, articulate, caring man like him?

She'd been thrilled to wake up in the hospital to find him standing by her bedside, looking ravaged with worry. That meant he cared, right?

Despite what he'd said the night before, Izzy believed his actions spoke louder than his words. He'd come running, and he'd stayed to help her out at home. That meant something, and no one could convince her otherwise, even him.

"You'll find your Lincoln one of these days," Molly said with a meaningful look at Izzy, as if she understood that questions remained to be answered between her and Cabot.

Izzy's family was probably as uncertain of what him being there meant as she was, and knowing them, they were abuzz about the fact that he was staying with her.

"Oh, I will," Izzy said, looking away from Cabot. "I have no doubt."

"Me either," Molly said. "Any man would be lucky to land the incredible Isabella Coleman."

"I couldn't agree more," Linc said.

"And you guys aren't the slightest bit biased, right?" she asked, amused by them.

"Not at all," Linc said. "We only speak the truth. Oh, and I meant to tell you, I brought the special balm from the store that works wonders on bruising." He jumped up from his seat to retrieve one of the bags they'd arrived with, withdrawing two tubs of the balm.

"Thank you. I need that. I'm one big bruise."

"Cameron swears that stuff is magic," he said of his daughter-in-law, who ought to know. She was known as the girl who hit Fred, the town moose, with her car during her first minutes in Butler.

"I'm in need of some serious magic. Everything still hurts."

"You're doing so much better than you were a week ago, honey," Molly said. "You'll be back to a hundred percent in no time."

Izzy both looked forward to that and dreaded it, because once she was restored to full health, there'd be no reason for Cabot to stay.

Molly and Linc left a short time later, promising to be back to visit again soon.

"I'm going to shower," Izzy told Cabot.

"Do you need any help wrapping your cast?" They'd rigged up a bag system that she used to keep her cast dry.

She wanted to say, *Yes, why don't you come in there with me?* But she wanted to wait until she wasn't black and blue from head to toe before she revealed herself to him. Hopefully, she'd get that chance. "I'm okay once I get myself out of the chair."

"That I can help with," he said, offering his arm.

She took hold of his arm and let him do most of the work in helping her up.

The ever-present pain took her breath away and made her knees weak under her.

Cabot put an arm around her waist. "I've got you."

Izzy leaned into him, warm and solid and the perfect height for her as he rested his chin on the top of her head. She wanted to wrap her arms around him and hold on to him forever. So that's what she did.

For a second, he went totally still before relaxing into her embrace.

That's all it was—an embrace—but Izzy enjoyed every second she spent wrapped up in him. He smelled like the perfect combination of citrus and spice, starch and fabric softener. Delicious.

"Ah, Iz?"

"Yes, Cabot?"

"I thought you were going to shower?"

"I am, but for right now, this is pretty good."

His grunt of laughter made her smile.

"Could I ask you something?"

"Sure," he said, sounding a bit wary.

"This feels pretty good, doesn't it, to hold each other this way?"

"It does."

"I liked the way you held me when we danced at the wedding."

"I loved dancing with you."

"I loved it, too. I also like talking to you and hearing about your work and your life in Boston and your family and how much you love your daughter. I like it all."

"Izzy..."

"I heard what you said last night, and I understand why you feel the way you do. Anyone would be angry and bitter after what was done to you. But I also know there's so much more to you than that. Sometimes when something is so big, so overwhelming, it's all you can see. I've already seen so much more than the bitterness and anger, which you've never shown me. I wouldn't have known it was there if you hadn't told me."

She held on for another full minute before she reluctantly released him and made her way slowly and painfully to the bathroom to shower.

CHAPTER FOUR

*"Although the world is full of suffering, it is full
also of the overcoming of it."* —Helen Keller

Long after Izzy walked away, Cabot stood rooted in
place in the kitchen, bowled over by what she'd said.
There's so much more to you...

He wasn't sure that was true. The anger was such a big part
of him that he didn't remember who he'd been before it. When
he'd first discovered that Deb had left with Mia, he'd felt nothing
but fear. Deb could be unpredictable, which he'd once found
attractive, until unpredictable became unstable. He'd worried
desperately for the safety of his daughter as days stretched into
weeks, months and then years without a sign of either of them.
All that time, he'd had to wonder if his daughter was even still
alive.

It'd been hell. The anger had kicked in after about a year,
when it became clear to him that Deb had taken Mia to punish
him because he'd come at her with hard-charging lawyers after
she filed for divorce. She'd known full well how much Cabot
had adored Mia. She'd known full well that he was the better
parent. And she'd taken their child from him anyway.

Some people might think he should let it go, especially now

that Mia was back in his life, but how did one "let go" of twenty-five years of desperate searching for the person they loved best in the world, who'd been intentionally kept from him by someone he used to love? You didn't just get over something like that or move on with your life like it never happened, even after it was resolved.

No, it stayed with you forever, permanently imprinted upon your soul, no matter how much you might wish otherwise.

Someone like Izzy, who was all light and sweetness and pure joy, deserved a man who wouldn't be like a live grenade in her life, waiting to explode at a moment's notice. No one needed that, especially Izzy, who'd already had her life explode once before when her father left their family. She didn't need to be living with a ticking time bomb who could blow at any second.

And yes, he'd had therapy about this issue. Lots of it. He'd talked it to death for years, but the anger remained just the same.

He was still standing in the kitchen when he heard the shower turn off. Shaking his head, he released a deep breath and went to find his laptop to log into work. That's what made sense to him, and he'd buried himself in work from the start of his ordeal, first working for one of his uncles in the family real estate business and later branching out into his own company. He'd grown his business into a multimillion-dollar enterprise fueled by rage.

Izzy didn't see that when she looked at him. No, she saw only the successful businessman, the doting father, the devoted brother, uncle and friend. She didn't see the rage that fed the entire operation, like a nuclear power plant that lived deep inside him. No one would know it was there if he didn't tell them, which was why he'd felt obligated to warn her.

He sat on her sofa and opened the laptop to check his email, but all he could think about was how surprised he'd been when she put her arms around him or how amazing it had felt to hold her. The information he'd given her last night hadn't scared her away from him. If anything, it had seemingly made her more determined to turn their friendship into something more.

What are you doing here?

Her question from the night before had kept him awake long after she'd gone to bed. What was he doing there? Of course she was confused. Out of one side of his mouth, he was telling her he had nothing to give a relationship, but out of the other was his insistence he be the one to care for her at home when she certainly had plenty of others who could've done that.

But she'd wanted it to be him.

He stared at the screen full of emails without seeing anything other than her face as she'd told her aunt and uncle that she wanted what they had. Her words had pierced his chest, stabbing him straight in the heart. Did he want her to have that with some other random guy? No, he did not. The thought of her with someone else filled him with panic.

"Well, then, you're going to have to step up and give her what she wants unless you want to hear about how happy she is with someone else."

"Cabot?"

He looked to his left and nearly stopped breathing at the sight of Izzy in a clingy robe. She had her hair wrapped in a towel, which put her gorgeous, flawless face on full display. Even with the lingering bruises on her face, she was stunning.

"Were you talking to someone?"

"Only myself."

"Do you reply to yourself?"

Forcing a smile for her, he said, "Sometimes."

"Are you okay?"

"I'm good. How was the shower?"

"Delightful. I'll never again take a shower for granted after going without for a week in the hospital."

"It's the little things that make us happy."

"Yes, it is," she said with a meaningful look. "The little things are the best things."

He put down his laptop and stood to go to her, knowing he had to either man up or get out of her home and her life. In the two seconds it took him to walk to her, he still wasn't sure what he was going to do.

"You said you're good, but you don't look so hot," she said. "What's wrong?"

"I've been sending you some mixed signals here. I see that now."

"I'm glad you do." Her lovely eyes glittered with amusement. "The signals have been decidedly mixed."

"It's not my intention to confuse you."

"And yet…"

He looked down at the floor, summoning courage that was in far shorter supply than the rage before he returned his gaze to her face. "I heard what you said before, about there being more to me than the bad stuff."

"There's *so* much more."

"I appreciate that you see that."

"I do. I have from the start. I thought you were amazing at the wedding, the way you didn't care at all if the whole world saw you weeping with happiness for your daughter and yourself."

Grunting out a laugh, he said, "That was mortifying."

She reached for his hand and linked their fingers. "No, it was *lovely*."

"If you say so."

"I do. I felt like I'd seen your heart that day, and I… I wanted…"

"What?" he asked, feeling as breathless as he sounded. "What did you want?"

"More. More time with you. More of everything we shared that day. Just more."

"I did, too. I couldn't stop thinking about you after the wedding. Or after our dinner in October. I'd find myself thinking of you first thing in the morning, during important meetings, at business dinners and late at night when I should've been sleeping. I'd be thinking about you, wondering where you were, what you were working on, if you were happy."

"Cabot," she said on a gasp. "*Why* didn't you call me?"

"I told you why last night."

She shook her head, took a step to close the distance between them and released his hand so she could wrap her arms around his neck. "You failed to scare me off," she whispered, her lips so close to his, he could almost taste them. He wanted to taste them.

"I see that."

"I'm not afraid of the anger that lives inside you. In fact, I wonder if you replaced it with a more productive emotion if it might eventually disappear altogether."

"What emotion did you have in mind?"

Her smile was truly a thing of beauty. "I'm thinking of a couple that might work, but I'd hate to tip my hand too soon. And besides, why tell when I can show?"

She brushed her lips over his, making his mind go blank of anything that wasn't about her and wanting her. His fingers dug into her hips before he remembered she was injured and lightened his grip. He wished he could haul her into his arms and kiss her the way he'd wanted to since the first time he laid eyes on her the night before Mia's wedding.

Who, he'd wondered, *was she? And how can I get her to talk to me?*

And now she was kissing him as if she hadn't heard a word he'd said about all the reasons this was a bad idea. He needed to retake control of this situation, but how could he do that when she had her arms around his neck and her lips pressed to his? If he moved, he risked hurting her, and besides, kissing her was the best thing ever. Why would he want to stop?

The thoughts raced through his mind, one after the other, as she kissed him with almost unbearable sweetness.

"I knew it," she whispered many minutes later.

"What did you know?"

"That kissing you would be amazing, even if my sore lip isn't quite ready for that." She released him and turned away, heading slowly and carefully to her room, as if she hadn't just completely rocked his world in every possible way.

He ought to leave. A work emergency could arise that would take him back to Boston, where everything made sense to him.

He wished he could call Emily without Izzy overhearing him. Since that wasn't an option, as soon as he could think again, he went to his laptop and wrote his sister an email.

Subject: Greetings from VT

How's it going? Things are good here. Izzy is a little better every day, getting around more than she was. Which is great, except she's decided we're going to be more than friends, and I'm not sure what to do about that. So. Help.

He sent the message before he could talk himself out of it and then forced himself to focus on work, pending issues and questions from his staff that had them at a standstill until he weighed in, and emails regarding city council business.

One was from the mayor. *Hey, Cabot, hope your friend is doing better and is on the mend. Just wondering if you'll be able to make Tuesday's meeting. We have a number of items on the agenda (enclosed in case you missed the email earlier this week) that we need you for. If you can't be here, we will move to postpone the zoning matters and school budget. Let me know when you get a chance. All the best, Lenore.*

They would've already advertised the agenda, which meant they couldn't change it.

Tuesday was in four days. If he left to go back to Boston, what reason would he have to come back? Someone else would come and stay with Izzy while he was gone, which would make it strange for him to come back and take over. He didn't want to leave. Not yet.

He wrote back to Lenore. *So sorry that I can't make it Tuesday. My friend is still in pretty rough shape and needs around-the-clock care.* He was going straight to hell for lying to Lenore, who was a good friend. *Sorry to leave you short, but if you can postpone, I should be able to make the meeting in two weeks. Fingers crossed. Cabot*

Again, he sent the message before he could find a dozen reasons not to, such as his belief that Izzy would be much better off if he got into his rental car and drove home to Boston, leaving her to get on with her life without him in it.

But would that be better for him?

Not at all.

"You're a selfish bastard," he whispered as an email from Emily popped up in his in-box. He clicked to open it.

His sister's email opened with a question. *What the hell is wrong with you?*

"You want the whole list?" he muttered.

When you heard Izzy had been badly hurt, I thought you were going to lose your mind trying to get to her. Remember that? I do, because you called me and told me you were losing it out of fear of losing her. Is this bringing back any memories for you?? Why are you doing what you do with her? When is it time to put the past where it belongs and live for the here and now? Granted, your past is horrible, and no one would blame you for avoiding relationships forever. But I think you like this woman, perhaps in a way you haven't liked anyone—even SHE who shall not be named. So are you going to let Izzy slip through your fingers so she can go find someone else to love while you carry on, tending to the wounds of the past while she's living a wonderful, fulfilling life with another man? Is that what you want?

Leave it to his sister to sum things up in a way that only a sibling could do, with zero sugarcoating.

You LIKE HER, Cabot. Apparently, she LIKES YOU, TOO. I have a feeling you'll regret it forever if you don't at least TRY to make it work with her. Remember how you felt when you weren't sure she was going to survive the accident??? Tap into that memory bank and ask yourself how you would've felt if she hadn't survived.

That possibility was too awful to contemplate, even knowing she was going to make a full recovery.

He hit Reply and started typing. *As always, thank you for telling it to me straight. I hear what you're saying, and you're right. I do like her. A lot.*

He sent the message, and she wrote back a minute later.

Don't blow it with her, Cab. You'll be so sorry if you do. I know it'll take a huge leap of faith in a situation that has no guarantees of working out. But I saw you with her at the wedding, and I liked the way you smiled that day—and not just because of Mia or the wedding.

It was Izzy, too. We all saw that and have been hoping we might see something come of it.

I hear you. Thank you. I'm trying to find the courage to try...

I have a feeling she'll be worth the effort. Keep me posted.

Cabot already knew Izzy would be worth the effort. He'd known that since last June and had been even more sure of it after their dinner in October. Emily had reminded him of just how frantic he'd been after hearing about the accident. Mia had called him, thinking he would want to know, and his only thought had been about getting to Vermont as fast as he possibly could. At no time during the seven-hour drive did he stop to wonder whether it would seem weird to her or her family if he showed up as if he had some sort of right to be there.

That hadn't mattered to him.

No, the only thing he'd cared about was seeing her and being with her.

Ever since Deb had disappeared with Mia, he'd been fanatical about the concept of *control*. He was in charge of his life, and nothing and no one was ever again going to catch him flat-footed the way Deb had when she'd bolted with Mia. Every single thing he did was predicated on him being *in control* of every situation, which was why he found it odd to realize that since he'd heard about Izzy's accident, he'd been anything but in control.

He'd been completely *out* of control, and that was so far from his comfort zone as to be laughable.

She had that effect on him, which was another reason to disentangle from what was happening between them.

Cabot couldn't afford to be out of control.

Izzy came out of her room, with her long auburn hair falling in sexy spiral curls around her shoulders. She had on an oatmeal-colored cowl-neck sweater with black leggings and had applied makeup for the first time since her accident. "How do I look?"

Cabot could only stare at her until he recovered the ability to speak. "You look even more beautiful than usual. How did you dry your hair?"

She smoothed her hands over her sweater. "I didn't wash it. Just did some curls. I haven't seen my father in a long time. I didn't want to look like hell in front of him."

He was deeply touched to realize she was anxious about seeing her father. "You couldn't look like hell if you tried."

"Haha, very funny. I've looked like death warmed over for days now."

Cabot shook his head as he moved closer to her. "No, you haven't."

"You're just being nice."

He ran a finger gently over the bruise on her right cheek that she'd covered with makeup. "Nah, you're always lovely, even with a bruise here or there."

"Thank you."

"When was the last time you saw him?"

"More than five years ago. I ran into him in Stowe. At first, I didn't recognize him, but he knew me. Said my name. It was shocking to realize I'd almost walked right past him."

The same might've happened between him and his daughter if they'd run into each other somewhere before their reunion, albeit for far different reasons.

"I was unprepared to see him. I didn't know what to say."

"That must've been unsettling."

"It was. I think I've seen him four times, total, in the twenty years since he left."

Cabot despised Mike Coleman with a fiery rage for what he'd done to his wife and children. What he would've given for the chance to raise his daughter, while Mike had walked away from his beautiful family. "Did you ever hear why he left?"

Izzy shrugged. "What does it matter?"

"I guess it doesn't." He took hold of her hands, brought them gently to his lips. "You don't have to see him today if you're not up to it."

"It's fine."

"Is it, though?"

"I tell myself it is. He wants to see that I'm all right, which is proof he still cares. That's the part that bothers me. That I care that he still cares. I sorta hate myself a little for that."

"No one would blame you for feeling that way."

Smiling, she shrugged again. "I blame me."

Before he could think of what he should say to that, the phone rang. Cabot released her hands and went to the kitchen to answer it.

"Hi, Cabot, this is Cameron Abbott, Will's wife."

"Oh, hi, Cameron."

"My sister-in-law Lucy and I are on the schedule for lunch delivery today, and we were just checking to make sure Izzy is up for the visit. I also wanted to mention that our friend Troy is in town from New York and tagging along with us today, but he can stay in the car if Izzy isn't up for extra guests."

"Hang on just a second, Cameron." Cabot relayed the information to Izzy.

"Oh, please tell them to come by, and their friend is welcome to join them."

He passed that on to Cameron.

"Great, thanks. We'll come by around noon, then."

"See you then." He put down the phone and joined Izzy on the sofa, where she'd settled. "Your family is quite something with their schedule."

"They really are. I'd tell them not to worry about me, but that'd be pointless."

"You're lucky to have them."

"And I know it. When I start to feel a little weird about seeing my dad, I think of how many wonderful people have been there for my siblings and me all along, and they make it so he can't hurt me, you know?"

"I do. That's a good way to look at it. I was wondering about his health since the transplant."

"I heard he's in remission, which is good news. We all give Gray so much credit for what he did. I'm not sure I could've done it."

"You would've so you didn't have his death on your conscience."

"That's why Gray did it." She glanced at Cabot. "You must have work to do."

"I have a meeting in fifteen minutes that's apt to take an hour or so."

"Do what you need to. I'm capable of entertaining myself."

He had numerous things that needed tending to, but since she'd kissed him earlier, the only thing he wanted to tend to was her.

CHAPTER FIVE

"Pleasure of love lasts but a moment. Pain of love lasts a lifetime."
—Bette Davis

*I*zzy tried not to listen to him on the phone with his office, but that was hard to do in a tiny house like hers. He spoke respectfully to his colleagues, asked their opinions, listened to what they had to say and made decisions only after he had all the relevant information. Friends and family had brought countless books and magazines to keep her entertained, but nothing was more interesting to her than Cabot.

She still couldn't believe the brazen way she'd kissed him and put him on notice that she wanted something more from him. Today would've already been classified as a great day if only she didn't have to think about seeing her father later. Why had she said he could come if thinking about the visit was going to upset her so much? Probably because it'd always been important to her and her brothers Grayson and Noah, as the eldest three, to be the bigger people in their dealings with him.

He might've left them and their five siblings, putting them into a desperate financial situation in addition to the emotional fallout, but they weren't going to ever let him see the damage he'd done to them. As high school students, the eldest three had

had nearly full-time jobs to help their mother support the family after Mike had disappeared for three years.

A lawyer their uncle Lincoln had hired had finally tracked him down, taken him to court and forced him to pay some child support. But it hadn't been nearly enough to support a family of nine people. Each of them had clawed and scraped their way through high school and college, some with scholarships and all with loans they'd be paying off for years to come. His departure had made their lives difficult in ways they were still processing well into adulthood.

They owed him *nothing*. So why was it when he'd called and asked to see her that she'd said yes? Sometimes being the bigger person wasn't easy. When Cabot had finished the phone meeting with his office, Izzy placed a call to her brother Grayson.

"Hey, Iz, how are you feeling?"

"A little better, actually."

"That's very good news. What's up?"

"So, um, Dad is coming by at two."

"Is he? I wondered if you'd hear from him when he didn't show at the hospital after asking if he could visit."

"I guess his doctor nixed the visit to the hospital because of his immune system."

"I wondered if he was just saying that to get out of having to do it."

"A valid question in light of his track record for making offers that never materialize."

How many times had he asked to see his children and then failed to show up after arranging a time? Too many times to count.

"I hate to say that he seems to be trying to make some amends since his illness forced him to confront his mortality," Grayson said.

"I suppose that's understandable from his point of view."

"And annoying from ours."

"Yeah."

"You don't have to see him. No one would blame you if you didn't."

"I know, but I figured I could give him half an hour and then go on with my life."

"As long as that's what you do. No looking back, you hear me?"

"Is that how you handled being the donor?"

"Yep. I did it and then tried to forget about it."

"How'd that go?"

"Pretty well because I have Emma and Simone to give me something more important to think about besides the man who'd disappointed me so profoundly."

"I can see how that would help."

"It does. By the way, I'm having lunch with Mom. Do you want me to tell her to steer clear of your place this afternoon?"

"That'd be great. I was going to call her."

"I'll tell her. And speaking of distractions, seems like you might have something better to think about lately, too."

Izzy glanced at Cabot, sitting at the desk in her office while typing on his laptop. "Maybe."

"You're not sure?"

"Not entirely."

"Interesting. We all figured there was something going on when he offered to stay with you."

"As did I."

"So there isn't? Something going on?"

"We'll see, won't we?"

"I know you can't talk with him right there, but now you're leaving me with more questions than I had before."

Izzy laughed. "Right there with you, brother."

"The plot thickens. Let me know how it goes with Dad?"

"I will. Don't worry. I'll be fine."

"And yet, I'll still worry."

"Because that's what you do as the big brother."

"Guilty as charged. Don't let him hurt you, Iz."

Touched by Grayson's concern, she said, "I won't. I promise."

"I'll come by later to check on you."

"I'll look forward to that."

Izzy ended the call feeling better after having spoken to the brother who'd been by her side through all of life's highs and lows. While she was also close to Noah, he tended to be more remote and self-contained, although a little less so since Brianna had come into his life. According to her younger siblings, who'd been staying with Noah while Izzy was in the hospital, the Noah they'd known before his ex-wife had done a number on him was reemerging since he'd fallen for the architect working with him to rebuild the Butler Inn.

Izzy was looking forward to getting to know Brianna and to spending time with her and Noah as a couple. And she couldn't wait to meet the son Noah hadn't known he had with his ex until recently. She was still wrapping her head around having a two-year-old nephew named Elliott.

Life could be so completely fucked up sometimes, she thought, ruminating over the many ways people hurt the ones they supposedly loved. Like what her father had done, what Cabot's ex-wife had done, what Noah's ex-wife had done. It was no wonder that Cabot had trouble trusting people after what he'd endured or that she'd struggled in relationships with men after being betrayed by her own father as well as her first true love. She did fine until the man of the moment wanted a commitment to more than just casual dating. That was usually the point where she wanted out.

Isabella Coleman didn't do commitment, which hadn't been a conscious choice on her part. It had sort of just turned out that way when one man after another exited her life after she'd refused to give them what they wanted. She hadn't been aware of the pattern until a close friend brought it to her attention after the latest of the promising men in her life was dispatched to the scrap heap of exes who'd failed to pin her down. Izzy had mourned the loss of every one of them, wishing they'd been as satisfied with the status quo as she had been and not pushed for more than she was capable of giving.

Once her friend had identified the pattern, Izzy had been forced to acknowledge that her father's betrayal had done more damage than she'd previously thought. Since then, she'd engaged in extensive therapy to "work out her daddy issues," as she jokingly referred to them in the hope of one day being capable of more than surface relationships.

Cabot had no way to know that he was the first man she'd wanted to take a real chance on since making some rather large discoveries about herself and then doing the work necessary to make substantive changes in how she approached men and romance and the possibility of happily ever after.

And then he'd never called her, even after asking to exchange numbers at the wedding.

For a time that day, she'd expected to spend the night with him, but that hadn't happened either. Unlike almost everyone else associated with the wedding, he hadn't stayed at the hotel where the reception took place. He'd walked her to the elevator, kissed her cheek, thanked her for a lovely day, declined her invitation to come up to her room for a nightcap and had walked out of the hotel to go home.

It had been a strange end to a wonderful day, and it had gotten even stranger when he never called her or returned the texts she'd sent him in the ensuing weeks. When work had taken her to Boston, she decided to give him one last chance by texting to say she'd be in town and to ask if he'd like to meet for dinner.

She'd been shocked when he replied to say he'd love that, as if they'd been in touch all along. Dinner had been fantastic, full of the witty conversation they'd enjoyed at the wedding, followed again by nothing.

Until the accident.

Truth be told, after nothing came of their dinner last October, she'd been determined to move on. She hadn't done all that work with the therapist to get at the root of her commitment issues only to be left trying to convince a man to give her a chance. And yes, the irony of that wasn't lost on her. After years of running from men who wanted more, she'd found a man who didn't seem to want anything.

Or did he?

Wasn't that the question of the year?

And she was right back to the question she'd asked him—what was he doing there? If he didn't want to be with her, why would he feel the need to stay with her after she was discharged from the hospital? The rush to the hospital was enough of a gesture based on what they'd shared prior to the accident. She would've totally understood if he'd headed back to Boston after she was discharged into the care of her mother or one of her siblings.

But nope, he'd insisted on being the one to care for her, and now, here they were.

If she'd heard this story from someone else, she'd think it was funny how two emotionally stunted people were stumbling around like a couple of idiots, trying to figure out what the hell they were doing. However, as one of the aforementioned emotionally stunted adults, she didn't think it was particularly funny.

Izzy was pulled out of her thoughts when Cameron, Lucy and their friend Troy Kennedy arrived with lunch. He was the epitome of tall, dark and handsome, with kind brown eyes. She'd met him before, at Cameron's and Lucy's weddings, but hadn't gotten the chance to talk to him.

"We made tomato soup and our own chicken salad wraps," Lucy announced.

"And we baked cookies," Cameron added as they unpacked containers.

"You guys are awesome," Izzy said. "Thank you so much."

"Are you kidding?" Cameron asked, her blonde hair piled in a messy bun. "You made us look like movie stars on our wedding days with the most incredible photos we've ever seen. This is the least we can do for you."

"Aw, you're too kind," Izzy said. "I had beautiful brides and grooms to work with."

"They were rather stunning," Troy said. "I'm glad to see you looking so well, Izzy."

"Thanks. I understand it was touch-and-go for a minute there."

Lucy, who had red hair and green eyes and was hugely pregnant, shuddered. "That was an awful phone call to receive." She was married to Izzy's cousin, Colton Abbott.

"Sorry to worry you all," Izzy said.

"We're just glad you're doing better," Cameron said.

"How's baby Chase doing?" she asked as she directed them to plates, bowls, spoons.

"He's delightful," Cameron said, smiling. "The sweetest baby boy ever."

"I can't wait to see him again. He's going to be due for some new photos by the time I'm back on my feet."

"The last ones were so amazing," Cameron said. "I wanted to frame every one of them."

"He's an adorable subject."

"We think so, too, but we're quite biased," Cameron said with a laugh.

"How're you feeling, Lucy?" Izzy asked.

"Like a beached whale, if I'm being honest, but I'm told that's what the ninth month is like."

"You're glowing," Cameron told her friend, who'd become her sister-in-law when they married brothers.

"If you say so. I'm so ready to get this baby out. I've given him free room and board for thirty-six weeks. It's time for him to quit being a freeloader and show his face."

Cameron and Izzy laughed while Troy rolled his eyes.

"I hate to tell you, pal, but the freeloading is just beginning," Cameron said.

"That's what I hear," Lucy said, frowning.

"Is Cabot joining us?" Cameron asked.

"He's on a work meeting in my office, but he said to start without him, and he'll catch up."

They enjoyed the delicious soup and wraps while swapping family gossip that was always plentiful with ten Abbotts and eight Colemans to dish about. Cameron told a hilarious story about Will and Colton's identical twin brothers, Lucas and Landon, pulling a fast one on their partners by getting identical haircuts, shaving their faces and wearing the exact same flannel shirts.

"What happened?" Troy asked, fascinated.

"Dani and Amanda went straight to the correct man and told them to stop acting like jackasses," Cameron said.

"You have to admit," Troy said, chuckling, "it's kinda funny they did that."

"*Everything* they do is funny," Lucy said, "but we can't let them know it. They're ridiculous as it is. We can't encourage them." Her face twisted into an odd expression as she laid her hand on her pregnant belly. "Ugh, Braxton-Hicks contractions are no joke."

"Ouch," Cameron said. "They're the worst. They feel so real."

"So what brings you to Butler, Troy?" Izzy asked.

"I wanted to see these guys, Emma, Simone, Ray and baby Chase, so I took a week off to do some skiing and visiting." Troy had been best friends with Cameron, Lucy and Lucy's sister Emma—who was now engaged to Grayson—when they all lived in New York City.

Izzy had heard how sad he'd been when they all moved to Vermont and left him "alone" in the city.

"He's staying with us," Cameron said, "so he's getting lots of baby Chase time."

"Which I love," Troy said. "He's very cute. And I also got to ski yesterday with Will and Colton, which was a blast."

"If you can keep up with them," Izzy said, "you can keep up with anyone."

"There's a reason I took today off from the slopes. Everything hurts after trying to keep up with them."

The back door opened. "Hello in there? Is it safe to come in?"

Izzy rolled her eyes. "Come in, Ness. It's safe."

"Oh, hey," Vanessa said to Lucy and Cameron before her gaze shifted to Troy and stuck there for a second. No one else would've noticed that, but Izzy did. "Sorry to interrupt. I can come back later."

"Nonsense." Cameron jumped up to get another bowl, plate and spoon. "Join us. We made a ton."

"Are you sure you don't mind?" Ness asked.

"Positive." Izzy reached out her right hand to her sister. "Come sit by me."

Vanessa put a plate on the counter. "I baked you some cookies."

"Thank you." Izzy was going to need a crowbar to get through the door with the way her family was feeding her. But she'd worry about that after she was fully recovered and able to get back to her active lifestyle. For now, she'd eat the cookies and not worry about the consequences.

Vanessa sat next to her and accepted the bowl of soup that Cameron handed her. "Thanks. This smells yummy."

"It's so good," Izzy told her. "Troy, this is my sister Vanessa Coleman. Vanessa, meet Troy, friend to Cameron, Lucy and Emma."

"Troy Kennedy," he said. "And it's nice to meet you."

"I feel like I've seen you before," Ness said.

"At the weddings," Lucy said.

"Ah, right. That's it."

They talked about skiing, life in Vermont versus life in New York City and the lack of cell service in Butler and how crazy-making that could be for people used to being tethered to phones.

"Every time I'm here," Troy said, "it's like a shock to my system being cut off from the rest of the world."

"Eh," Cameron said, "you get used to it."

"I don't think I ever would," Troy said.

"When I first moved to Boston after growing up here," Vanessa said, "I had trouble getting used to being constantly reachable in multiple formats—texts, calls, social media, etc. It was a bit overwhelming. Still is, to be honest."

"That's interesting," Troy said. "I never would've thought of it that way."

Vanessa shrugged. "It's all what you're used to, I guess." She had light brown hair and lovely hazel eyes in a shade similar to Izzy's.

"Indeed," Troy said.

Izzy glanced at Cameron, who raised a brow in her direction, confirming Izzy wasn't the only one noticing a spark of potential interest between the two of them. Nothing would make Izzy happier than for her delightful younger sister to find someone special.

Cabot came into the kitchen. "Sorry to be late for lunch," he said in a teasing tone.

Cameron introduced him to Troy, and the two men shook hands.

"Pleasure to meet you," Cabot said.

"Likewise," Troy said before returning to his seat. "So you're Mia's father, right?"

"That's right," Cabot said, smiling as he helped himself to some of the soup while Cameron put a sandwich on a plate for him.

Chairs were moved to make room for him at the table.

While being injured totally sucked, Izzy had to admit that the social gatherings that'd followed her accident were rather fun. Normally at this time of the year, when the holidays were over and it was freezing outside, everyone hunkered down for the winter until the sap started to run and the family was recruited to help at Colton's sugaring facility on Butler Mountain.

She was also thrilled to have Vanessa, Ally and Henry in town for the time being, while Sarah had gone back to nursing school in Boston, and Jackson had also returned to his job in the city. Noah had mentioned something about Vanessa leaving her job due to a problem with one of the men she'd worked with. Izzy wanted to know more about that, so she hoped she got a chance to speak to Ness alone before she left.

They passed a lovely hour with their visitors until Cameron said she needed to get back to work. She and Lucy ran the store's website and e-commerce operation.

"And I need to get back to the mountain to make sure Colton hasn't burned the place down while I was gone," Lucy said. "He requires constant supervision."

"Can you imagine what his kid is going to be like?" Troy asked, smiling.

"I try not to think about it too much," Lucy said.

"You picked a good week to ski, Troy," Cabot said. "I hear we're in for some fresh powder tonight into tomorrow."

"That means a foot of snow is coming," Vanessa said. "It's almost never less than that."

"Damn," Troy said. "That's a lot of snow." To Vanessa, he said, "Do you ski?"

"I know how."

"Maybe you'd like to join me on the mountain this week."

"Sure, that'd be fun."

"I'll get your number from the girls and give you a call."

"Sounds good."

Izzy wanted to jump up and down and clap with excitement, but since she couldn't do that, she celebrated on the inside. She loved that he'd asked her right in front of everyone, like it was no big deal. Confidence in a man was such a turn-on for her, and Troy Kennedy had just shown his cards to the entire group. Izzy liked that.

"Thank you all so much for the company and the delicious lunch," Izzy said. "I so appreciate it."

"We're glad to see you doing better," Cameron said when she kissed Izzy's cheek.

"What she said," Lucy said, bending to do the same, but stopping midway. "Ouch. *Ugh*, these freaking fake contractions are ridiculous."

"I had them *so bad*," Cameron said. "I feel for you. They're the worst."

Izzy extended her right hand to Lucy to save her from bending. "Thanks again. Take care of yourself."

"Will do. Bruiser here is clearly in charge."

"Nice to see you again, Izzy," Troy said.

"You, too. Enjoy your week in town."

"I will."

Cabot saw them out and then got busy putting dishes in the dishwasher. "I'm going back to the office, unless you ladies need anything."

"We're good," Izzy said for herself and her sister. "Thank you."

"All right. Call me if you need me."

"Will do."

"Nice to see you, Vanessa."

"You, too. Thanks for taking such good care of Iz."

"That's a pleasure."

CHAPTER SIX

"You will never know true happiness until you have truly loved, and you will never understand what pain really is until you have lost it."
— Unknown

*V*anessa raised her brows, her expression full of intrigue. "A pleasure, is it?" she asked after he'd left the room.

"Oh, hush."

"How are things in the love shack?"

"Very hot. I mean between my busted arm, my surgically repaired abdomen and split lip, we're just getting busy nonstop. Around the clock."

"Haha, I'm glad to see your sarcasm was unaffected by the accident."

"Let's talk about Troy asking you out right in front of everyone."

"He didn't ask me out. He asked me to ski."

"He asked you *out*, you nitwit."

"Whatever you say, and nice deflection off you onto me."

"Your situation is much more interesting than mine. Trust me on that."

Ness looked over her shoulder to make sure they were alone. "So *nothing* is happening on the Cabot front?"

"Nothing... much."

"Mom said he absolutely *insisted* on being the one to care for you at home."

"Yep."

"That sounds like a man who's already in a relationship, whether he realizes it or not."

The comment made Izzy question everything. Was it true that she and Cabot were already in a relationship? "I, uh, I don't know if that's true."

"Not every relationship begins the same way, Iz. Some are all in from the word go, others are fits and starts, but they still count as a relationship. Look at Noah and Brianna. They couldn't stand each other, were fighting every day at work until Mrs. Hendricks forced them to spend time together outside of work, and everything changed. Noah said later that looking back, he realized it had started between them long before the night Mrs. Hendricks intervened. All the fighting and stuff... That was part of it."

"I'm so happy for him. No one deserves it more."

"We all deserve love and happiness and good things."

"Yes, we do." Izzy put her uninjured right arm around her sister. "Tell me what happened at work."

"Ugh, do I gotta?"

"Only if you want to."

"The usual misogyny with a successful sales rep getting too familiar with one of the admins, and which one is more valuable to the company?"

"You were every bit as valuable."

"They didn't think so. When I reported it to HR, he tried to get me fired, and I ended up quitting so I'd never have to see his disgusting face again."

"I hope you've talked to Gray about this."

"Not yet," Ness said with a sigh. "It's all too much. I can't even think about it without feeling like complete shit."

"Which is why you need to do something about it so you don't have to feel that way. No one should be treated that way in their place of employment. You were harassed, Ness. You quit because of a hostile work environment. If nothing else, a letter from your attorney brother might lead to a large severance package that would allow you to figure out what's next without having to worry about money."

"True." She rested her head gently on Izzy's shoulder. "It's so exhausting dealing with entitled men."

"Yes, it is. Why do you think I became self-employed long before I could actually afford it?"

"That was why?"

"Yep. There was a guy at my agency who couldn't take no for an answer, and when I reported him, I was told I needed to find a way to work in harmony with my colleagues."

"What the hell is wrong with people?"

"That's a very good question with an answer so long, it would take us all day to list everything that's wrong. I just got so tired of having to fend him off, but I did get even."

Vanessa raised her head and turned to face Izzy. "Do tell."

"About a week after my last day at the office, I went to his house one evening."

"Stop it! You did not!"

"I did. I took a friend with me in case it turned bad, but I went right up to his front door and rang the bell. His wife came to the door. I said, 'I'm Isabella Coleman, and I used to work with Tim. Is he here?'"

"She said, 'Yes, he is, come in.' I said I'd prefer to wait outside because there was no way I was going inside that house. While she went to get him, his little kids came to see who was there, and I met his daughter and two sons."

"Oh my God, Iz. You're such a badass!"

"My knees were quivering the whole time. Part of me felt like a deranged lunatic to be showing up there like that, but I wanted him to know I could do damage to him, too."

"So what happened? Did you see him?"

"Yep. He came to the front porch, where I was having an animated conversation with his kids, and went absolutely pale at the sight of me."

"This is the best thing I've ever heard," Vanessa said, laughing. "Keep going."

"He said, 'Wh-what're you doing here?' I said, 'Looking for you.' He glanced over his shoulder where his wife was watching and then back at me. 'What do you want?' he asked. I handed him the letter I'd written about the reasons I'd left the firm and detailed how he'd sexually harassed me for months. I'd documented every instance with the date and time and the particulars of exactly what he said to me. I put him on notice that I could file a civil suit at any moment against him and his employer and that I wouldn't hesitate to do so if I heard so much as one word from my former coworkers about him harassing anyone else the way he'd harassed me."

"You're my hero, Iz. Truly."

"Nah, I was just fed up with his shit and wanted to take back some of the power I'd ceded to him."

"What did he say?"

"I didn't give him a chance to say anything else. I just said, 'You all have a nice evening,' and I left. But I heard later he got fired for fudging his sales numbers, and his wife left him after she caught him messing around with another woman. Some men just can't change their ways, no matter how many warnings they receive."

"It's ridiculous. At what point do they change from sweet young boys to predators who think women are there for their entertainment?"

"I'm not sure when, but it happens far too often."

"Yes, it does. After hearing what you did, I'm going to talk to Gray about the options with my situation. You confronted the guy *in front of his wife and kids*! I can sic a lawyer on mine."

"That's my girl."

"Now tell me all you know about Mr. Tall, Dark and Dreamy."

"So you noticed he was dreamy, huh?"

"Shut up and start talking."

Laughing, Izzy said, "I only know him through Cam, Lucy and Emma, who were his best friends in the city until they all moved up here. They were all sad to leave him behind when they left."

"What does he do?"

"I believe he's an attorney."

"Interesting. That's all you've got?"

"That's about it, but I'm sure Emma could fill you in if you wanted more info."

"Probably."

"I was thrilled when he asked you to go skiing right in front of everyone. I love that kind of confidence in a guy when he's a good one and not some icky SOB."

"It was kind of surprising when he came right out and asked me that."

"Confidence is sexy."

"If you say so."

"I say so, and as I'm the older and wiser sister, you have to listen to me."

"Okay, then."

"So, Dad is coming around two."

Ness glanced at the clock on the stove. "Thanks for the warning so I can get out of here."

"Why?" Izzy asked in a teasing tone. "You don't want to see him?"

"Not even kinda. Do you?"

"Not really, but he asked nicely, so I agreed. I figure it's no biggie to give him half an hour of my time."

"It's way more than he deserves."

"Probably."

"*Definitely*. You want me to stay so you don't have to see him alone?"

"That's okay. Cabot will be here."

"You're sure?"

"I am, but if you wouldn't mind giving me a hand up, I'd like to use the bathroom and move to the sofa before he comes."

"I gotcha." Ness helped her up and walked her slowly to the bathroom.

"I'm stiff from sitting too long."

"Do you need meds or anything?"

"I'm trying to go without them."

"And how's that working out?"

Izzy grimaced. "I think I'd like one."

"I'll get it for you."

"They're on the counter next to the sink."

"You need help in there?"

"Fortunately, I can do that myself." Although it wasn't easy with only one working arm. Thankfully, her right hand was her dominant hand. She couldn't fathom how she would've functioned if her right arm had been broken. After she used the facilities and struggled her way back into the stretchy leggings that were easier than anything with zippers, she stood facing the mirror, looking at what her father would see when he arrived.

Would it bother him that her face was so badly bruised, or her lip swollen from connecting with the steering wheel—or so she was told. Izzy didn't remember much about the accident itself beyond knowing the car was in a skid she couldn't control.

Ness was right. She probably shouldn't have agreed to see him, but after having served as the family's peacemaker for most of her life, that was a hard habit to break. Yes, some things were definitely unforgivable, and Mike Coleman's transgressions certainly fell into that category. Seeing him didn't mean she forgave him, but she'd decided a long time ago to let go of the damage he'd done to her life and the lives of her mother and siblings. That baggage was just too heavy for her to carry around forever.

Letting it go had been a process that had taken several years to fully execute, but she'd done the work and was better for it. But that didn't mean the others felt the same way she did. Most of them wouldn't have crossed the street to see him. Izzy had found that among the eight of them were eight different opinions when it came to Mike. The four eldest—Grayson, Noah, herself and Vanessa—tended to be much more bitter than their younger siblings, the youngest of whom barely remembered him living with them.

But they all recalled the struggle to get by without his income and presence.

The older four had been more like parents than siblings to the younger ones, and that, too, had caused its own set of challenges. How many times had one of them heard "you're not my mother" or "you're not my father" from a younger sibling who didn't want to hear it from an older one? Too many to count.

Life in their home had not been easy after Mike left, and the fallout was still part of their lives more than twenty years later.

Ness knocked on the bathroom door. "You okay in there, Iz?"

"Yep." She opened the door and greeted her sister with a smile. "You'd better get out of here if you don't want to run into Mike."

"I'm out."

"Keep me posted on everything, especially skiing with Troy."

Ness rolled her eyes. "Will do. Don't tell anyone about that, okay?"

"Uh, I hate to say that it happened in front of Cameron and Lucy, so it might be too late to contain it. Not that I think they'll tell the world, but as you well know, in our family, they only have to tell one person for it to be all over town."

"Ugh, and you wonder why I moved to Boston for college and never came back?"

"I don't actually wonder."

The sisters shared a laugh and a gentle hug.

"Thanks for not kicking it in that accident," Ness said, sounding a bit tearful. "I wouldn't know what to do without you."

"I'm not going anywhere."

"Thank goodness for that."

Izzy shuffled along behind Ness as she walked to the door.

"Go sit down," Ness said. "I can see myself out."

"I'm fine. Don't worry. Thanks for the cookies and the visit."

"You got it. I'm just hanging out at Noah's and job hunting. Call me if you need anything."

"Will do."

Vanessa started to walk out, but stopped and turned to face

Izzy, her expression fierce. "Don't let *him* do anything to hurt you. Do you hear me?"

"I do. Don't worry. I'll be fine."

"I'll worry. Call me later."

"I will."

Vanessa walked out and got into the small Toyota SUV that had once belonged to their late grandmother, Sarah. Their grandfather, Elmer, kept it running in case anyone needed it. In a family the size of theirs, someone always needed it.

Izzy waved to Vanessa and turned away from the door to find Cabot entering the kitchen.

"Did you have a nice visit with your sister?"

"I did."

"I think it's interesting how you and your siblings all have very different looks, but still resemble each other."

"We've heard that all our lives. Teachers have said they'd know a Coleman anywhere even if we all had our own individual look. They probably had a warning system in place any time another Coleman was going to be in their class."

"That's funny," he said, chuckling. "Were you a bunch of hellions, then?"

"Hellions is a strong word, but there was a certain lack of supervision since our dad was gone and our mom was working so much. The younger ones ran a little bit wild, but none of us was ever in any real trouble or anything."

"Which is a freaking miracle, when you think about it."

"Yeah."

"Your father is due soon."

"Uh-huh."

"You feeling okay about that?"

"I guess. It is what it is."

He tipped his head and raised a brow.

"Took me a lot of therapy to be able to say, 'it is what it is.'"

"Thank God for therapy, huh?"

"You know it. I wish some of my siblings would get some to deal with the residual issues from childhood. There's still a lot of anger."

"Does that ever really go away in a situation like yours or mine?"

"Not entirely, but it does get easier to manage the further from it you get."

"Does it, though?" He shrugged. "Sometimes I feel as furious as I did the day I finally realized they weren't missing, but that Deb had taken off with Mia. That fire has burned inside me for so long, I can't picture life without it."

"Have you tried?"

"What do you mean?"

"Have you tried to picture your life without it? Have you tried to imagine just letting it go and putting it in the past as something that happened to you but no longer defines you?"

"What are these words you speak of? Let it go? How does that work?"

Smiling, Izzy said, "I'd be happy to give you some pointers later, if you're interested."

"I'm very interested."

The three-word sentence and the way he said it only added to Izzy's confusion where he was concerned. Was he interested in pointers on how to let go of stuff from the past, or was he interested in *her?* The question would have to wait, however, because a knock on the door indicated her father had arrived right on time.

"You want me to hang with you for this?"

"Nah, go on back to work. I'll be fine."

He kissed her forehead. "If you're not fine, give me a yell."

As she watched him walk away, Izzy had so many questions. More than she'd had earlier, if that was possible.

CHAPTER SEVEN

"Don't feel sad over someone who gave up on you, feel sorry for them because they gave up on someone who would have never given up on them." —Frank Ocean

Izzy shuffled to the door and opened it to her dad, startled by the changes in him since she'd last seen him.

He'd lost most of his blondish-gray hair, and his eyebrows were wisps, as if maybe they were growing back after his cancer treatment.

"Come in."

"Thank you. It's nice to see you."

She refused to say it was nice to see him, too. There were some things she just couldn't give him. Not anymore. "It's nice to be seen after a near miss."

"I know what you mean."

"You look well."

"No, I don't, but it beats the alternative."

"Yes, I suppose so."

He took off his coat, hung it over one of her kitchen chairs and took a measuring look at her. "You're feeling okay?"

"Better than I was, but a ways to go. Can I offer you something? I have coffee and water, and I think there's some soda in the fridge."

"Water would be great, but I can help myself."

Izzy directed him to the cabinets, the contents of which her mother knew by heart. This was the first time her father had visited her home of eight years.

"I love your place," he said when he was settled next to her on the sofa, bringing water for them both.

"Thanks."

"Are those yours?" he asked of the framed photos on the wall.

"Yep, it's cheaper to frame my own stuff than to buy other people's work."

"Your work is extraordinary, Isabella." He'd never called her Izzy. Only Isabella. She'd forgotten that little detail.

"Thank you."

"How long will you be out of work?"

"Could be three months."

He winced. "Will you be all right?"

She wanted to ask where that concern had been when he'd left his family without a financial safety net, but she stifled that thought. "I'm okay. I have some money saved for rainy days."

"That's smart."

"Yes, Uncle Linc has always preached savings to all of us, for something just like this."

"Good old Uncle Linc," Mike said with an edge to his voice Izzy didn't appreciate. If he said one negative word about the uncle who'd been there for them when their own father wasn't, Izzy wouldn't be responsible for her actions. "How is he?"

"He's very good. He recently reconnected with his siblings and got to see his father before he passed."

"I never knew why he was on the outs with them."

"Doesn't matter now, but it wasn't his doing."

"How's your mother?"

"She's wonderful."

"That's good. I'm glad to hear it. She deserves to be happy."

"Yes, she does, and her boyfriend, Ray, makes her very happy."

"Oh, I hadn't heard that she was seeing someone."

"Has been for a while now."

"That's great news."

He seemed far more excited about that than Izzy would've thought.

"I'm engaged," he said.

"Oh, well, congratulations."

"Thank you. Ellen has been wonderful through my illness. She was so supportive and loving. I got lucky when I found her."

"Does she know about us?"

"Yes, of course she does."

"Does she wonder why you don't see us?"

"I, uh, told her there'd been some issues, and it was better this way."

"Maybe you ought to tell her the truth before you marry her."

He didn't like that. Too bad.

"The thing is, I was wondering… Your mother never signed the divorce papers, and it would be helpful—to both of us, that is —if she'd do that one of these days."

"Is that why you're here pretending to be concerned about me? Because you want something from her?"

"Of course not," he said indignantly. "I wanted to see you and make sure you're all right."

"I'm fine. Thanks for coming by."

The French doors to the office opened, and Cabot came out.

Mike stood and extended his hand to Cabot. "Mike Coleman."

Only because he was too polite not to, Cabot shook his hand. "Cabot Lodge."

"He was just leaving," Izzy told Cabot.

"I'll show you out," Cabot said.

Mike glanced at Izzy, as if there was something else he wanted to say to ensure she understood his true motivation for visiting. Thankfully, he thought better of it. "It was real good to see you, Isabella."

"Thank you." What else could she say? She wasn't about to tell him it'd been good to see him, because it hadn't. She was such a fool for continuing to hope, after all this time, that he might become a better man. Clearly, that was never going to happen.

The irony of the two men currently in her house wasn't lost on her—one was a father who'd left, and the other was a father who'd been left. They couldn't be more opposite.

Cabot was cordial to him as he escorted him out, closing the door behind Mike and returning to her.

Izzy was furious about the tears burning her eyes. The last freaking thing she wanted was to shed any more tears over the man who'd fathered and abandoned her.

"What happened?" Cabot asked when he sat next to her and took hold of her hand.

"Can we talk about it later?"

"Of course. What can I do for you?"

"Help me up? I think I'd like to lie down for a while before dinner."

"You got it." He carefully helped her up, held her until she was steady and then walked with her to the bedroom.

Izzy sat gently on the bed, giving the pain time to recede and adjust to the movement.

Cabot helped her to get settled on the bed and then covered her with the throw blanket she kept across the foot of her bed. "What else can I do?"

"Keep me company?" She patted the other side of the bed.

"I can do that." He kicked off his shoes and walked around to the other side. When he was settled, moving carefully so he wouldn't jostle her, he took hold of her hand again.

After a long period of silence, Izzy said, "I never want to see him again."

"Aw, Izzy. I'm sorry."

"It infuriates me that he can still do this to me more than twenty years later, as if I'm fourteen again, and my dad has just let us know he'd rather be anywhere than with us."

"That pain never really goes away. You just learn to live with it."

"Yes," she said, sighing. "That's true. I was thinking that you two are the exact opposite as fathers—one who left and one who was left."

"I never would've left Mia, even if it meant staying with Deb, who made me miserable after the first year or so. I would've done whatever I had to in order to be there for my daughter."

"She was always lucky to have you, even during the years you spent apart."

"Thank you for saying so, but that doesn't change the fact that she grew up without a father in her life, which is the part that makes me the angriest. That didn't have to happen."

"No, it didn't, but you're making it up to her now, and she obviously adores you."

"You think so?"

"I know so. I saw it with my own eyes at the wedding and since you've been here. She's so happy to have you close by."

"I love having her right down the road. I'm thinking about buying a place up here so I can spend more time here."

His words hit Izzy like a punch to her wounded gut. If he was thinking about buying a place in Vermont, did that mean he really wasn't interested in a relationship with her? If he was, he wouldn't need his own place. Trying to figure out what he was thinking was adding to her exhaustion. Here he was lying on her bed, holding her hand, taking care of her, and what did it all mean?

"Would that be okay with you? If I spent more time here?"

"What's it got to do with me? It's about you being with your daughter."

"And you."

Izzy closed her eyes. "I can't figure you out, Cabot."

"What do you mean?"

"I just… I can't make sense of what we're doing. You tell me you don't do relationships, but it sort of feels like we might be in one. Then you say you want to buy a place up here so you can be closer to Mia—and me."

"Of course you'd be part of me wanting to spend more time here."

"But this isn't a relationship, right?"

"I, um, I mean it could be?"

"Are you trying to talk yourself into it?" Izzy opened her eyes. "Because that's just what every girl wants."

"I told you I'm a mess."

"No, you're not. You've just convinced yourself that you are so you have an excuse to avoid things like this," she said, giving their joined hands a squeeze to make her point.

"I thought you'd see it as a good sign that I want to buy a place up here."

"Cabot, if you're *with* me, you wouldn't need your own place here," she said, releasing a deep sigh.

"Oh, well, I wouldn't want to impose on you."

"If I suddenly start screaming, I want you to know you've driven me to it."

"I'm sorry. I tried to tell you I suck at this."

"No, you don't. You're just out of practice. Let me make this easy on you, okay?"

"That'd be good."

"I like you. I think you like me. I want to be with you. I think maybe you'd like to be with me. So why don't we just give it a whirl and see what we think of it while we have this time together?"

Cabot glanced at their joined hands. "My greatest concern would be that I'd hurt you somehow because, despite how it might appear on the outside, I'm still super fucked up on the inside."

"I don't think that's as true as you think it is. You've been such a good friend to me since the accident, and all I see is a man who gives of himself to others. I've read about your philanthropy and your youth mentoring program in Boston. I've seen how you've devoted yourself to rebuilding your relationship with your daughter. Is there damage from things that happened in the past? Sure, but at our age, we all have that."

He seemed to be thinking about what she said.

"But here's the thing, Cabot. I'm not going to try to talk you into something you don't want. I fully respect your right to say this isn't for you, even if I'll be sorry we didn't get a chance to see what it might be."

"I want to try. I'm just not sure I can."

"Only you can decide that, but I need to draw a line in the sand."

He looked up at her. "What do you mean?"

"If you don't want this with me, I'll be sad about it, but I'll get over it. If you stay for a couple more weeks, I may not get over it so quickly. And frankly, I'd rather not put myself through that. So, you need to decide. Either you're in or you're out. If you're out, you have to go. I can't do this to myself."

"I don't want to go."

Izzy raised a brow. "Okay..."

"Since we met last June, I've thought of you so often, and the thing I kept coming back to is that for the first time since everything happened, I'd found someone who made me wish my life could be different."

"It *can* be, Cabot. But only you can open that door. I can't force it open for you."

"The door cracked open in June, a little more so in October, and it's been wide open since I heard you'd been so badly hurt, and all I knew was I needed to get to you as quickly as possible. The door is wide open, Izzy, and that scares the crap out of me."

She released his hand and placed hers on his face. "You don't need to be afraid of me."

"Yes, I do."

Shaking her head, she said, "No. Never." She drew him closer to her, and he took the hint, kissing her softly and carefully so as not to hurt her healing lip. "I can't wait for my damned lip to heal so I can do that properly."

His smile made his eyes sparkle, which was a nice look on him. "I'm looking forward to that."

"Are you? Really?"

"Yes, really. You're so brave and confident. I wish I could be more like you."

"You're brave and confident. Look at the business you've built."

"I'm good with the business stuff. It's the personal side that needs work."

"Then we'll work on it together. You'll be like this place was when I first bought it. A true fixer-upper."

Laughing, he said, "That about sums me up." He reached over to lightly caress her face. "I want you to know something…" After a deep breath, he seemed to struggle with his emotions. "There's been no one else, in all these years, who made me want the things that you do."

Izzy's heart soared at the words she'd longed to hear from him. "All you had to do was say so."

"Turns out that's easier said than done."

"Nah, you've got this. You're doing great so far. You can tell me anything, and I promise I want to hear it."

"It's that simple?"

"Yep."

"I didn't mean to make this so difficult."

"It's okay."

"No, it isn't, but I hope you'll let me try to explain it a little."

"I'm here all day."

Smiling, he took her hand again. "When I heard about the accident and how bad it had been, all I could think about was how stupid I'd been this last year, squandering the two chances you'd given me to start something with you. But then when I got here and spent time with you and realized everything I'd felt then was still there, only *more* so, I didn't know what to do about it. It'd been so long since I'd wanted anything like this that I'd forgotten how it works."

"You haven't forgotten. You're just out of practice."

"What if I turn out to be the worst boyfriend you've ever had?"

She snorted out a laugh. "That's not possible."

"No?"

"If you can refrain from cheating on me with my close friend, you'll never reach that distinction."

"That actually happened? To *you*?"

Brows furrowed in confusion at his meaning, she said, "Yep."

"I can't believe anyone who was lucky enough to have you in their life would be that stupid."

Her heart gave a giddy little lurch that made her feel breathless and hopeful and so many other things that she couldn't process them all. "See? You'll never be the worst boyfriend I ever had."

"I want to be the best."

"That's a good place to start."

CHAPTER EIGHT

"It's hard asking someone with a broken heart to fall in love again."
—Eric Kripke

ours later, Cabot was still floating on air thinking about the conversation with Izzy and what they'd agreed to. He felt like he'd staggered his way, like a drunken sailor, into committing to more than just friendship with her, nearly bungling it beyond repair before she finally showed him the way forward.

She was like a lighthouse beacon, guiding him out of the darkness that had been part of him for so long, he didn't recall life without it.

He couldn't remember ever feeling this kind of excitement or what it was like to be falling into something that was starting to feel a lot like love, which he'd studiously avoided since his marriage ended in disaster. It hadn't been like this with Deb. They'd jumped straight into bed and were married before he'd woken up to realize they had nothing in common, and their marriage was already on the road to failure.

They'd been young and stupid, but before they could go their separate ways, Mia had arrived. For a time, he'd thought they might fix what was wrong between them, but when they realized that was never going to happen, Deb had filed for divorce. That's when things between them started getting ugly.

He'd handled it badly. He'd never deny that. For years after she left with Mia, he'd relived those months, cringing over some of the things he'd said to her, his threats of harsh legal action. Those threats had driven her to run. It'd taken him a few years to understand that he wasn't blameless in what'd happened, not that he'd deserved to be kept from his child for all that time. He hadn't done anything to deserve that special brand of torture.

God, he hadn't thought of this shit in so long. Since Mia had come back into his life, with the caveat that all charges against her mother be dropped, Cabot had focused ruthlessly on the future rather than dwelling on a past he couldn't change. But his feelings for Izzy had forced him to confront mistakes he didn't want to make again. She was too important, too precious, too... everything.

While she napped, he'd gone to the grocery store to get what he needed to make vegan tacos with portobello mushrooms for Wade and Mia. He'd looked up the recipe online and was fairly confident he could pull it off. He and Izzy would have some of the mountain of food her family had brought them over the last few days.

As he cooked dinner for his daughter and her husband, Cabot tried to keep his thoughts in the present, which was a rather nice place to be. Apparently, he had a new girlfriend for the first time in decades. His daughter was back in his life and happily married to a man Cabot would've hand-picked for her. Soon enough, she would probably make him a grandfather, and he'd have the chance to watch her children grow up.

The knife he was using to chop the portobello suspended in midair when another thought occurred to him. Did Izzy want children? His mouth went dry, and a bead of sweat appeared on his brow. He used his sleeve to wipe it away and noticed his hand was trembling.

Holy shit. The thought had never crossed his mind. He was too old for that now. Wasn't he? Men far older than he was had children all the time, but he was so far past that time in his life that the thought of starting over with children at his age was nearly laughable. Except he'd committed to a relationship with a woman twelve years his junior who didn't have children.

Cabot sat down hard in a kitchen chair, rattled to his core by questions only Izzy could answer. He didn't want to wake her, but he needed to know. And what would he do if she said she wanted kids?

He had no idea.

AFTER VANESSA LEFT IZZY'S, SHE DID A BUNCH OF ERRANDS before she ended up at Grayson's home. She needed to *act* before she lost the nerve she'd worked up while with her older sister. Izzy had always been a source of strength and wisdom to Vanessa and their other siblings. After hearing about Izzy's accident, she, Sarah, Ally and Henry had jumped into Ally's car and headed for Vermont, driving for hours without knowing if Izzy would survive her injuries.

That'd been the longest night of Vanessa's life as she tried to picture a world without her older sister. She couldn't and was so, so thankful Izzy had come through the accident with injuries that would heal in time. It'd been a long time since Vanessa had prayed for anything the way she had for her sister during that endless drive to Vermont.

Putting four Colemans in any situation usually resulted in laughs and jeers and nonstop sibling nonsense. Not that night. They'd ridden in terrified silence for four hours.

Vanessa shook off those dreadful memories as she pulled into Gray's driveway at the restored church he, Emma and Simone called home. Emma's dad, Ray, had an apartment over the garage in back, but he was spending most of his time with Vanessa's mom these days. She was so happy for her mom to have found a great guy like Ray after so many years alone. No one in the world deserved a happy second chance more than Hannah Coleman did.

She trudged through sloppy snow and ice to Gray's mudroom door, where she rang the bell.

Her eldest sibling came to the door and smiled when he saw her there. "Hey," he said. "This is a nice surprise. Come in."

"Hope I'm not disturbing you."

"Of course not."

In the warm, cozy kitchen, Ray was helping Simone with her homework while Gray stood watch over a pot on the stove.

"Hey, guys," Vanessa said.

"Good to see you, Ness," Ray said.

"Hi," Simone said with a shy smile. She was eleven, with curly red hair and green eyes, and looked much more like her aunt Lucy than her mom, Emma, who was blonde.

"Nice to see you both," Vanessa said.

"What's going on?" Gray asked as he took her coat and hung it on the back of a chair.

"I need your professional advice."

"Carry on, citizens," Gray said to Ray and Simone, before leading the way through the wide family room that made up the center of the unique home. "Step into my office."

"This house is amazing."

"We love it, except for how all the heat ends up there." He pointed to the twenty-foot ceiling. "We may have to close that off at some point if we don't want to freeze to death down here."

"I never would've thought of that."

"We didn't either, until we spent a winter here. Thank goodness for the woodstove, but we go through some kind of wood heating this place."

"I'll bet."

He closed the French doors that sealed off his office.

"This is nice," Vanessa said.

"I love working from home. It's the best."

"You got enough to do in this sleepy town?"

"More than enough. Being general counsel to the store is a nearly full-time job alone, and now Mom's roped me into being the town solicitor. I've got my hands full."

"It's great that you were able to move home and figure out a life for yourself here."

"Is that what you want to do, too?"

Vanessa shrugged. "It's starting to look pretty good to me."

"I heard you quit your job. What's up with that?"

"That's what I wanted to talk to you about." Vanessa took a deep breath and then dove into the story of the coworker who'd made her life miserable at her job. "He's one of their top salespeople, so when I complained to HR about him being inappropriate, it fell on deaf ears. He tried to turn it around on me, that I was hitting on him, which was revolting."

Grayson had taken notes as she walked him through what'd happened.

"I finally quit rather than have to fend him off every day, but I documented every single thing that happened. I can provide dates, times, exact words and reports to HR that went nowhere. I have it all."

"That's excellent."

"My brother the lawyer taught me well."

"You have the grounds for a gigantic lawsuit here, Ness. You realize that, don't you?"

"That's what everyone tells me."

"Is that what you want to do?"

She released a deep sigh. "Part of me wants to forget that place and that asshole exist. The other part of me doesn't want them to get away with it. People shouldn't feel intimidated to go to work or have to fend off unwelcome advances from coworkers who outrank them."

"No, they absolutely shouldn't." He put down his pen and rested his elbows on the desk. "Here's what I think we should do. I could reach out to the company's general counsel and let them know we have the makings of a world-class lawsuit and the wherewithal to see it through. I'd need your documentation to make my case to their counsel. I have a feeling they'll be very eager to settle when they hear what we have."

"Settle. What would that entail?"

"A severance package for you that includes two years' salary, a cash bonus to be determined and all your benefits continued until you accept a new position. Something like that."

"What about him? What happens to him?"

"We could suggest they part company with him."

"They won't. He brings in too much money for them."

"They will if we make that a condition of the settlement."

"You really think they'd go for it?"

"If I had to guess, their goal would be to avoid a public lawsuit that'd bring negative publicity to their company. Getting rid of him would be a lesser price to pay in the grand scheme of things."

"Wow. It never occurred to me that I might be able to do something like this."

"You suffered sexual harassment in a hostile work environment that your company's HR officials were aware of and ignored. That's a lawsuit looking for a place to happen, but only if you want to go that route."

Vanessa thought about Izzy showing up at the home of the man who'd hassled her and how brave she'd been. "Yes, I think I want to do it."

Grayson stood, went to his file cabinet and withdrew a packet of paper that he handed to her. "My standard retention letter. If you give me a dollar and sign that, I'll be officially retained to represent you."

"I need to give you more than a dollar!"

"I'd do this for free, Ness. The dollar is a formality."

"Are you sure?"

"Absolutely. No one messes with my sister and gets away with it."

Moved by his support, she flipped to the last page of the document and signed her name. She didn't need to read it to know she was getting the best possible attorney to represent her. Then she fished a dollar out of her wallet and handed it over with the document.

"Next, I need the documentation of everything that happened."

Firing up her cell phone, which was mostly useless in Butler, she found the list of events she'd begun keeping more than a year ago in her Notes app. "What's the Wi-Fi info?"

After he gave her the log-in and password, she signed in and emailed the list to him.

His laptop chimed to indicate a new message.

Vanessa watched as he scrolled through the information, his eyes widening several times at the sheer outrageousness of it.

"I'm so sorry you had to deal with this, Ness," he said softly. "I'd bet anything you're not the first woman to be hassled by this guy."

"I'm sure I'm not. I think there're others in the company, but they keep quiet because they need the job. I mean, I needed it, too, but not that badly."

"I'll reach out to their counsel tomorrow and see what we can do for you."

"Thank you so much, Gray. I appreciate this more than you'll ever know."

"I'm very happy to take care of this for you, but I wish you'd told me about it a long time ago."

"I thought I was handling it, you know?"

"Yeah," he said, sighing. "I get it."

"I'll let you get back to your family."

Gray stood up, came around the desk and reached a hand out to her.

Vanessa took it and stood.

He hugged her. "You're my family, too. You always will be."

She held on tight to the older brother who had been a rock for her and their other siblings. "Thank you for always being there for us."

"That's my job as the oldest and wisest."

"Haha, you had to ruin it."

"That's also my job," he said, releasing her. "Did you see Iz today?"

"I did. She's still black and blue, but seems to be moving around a little better than she was. When I left, she was waiting for Dad to show up."

"Ugh. She told me she'd heard from him."

"I guess he just wants to see that she's okay."

"Now that he has my bone marrow, I wish he'd go away and leave us all alone."

"Me, too."

He opened the French doors and gestured for her to lead the way to the kitchen. "I'll check on Iz later to see what happened with *him*."

"I'm sure she handled him just fine."

"Probably, but seeing him is still tough, even after all this time."

"I hate that he's still upsetting us."

"I know. It's such bullshit."

When they stepped into the kitchen, Vanessa immediately noticed Emma had arrived with Troy Kennedy, who smiled widely when he saw Vanessa.

"We meet again," he said.

"So it seems."

"I heard you guys met at Izzy's, and you're going skiing," Emma said as she accepted a kiss from Grayson.

Troy had told Emma about meeting her. What did that mean? And why did she care? The man was incredibly handsome, but he probably knew it.

"Did you tell him you're not much of a skier?" Grayson asked Vanessa.

"I didn't have the heart to tell him."

"She's never progressed much past the bunny slope, despite significant effort on the part of many siblings and cousins."

"I suck at it," Vanessa said bluntly.

"Then we'll do something else," Troy said, laser-focused on her.

Vanessa felt her face get warm. "Sure. Anything is better than skiing."

"You should've said so."

"But you're here to ski."

"I'm here to see friends and escape work for a few days. I don't care what I do as long as it doesn't involve a computer or a deposition."

"I hear that," Gray said. "I used to be chained to that crap." He put his arm around Emma, who snuggled into his embrace. "Everything is so much better now."

"I see that," Troy said. "You're all happier than pigs in shit up here in the boonies."

"Um, Mr. Troy," Simone said. "'Shit' is a swear word, so you owe me a dollar."

"You didn't have to repeat the word, madam," Emma said to her daughter.

Troy got out his wallet and retrieved a five-dollar bill that he handed over to Simone. "That's a down payment on four more swears. I'm out of the habit of being around kids since you moved away and left me, so I have a feeling I'm going to slip up again before the week is out."

"I'll start a tab for you," Simone said.

"How does she know about starting tabs?" Troy asked Emma.

"She knows everything. It's kinda scary, actually."

"My baby is the smartest girl in the history of smart girls," Ray said, earning a warm smile from his granddaughter.

"Thanks, Pop."

"I need to get going," Ray said as he stood. "Hannah and I are going out to dinner."

"Where're you going?" Emma asked her father.

"Not sure yet. We like to get in the truck and drive until we find something interesting."

That sounded lovely to Vanessa. "Hey, Ray?" she said.

"Yes, ma'am?"

"You make her really happy, which she very much deserves. Thank you for that."

"Aw, thank you, honey. I love being with her, and making her happy is my only goal."

"We appreciate it," Vanessa said, glancing at Gray.

"We sure do," her brother said.

"Means the world to us that you kids approve," Ray said gruffly.

"We definitely approve," Vanessa said.

"We do, too, Dad," Emma said. "It's wonderful to see two

people who've been through a lot having this marvelous second chance with each other."

"As long as we're putting it all out there, I may as well tell you that you can rent out your garage apartment starting in February."

"And where will you be going, young man?" Emma asked in her sternest mom voice, hands on hips for effect.

"Very funny. You know exactly where to find me."

"I'll take the apartment," Vanessa said on an impulse. "If you don't mind having me underfoot."

"We'd love that," Emma said. "Consider it yours."

She had no idea what she was going to do for work, but she'd figure something out in the next couple of weeks. All she knew for certain was that she didn't want to go back to Boston. After more than a decade there, she'd had enough of city life. Her sublet apartment lease was up in April, and she'd been debating what she wanted to do since quitting her job.

Hearing the apartment at Gray's was opening up had sparked a decision, which was a huge relief.

Ray hugged her, Emma and Simone, shook hands with Gray and Troy and said his goodbyes.

"I love that he and your mom are moving in together," Emma said to Gray. "Don't you?"

"Yes, it's great, and merely a formality since he's practically living there already."

"What *is it* about this place that has people falling in love left and right?" Troy asked. "Everyone I know who's come up here has found true love."

"Not me," Simone said.

"Hahaha." Troy patted her curly red head. "Your day is coming, sweetheart. I have no doubt about that."

"All the boys in my class are stupid," Simone said.

"That's why you have to look at slightly older men," Troy advised. "You need someone more mature, and since boys mature way slower than girls, maybe check out the ninth-grade boys."

"Troy!" Emma said. "She is *not* going to check out high school boys. She's in fifth grade!"

"I'm just saying… That would be her sweet spot. She's probably too mature for them, too."

As Emma glared at him, Vanessa rocked with silent laughter.

"I'll take that under consideration," Simone said.

"You will not," Grayson said. "I'll bring out my shotgun for any boy who dares show his face around here."

"Oh, please," Simone said. "You will not. You'd get disbarred."

"I'll risk it to keep the boys away from my girl."

"Grow up, Gray," Simone said. "I'm going to date eventually, so you'd better prepare yourself."

"I can't," Gray said, adding to Emma, "Make her stop saying these things to me."

While Emma wrapped her arms around Grayson, she said, "Simone, stop upsetting your dad this way."

Laughter exploded out of Vanessa. She laughed so hard, she couldn't breathe. "I love you so much, Simone. You remind me of me and our other sisters telling Grayson to stop glaring at the boys who came to the house. I can give you some pointers for how to work around him when the time comes."

"Good to know," Simone said. "I think he's going to be a problem."

"You think right," Gray said.

"Can you guys stay for dinner?" Emma asked Vanessa and Troy. "I made a ton of chicken chili, although I'll warn you it's a new recipe, so I have no idea how it came out."

"I took a little sample earlier," Gray said. "It's awesome."

"Well, there you have it," Emma said. "Can you stay?"

"If you're sure it's no problem, I'd love to," Vanessa said.

"What she said," Troy said, using his thumb to point to Vanessa.

"Excellent," Emma said. "It's a party!"

CHAPTER NINE

"You weren't just a star to me. You were my whole damn sky."
—Unknown

*I*zzy forced herself to put on a happy face for Cabot, Mia and Wade during dinner, but she felt sick on the inside over the visit with her father. More than anything, she hated that he could still make her feel like shit all these years later. That was like his superpower or something, making his kids feel like shit every time they saw him or had contact with him.

"What do you think, Izzy?" Mia asked.

"I'm sorry," Izzy said. "What did you say?"

"I said Dad ought to move to Vermont so he can live near us."

"He said something about getting a place up here," Izzy said, "but I told him he can use my house as his Vermont base."

"That sounds promising." Mia's gaze darted between her and Cabot. "Anything you want to tell your daughter, Pops?"

Cabot smiled as he held out a hand to Izzy.

She put her right hand in his, sighing when he curled his fingers around hers.

"It seems I've got myself a girlfriend," Cabot said.

Mia squealed as she clapped and cheered. "I told you!" she said to her husband. "Now pay up!"

"You bet on whether we were together?" Cabot asked.

"Yep, and he lost. He said he thought you were 'just friends.' I said it was more than that, and I was right!"

"And she *loves* to be right," Wade said, amused by his wife. "It's her favorite thing."

"That's a woman thing, son," Cabot said.

"Oh, stuff it," Mia said to her father. "It's because we are, in fact, usually right."

"Do you hear the way she's talking to her old man?" Cabot asked Izzy.

"I do, and I think her old man, who isn't that old, loves the way she talks to him."

"Yes, he does." Cabot seemed as content as Izzy had ever seen him. "He loves it all." He glanced at her as he said that, and Izzy forgot all about her deadbeat dad and anything that wasn't Cabot, how much she cared for him and how excited she was to be starting something meaningful with him.

She fully appreciated how difficult it was for him to commit —and why—so she was determined to show him something better than anything he could've imagined for himself. He had only his failed marriage and the ensuing nightmare with Mia for reference. He'd never been in a successful relationship. She'd been in several that, while they hadn't lasted forever, had brought her joy for a time. Only one of them had ended "badly." The rest fizzled out quietly, but had shown her the difference between good and bad.

Izzy understood the goal and wanted to show him what was possible.

"So how will this work between you crazy kids with Dad living in Boston and Izzy living in Vermont?" Mia asked over dinner.

Izzy had been impressed by the lengths Cabot had gone to make a vegan dinner that Mia and Wade would enjoy. "We haven't gotten that far yet," she said between bites of her cousin Hannah's tasty lasagna.

"We only sort of made it official today," Cabot added.

"Is that right?" Mia raised a brow. "And the fact that you've already been here almost two weeks doesn't count?"

Cabot gave Izzy a deer-in-headlights look.

"She's your daughter," Izzy said.

"She's ten steps ahead of me," Cabot said.

"Don't feel bad," Wade said. "She's usually twenty steps ahead of me."

"Oh, hush," Mia said. "Both of you. I love that Dad met Izzy through us and that he's hanging out in Vermont, but I also know he can't do that forever. What about the council?"

"I've been thinking about resigning from that."

"You have?" Mia and Izzy said in stereo.

Cabot nodded. "For a while now. I've done three terms, and I'm up for reelection this fall. I think I'm going to let someone else take it on. It's a lot on top of a very demanding work life. That frantic schedule suited me when I didn't have anything better to do." His gaze encompassed both Izzy and Mia. "But now I have other things in my life that I didn't have before. If I didn't have the council to deal with, I could work remotely from anywhere, even the cell phone disaster land known as Butler."

"We have cell service at our house," Mia reminded him.

"Ah, yes, you found the one square block in Butler that has service," Cabot said.

"Don't forget Colton's mountain, too," Wade said. "They have the best service up there."

"Good to know," Cabot said. "Maybe I can rent office space on the mountain from Colton."

"He'd be down for that," Wade said, "but you'd have to be willing to see him walking around naked up there."

"Uh... naked?"

Izzy cracked up. "You never know what you'll get when Colton's involved. Just ask Lucy. She'll tell you."

"He's feral," Wade said bluntly. "We left him alone up there for too long, and now he's ruined. We're still amazed that he got a very nice woman to actually marry him."

"And procreate with him," Mia added.

"I can't imagine what Colton's child will be like." Wade

laughed along with the others. "Lucy will have her hands full with the two of them."

Wade glanced out the window. "The snow is really coming down out there."

"Supposed to get a foot tonight," Izzy said.

"You guys are so casual about a foot of snow," Cabot said.

Mia laughed. "We're Vermonters. Flatlanders can never understand how blasé we are about snow that would cripple other places. We're used to it."

"Maybe you guys ought to get home before it gets much worse," Cabot said.

"Are you kicking us out, Pops?" Mia asked.

"Not at all. I just worry about you driving in this weather," he said, looking at Izzy, "especially after recent events."

"We'll be fine," Wade said, "but we should go soon. I've got an early meeting with one of our suppliers, who's coming up from Rutland."

"In Boston, everything would already be canceled for tomorrow," Cabot said.

"You're not in Boston anymore, Toto," Izzy said, smiling at him.

"I guess not."

"Mia, don't forget you have something you wanted to tell your dad," Wade said.

"Oh, right! So I'm changing my name—again."

"To what?" Cabot asked, confused.

"I never got the chance to be a Lodge, so my legal name going forward will be Mia Lodge Abbott, and I plan to go by the full name."

For a moment, Cabot was too undone to speak. "That's amazing, honey. I'm honored that you're taking my name along with Wade's."

She put her hand on top of Cabot's as Izzy placed a hand on his knee. "It should've been my name all along."

"Yes, it should have."

Wade and Mia left a short time later, taking dinner leftovers and the vegan cookies Cabot had made for them to enjoy at home. Mia was excited to not have to cook the next night and had kissed her father on the cheek before she left. "Thank you for all the trouble you went to making a special dinner for us."

"Completely my pleasure," Cabot had said, hugging her.

"You're very cute with your daughter," Izzy said when they were settled on the sofa in front of the woodstove Cabot had kept burning all day.

"She's just the most delightful person. I have to give Deb credit for raising such a lovely young woman."

"It's amazing that you can give her credit for anything."

"I can hate what she did while acknowledging the daughter she raised is magnificent."

"She obviously adores you."

"That makes me feel so lucky. I'm well aware that it could've gone either way. She could've come to Boston, met me and gone on with her life."

"Knowing Mia just a little bit, I don't think she ever could've done that after finding out the truth about you and what'd happened years ago. Does she talk to her mother?"

"Rarely, although Deb tries frequently. She has a lot of unresolved issues with her. Deb told her a lot of lies over the years and did things like set her up with a fake Social Security number that nearly tanked her relationship with Wade when the truth came out. We've talked a little about our feelings toward Deb, but we don't really dwell on that."

"Yeah, I suppose that's counterproductive to building your own relationship with Mia."

"It is, but sometimes I wonder about what she's not saying and whether she's dealing with it all."

"I'm sure she talks to Wade about it."

"I hope so. How about her changing her name? Just when I think I couldn't love her more..."

"It's wonderful."

"I almost broke down when she told me that."

"I know. I could tell you were trying not to."

"It rights another terrible wrong."

"Yes, it certainly does."

He turned to face her and reached for her hand. "As much as I love talking about my daughter, now I want to talk about my new girlfriend."

Smiling, Izzy said, "What about her?"

"Everything about her. I want to know everything."

"That might take a while."

"It seems like we're going to be snowed in, so what better time for you to tell me all about the lovely Isabella Coleman?"

"What do you want to know?"

"Your favorite color, favorite food, favorite sibling, favorite everything. To start with."

"Let's see... Navy blue, Mexican, I don't have a favorite sibling. My favorite book is *Twilight*. I was Team Jacob all the way."

"I have no idea what that means."

"It's okay." She laughed at the face he made. "You don't need to know."

"That was about vampires, right?"

"Yep."

"I don't understand the allure."

"That's because you're very practical and literal."

"My sister Emily says I was born without the suspension-of-disbelief button."

"That sounds about right. You have to suspend disbelief to buy into vampires."

"See? That's a problem for me."

"We'll watch the movies, and then you'll understand."

"If you say so. Could I ask you something else, something a little more... important?"

"Sure."

"What are your thoughts about having kids?"

The question surprised the hell out of her. "Uh, well, I'm not sure."

"Is that something you want?"

"Maybe?" She took a second to get her thoughts together. "Growing up as the oldest girl in a big family, in which the father took off when I was fourteen, I did a lot of parenting long before I should've had to. That sort of made it so I didn't want kids of my own for a long time."

"And now?"

"I think about it. Sometimes. It's not like I'm dying to go there any time soon, but the older I get, the more I seem to think about the time getting away from me."

"You're still a spring chicken."

"Tell that to my moldy eggs."

She loved the sound of his laugh and loved being the one to make it happen. He was so serious all the time that seeing him relax and enjoy himself was such a pleasure. "What about you? Where do you stand on that issue?"

"Well, I have a twenty-seven-year-old daughter."

"Whom you didn't get to raise. Wouldn't it be fun to get to do that?"

"I'm going to be forty-eight in March. I'm getting kind of long in the tooth to be starting a new family."

"Eh, age is a number. You've got a lot of years left, and you should spend them doing things that bring you joy."

"I'm going to be honest with you."

"I would hope so. That's sort of critical to making something like this work."

"I want to make this work, which is why I want to be honest." He looked down at the floor for a second before returning his gaze to her. "Before I met you, the thought of having more kids never occurred to me."

"And now?" she asked, holding her breath.

"I guess I wouldn't rule it out if it was something you really wanted."

"The only way I'd have one was if I knew I could have two. After growing up in a big family, I'd want my child to have at least one sibling."

"I get that, and I agree. I wouldn't have survived everything that happened without my siblings."

"Same. We've been there for each other through everything." She gave him a cute little side-eye. "So have we gone from deciding to be together to talking about kids, all in the same day?"

"I believe we have."

"That has to break some sort of land-speed record."

"I'm twelve years older than you, Izzy. I've got no time to waste if you're wanting me to father your children."

She waved a hand in front of her face. "You're going to need to give me a minute to catch up to you, stud."

Smiling, he released her hand so he could caress her face. "I'm happy to give you all the time you need, but you're hitching your cart to an older man with a lot of baggage. I want to do this right and be open with you."

"You're doing a great job with that so far."

"You make it easy. I feel like I can talk to you about anything, and it'll be okay."

"It will be."

He kissed both her cheeks, the end of her nose and then her lips, being careful to avoid her injured bottom lip. "You're doing quite a number on me, Ms. Coleman."

"How so, Mr. Lodge?"

"You're making me want things I thought would never happen for me again."

"What sort of things?"

"You know."

"Tell me anyway."

"Love and babies and happily ever after to start with."

"That's a lot to start with."

"Uh-huh." He bent his head to place a kiss on her neck.

Izzy tipped her head to give him better access, wishing she felt well enough to show him what he meant to her. But what they'd shared thus far was enough.

For now, anyway.

On the way home, Mia was lost in thoughts that swirled through her mind every time she saw the father who'd been missing from her life for so long. Spending time with him was such a pleasure. Things as pedestrian as sharing a meal took on greater significance because she was with him after wondering about him for so many years.

"Whatcha thinking about over there?" Wade asked as he drove them home slowly through the accumulating snow.

"Just about how cool it is that my dad made us a vegan dinner and that I can see him any time I want now. It never gets old."

"I'm so glad you found him and that he turned out to be such a great guy."

"He's so great, and that just adds to my confusion about why my mother did what she did. I can't reconcile the man she says wasn't good for us with the man I've come to know."

"You should ask her about that."

"I hate the idea of dragging up all that crap again." She'd struggled with her relationship with her mother over the last year and had spoken to her only sporadically. Deb was pushing her for more, even threatening to come to Vermont to see her if that's what it took, but Mia had resisted her mother's overtures. If she was being truthful, she was so freaking angry with her mother that she wasn't sure she would ever get past it.

"It's only natural that you have questions, honey. Anyone would. She owes you an explanation."

"Part of me feels it doesn't matter. She did what she did for reasons she must've felt were important, but the bottom line is now I have my dad, and I really, really love him. I don't want to hear what she has to say about him. I just don't."

"Which makes all the sense. She must know she's very lucky not to be in jail right now, and she has you to thank for demanding they drop the charges before you'd see Cabot. She owes you everything."

"I wish I had the guts to come right out and ask her the things I want to know."

"You have the guts. You're the gutsiest woman I've ever known. Look at how you brought down a whole drug operation, almost single-handedly."

"That was easy compared to asking my mother about stuff

that happened in the past that I know she doesn't want to talk about."

"Too bad if she doesn't want to talk about it. She owes you the truth, Mia."

"I know."

"Why don't you write it all down and maybe send her an email so you don't have to actually talk to her about it? That might be easier, no?"

"That might work," Mia said, perking up at the idea of getting the answers she craved without having to confront her mother. "She's been saying she wants to come visit us and to meet you, but I've been holding her off because I have all these questions."

"So write to her and tell her you have questions that need answers before you can consent to a visit."

"I'll think about that. Thank you for listening to me for the umpteenth time on this same topic."

"I'm happy to listen to you on any topic at any time."

When they got home a short time later, they trudged through the snow into the house they were slowly but surely restoring and making their own. They kicked off their boots and hung coats on hooks in the mudroom.

The kitchen had been fully renovated, and the family room was almost finished. Next, they'd move upstairs to redo the en suite bathroom as well as knock some walls down to make bigger bedrooms for their future children. Despite the chaos of living in a work zone, Mia had never loved any house more than she did that one, mostly because she got to live there with him.

"Hey, Wade?"

He turned to her, sweet, sexy and adorable with cheeks red from the cold and hair mussed from the knit cap he wore every-where this time of year. "Yeah?"

"I just want you to know how much I love you and our life. I can't figure out how I ever survived before I had you and this."

Wade put his arms around her and held on tight. "I wonder the same thing. All that time when I knew you were out there somewhere... I thought I'd go mad from wanting you and from worrying about you."

"Same for me. After the first time we met, you were all I thought about."

"When you weren't conspiring to bring down a drug kingpin, that is."

"Other than that," she said, laughing. "Sometimes when I think about all that, I can't believe I made it as long as I did wishing I could be with you."

"Don't think about the bad stuff, love. All that matters is the here and now, which is as perfect as perfect gets."

"It is perfect, and I'm so damned thankful for that—and for you."

Wade kissed her with the sweet tenderness that was so much a part of their life together. Everything about this was different from what she'd had with Brody, when she'd lived in fear of him most of the time. "Let's go to bed."

She took hold of the hand he offered and followed him upstairs.

CHAPTER TEN

"The thing about love was that it caught you unawares, turned up in the most unexpected places, even when you weren't looking for it."
—Sarra Manning

*A*fter a delightful dinner, Vanessa left at the same time as Troy, following him out of Grayson and Emma's as they stood at the door, watching them go.

"You want to grab a drink?" Troy asked her.

"I'd love to, but there's nowhere to do that here, and it's snowing too hard to go elsewhere."

"What do you guys do for fun in situations like that?"

"Uh, well… You want to come back to my brother's house for a drink? I can't promise there won't be random Colemans underfoot there, though."

"Sure, lead the way."

"We have to go slow. Even though I grew up in this, driving in the snow still freaks me out, especially after Izzy's accident."

"No worries. I'm not looking to drive off any mountains tonight either."

"Yeah, let's not do that."

As she got into her car, she had to tell herself to calm the hell down and stop acting the fool over a handsome man who was paying attention to her. It wasn't as if that'd never happened before, but she liked this one. He was smart and funny and obviously well loved by people she liked and respected.

That Cameron, Lucy and Emma considered him such a good friend helped to cut out a lot of the uncertainty that came from meeting a new guy and trying to discover the truth about him. So many of them were self-absorbed jerks, and usually by the time she saw their true colors, she'd started to get hopeful that this one might be different.

They were all the same.

Except, she thought, some of the men in her family, such as Grayson and Noah, who was now happily in love with Brianna, and thank goodness for that. They'd sort of lost Noah for a few years when he went off the grid after the split from his ex-wife. Having him back, laughing and smiling, was such a relief.

Vanessa drove more slowly than she had in years, inching her way across town to Noah's, aware of Troy following her in a Mercedes SUV. Izzy's accident had scared the crap out of her and the rest of their family and had given them all new respect for the dangers of driving in the mountains this time of year. It was easy to become complacent about the risks of ice and snow, but Izzy's near miss had been a reminder to all of them to proceed with caution.

She pulled up outside of Noah's and parked to make room for Troy behind her. Nervous butterflies flittered about in her belly as she met up with him outside the cars and led the way into her brother's house, where only a light on the second floor was illuminated. She hoped that meant everyone else had gone to bed already.

Ally was working from home at Noah's for a marketing firm in Boston, and Henry had been talking about going back to Boston, so they might have already left in a car they'd planned to rent to get back to the city. Noah and Brianna spent most nights at her place since they had it to themselves.

Vanessa turned on a light in the mudroom.

Troy came in behind her, removing boots and hanging his coat next to hers. "I can't believe how much colder it is up here than it is in the city."

"You'd think I'd be used to it by now. You'd be wrong. I've always hated being cold."

"That must've been tough growing up with such long winters."

"It was." Keeping the woodstove going at home had been a constant thing from October to May every year, with everyone involved in the splitting and hauling of wood. She hadn't thought about that in a long time. She opened the cabinet where Noah and others had stashed various kinds of alcohol in recent weeks. "We have vodka, bourbon and red wine," she said.

"I'll do a little bit of bourbon."

"That sounds good to me, too." She poured them each a cocktail glass and led the way into Noah's living room, where someone had stoked the woodstove. "Ah, warmth."

"Feels good." He sat next to her on the sofa in front of the stove. "So your brother lives here?"

"He keeps his clothes here mostly these days. He's all but living with Brianna in a house she rents in town. They're working together to rebuild the Butler Inn. That's how they met."

"I was checking that out earlier when I stopped by the store to see Cam and Lucy. It looks great."

"It's coming along. I know he's relieved to have gotten the exterior finished before the serious cold set in. They're working on the inside now—with heat."

"I'm too much of a flatlander, as the girls call me, to work outside in the winter, especially up here."

"I couldn't do it. No way. I'm not sure how I ended up with such thin blood growing up in the mountains, but there you have it."

"Is that why you don't ski? You hate the cold?"

"That's one reason. I also just suck at that and ice skating. I have crappy balance—and I hate the cold."

His low chuckle sent a tingle of sensation down her spine, which was odd because most of the time, men didn't affect her that way. Or any way, for that matter. She'd yet to meet one who wasn't like all the others, just looking to get laid and willing to do the minimal amount of work to reach that goal.

"Let me ask you something, Troy Kennedy."

"Yes, Vanessa Coleman?"

"What's your game? What're you looking for? What do you see happening here?"

"Uh, well, that's direct," he said with a nervous-sounding laugh.

"I'm thirty-two years old. There's nothing I haven't seen when it comes to guys and dating and all the bullshit that goes along with it. So I guess I believe in cutting to the chase to save us both a lot of time."

"It's an interesting approach." He put his glass on the coffee table and turned to face her. "Do you want to know the first thing I thought when I saw you at Izzy's?"

"Um, well, I guess so."

Smiling, he said, "My very first thought was, 'She's the most beautiful woman I've ever seen in my entire life.'"

"Oh, shut up. That is not true."

"Swear to God. No bullshit, no lines, no lies. That was my very first thought."

"If you say so," Vanessa replied, her heart racing at the intense way he looked at her.

"I say so."

"So what does that mean?"

"I don't know yet. Do you?"

"No! I just met you today!"

"Would you maybe be interested in getting to know me better?"

As she eyed his ridiculously handsome face, Vanessa wanted things she hadn't allowed herself to want in a very long time. "Maybe."

"Hmmm, that's not a definitive yes."

"No, it isn't. I've learned to be skeptical when things seem too good to be true."

"Ouch," he said, laughing.

"Sorry, I don't mean to wound your fragile ego."

"It's okay," he said, his eyes alight with amusement. "I can take it. Will you have dinner with me tomorrow night?"

"Hold that thought." Vanessa got up, went into the kitchen, wrote down the phone number at Noah's and returned to the sofa. She handed him the slip of paper. "Call me tomorrow around two, and I'll let you know."

Troy took the paper, folded it in half and stashed it in his shirt pocket. "Hopefully, it'll be safe there," he said, patting his chest over the pocket. "I'd hate to lose that."

Vanessa rolled her eyes at him. "I'm sure you could hunt down Noah Coleman's phone number if you were dumb enough to lose that."

"I see I have my work cut out to convince you I'm not full of bullshit."

"Yes, you do, and I'm sorry. It's not your fault that I need to be convinced, but alas, here we are."

"I get it. I've been on the receiving end of some bullshit myself. It gets old after a while."

"It does. I'm sick of it. So sick of it that the idea of remaining single for the rest of my life is looking really good to me at this point."

"That'd be a crying shame—and that's not a line. I swear."

"You're very charming. I'll give you that. And you have good references as the friend of people I like and respect."

"I love those girls like they're my sisters, and Simone is my niece."

"Do you have sisters of your own?"

He shook his head. "Two brothers, but the three of them *are* my sisters. I miss them all so much since they left the city."

"That must've sucked."

"It really did, even though I was super happy for each of them. Will, Colton and Grayson are all good guys, and they've become my friends, too."

"They're the best. Any woman would be lucky to be with any of my brothers and cousins."

"So it seems. I joke that there's something in the water up

here. First Cam comes to build a website for the store and meets Will after she crashed into Fred the moose."

Vanessa laughed, remembering Cam's auspicious arrival in Butler. "She will forever be known as the girl who hit Fred."

"I'd been on the phone with her right before it happened. Scared me so bad when I heard about the accident."

"Luckily, Fred forgave her, and they're great friends now."

"Very true, and we talk about her friendship with a full-grown bull moose as if that's not the weirdest thing ever."

"You have to know Fred to get why it's not weird."

"So I'm told. He came strolling into Cam and Will's wedding reception like an invited guest."

"That was epic."

"How did I miss seeing you there?"

"Not sure."

"Are you sure you were there? I would've remembered you."

"I'm sure."

"Huh, well, I must've been busy dancing with Simone and missed you."

That sparked a memory for Vanessa. "I remember you dancing with her. I remember thinking you two were very cute together."

"I love her so much. True confession?"

"Sure."

"For a while, I sort of entertained the idea of something with Emma, and part of the reason why that was so appealing to me was because I'd get to be with Simone every day, too."

"That puts some extra points in your column."

"Is that right?"

"Yep. That's the kind of honesty I find refreshing. Most guys never would've admitted to liking someone else, because they'd think that would hurt their chances with the flavor of the month."

He raised a brow, which only made him sexier. "Did you just refer to yourself as the flavor of the month?"

"Metaphorically speaking, of course."

"Of course. You're very witty, Vanessa Coleman."

"That comes from holding my own with seven siblings and ten close first cousins. It was a madhouse around here."

"That sounds kinda fun, actually."

"It was, for the most part. After my dad left, it was rough for the Colemans. My aunt, uncle and grandparents stepped up for us where they could, but nothing was ever really the same after that."

"How old were you?"

"Almost twelve."

"Old enough to remember before and after."

"Yes." She glanced at him, uncertain of how much she wanted to share. But what the hell? She might never see him again after this week. "I started having a significant challenge with anxiety after he left. It's something I still grapple with, although medication helps."

"I'm really sorry you went through that and are still dealing with it to this day."

"That which doesn't kill you, right?"

"Yeah, but some things… They just shouldn't happen."

"No, they shouldn't. So, what's your baggage, other than your best friends falling in love with Vermonters and leaving you to fend for yourself in the big city?"

"That's not enough?"

"Nope."

"I lost one of my brothers to a drug overdose eight years ago. That was rough."

"Oh God, Troy. I'm so sorry."

"Thanks. It was an awful thing from start to finish, and I felt guilty after he died because at least I didn't have to dread him overdosing anymore, you know?"

"I understand what you mean. That dread must've been so hard to live with."

"It was awful. Debilitating at times. I almost flunked out of my third year of law school after my brother died, but a professor I'd gotten to know went to bat for me. Only because of him was I able to get through that year."

"What was his name? Your brother?"

"Michael."

"And he was older than you?"

"Yeah, three years older."

"Were you close?"

"Growing up, the three of us were inseparable. Our other brother, Logan, was between us in age."

"And you're still close to him?"

"More than ever after we lost Michael."

"Where is he?"

"He lives in Seattle and works for Microsoft. He's a computer whiz kid. Has been for as long as I can remember."

"Where did you guys grow up?"

"Stamford, Connecticut."

"That's Yankees territory, right?"

"Damned straight."

"Ew. I knew you were too good to be true."

"Spoken like a Red Sox fan."

"You know it."

"Well, even the most beautiful woman I've ever seen can still have significant flaws. That's good to know."

Vanessa used a couch pillow to smack him in the chest.

He dodged the pillow, which caused her to lose her balance. Troy steadied her with his hands on her shoulders. For an endless moment, they stared at each other, during which something electric zinged between them, an attraction she'd rarely experienced for any man.

He released her. "I, ah, should probably go."

Oddly disappointed that he was leaving, Vanessa got up to walk him out. At the door to the mudroom, he stopped her. "Stay in here. It's cold out there." He kissed her forehead. "Tonight was fun."

"Yes, it was."

"I'll call you tomorrow. Two o'clock, right?"

"Yep." She stayed in the kitchen while he put on his coat and boots. "Hey, Troy?"

"Yes, ma'am?"

"Drive carefully in the snow."

"I will." He left her with a smile and a wave.

After he drove off, she locked the doors and went upstairs to get ready for bed. Noah had told her and Ally and their brothers to hang out for as long as they wanted to. Since she had no good reason to get back to Boston, Vanessa had decided to enjoy some time at home and help out where needed with Izzy.

Cabot was taking good care of her sister, and now Troy had entered the scene.

She didn't recall Butler being this exciting when she used to live there. That made her giggle to herself as she brushed her teeth. Calling Butler "exciting" was an oxymoron.

In bed, she pulled two down comforters over herself and shivered until her body heat kicked in. Thinking about Troy Kennedy helped to warm her. The man was too handsome and too nice and too everything to be believed.

She really hoped he was as great as he seemed, because she already couldn't wait to see him again.

CHAPTER ELEVEN

*"If you have made mistakes... there is always another chance for you...
you may have a fresh start any moment you choose, for this thing we
call 'Failure' is not the falling down, but the staying down."*
—Mary Pickford

*I*zzy dreamed of driving off a mountain, sliding into a dark abyss and crashing into some unseen object. The imaginary crash caused her to jolt, which set off a wave of pain that woke her. There was nothing imaginary about the pain, that was for sure. She gritted her teeth, hoping it would subside, but everything hurt.

She sat up slowly and painfully, taking a minute to catch her breath before putting on a robe and making her way to the kitchen for a painkiller. She'd asked Cabot to keep them there so she'd have to make the effort to take one. The thought of getting addicted to the drugs scared the hell out of her, so she was being very conservative about taking the prescription stuff.

She poured herself a glass of water and took half a pill, hoping it would be enough to take the edge off so she could get back to sleep. Standing before the kitchen window, she watched the snow come down and estimated at least a foot had already fallen.

"Hey," Cabot said when he joined her in the kitchen. "Are you okay?"

"I had a dream about driving a car off a mountain and woke up in pain."

"Normally, I'd tell you that couldn't happen, but…"

She turned to smile at him. "Want to know something?"

He came to her, put his arms around her and drew her carefully into his warm embrace. "I want to know everything."

"I never thought a T-shirt and flannel pajama pants were sexy on a man until I saw them on you."

His low rumble of laughter filled her with a feeling of happiness and contentment. "I never knew bruises could be so sexy until I saw them on you."

"That might be a reach."

"I wish you knew how many nights I lay awake wishing I could be with you like this."

She held on tighter to him. "Oh, Cabot, why didn't you call me?"

"I just couldn't make myself do it. I was afraid I'd end up hurting you. I still am."

"There'll be times when you'll hurt me and I'll hurt you, but I'll never be cruel to you the way she was. I promise you that."

"And I will never be cruel to you either. If she taught me anything, it was what *not* to do." He pulled back from her, tucked a strand of her hair behind her ear and gave her a gentle kiss.

She couldn't wait for her damned lip to heal so there could be more kissing.

"Let's get you back to bed."

"Will you come with me?"

"Um, sure, if you want me to."

"I do." She kept ahold of his hand as she walked slowly back to her room, releasing him only when she was seated on the mattress to catch her breath before she made her way into bed. "God, this sucks. When am I going to feel better?"

"You're so much better than you were a week ago," he said when he got in next to her.

Izzy couldn't believe Cabot was finally in her bed, where

she'd wanted him since she first met him last June. She turned on her side to face him, waited for the predictable blast of pain and breathed through it. When she opened her eyes, she saw him watching her with concern. She could see his face thanks to the faint glow of a night-light her mom had brought over after Izzy got home from the hospital.

"Are you okay?" he asked, running his hand over her shoulder.

"Yeah, it hurts just to move, which is a drag."

"In a couple of weeks, you'll be back to normal, and this will all be a bad memory."

"Not all of it."

"No?"

"Nope. There was this guy I liked for a long time, you see, who came running to be with me in the hospital and then put his life on hold to take care of me at home. Not that I wanted to crash my car or anything, but it did help me out on another front."

"You're not thanking your accident by any chance, are you?"

"Maybe just a little. I hadn't been successful in getting you into my bed until after I crashed my car."

"Thank you for giving me another chance after I blew the first two so badly."

"You didn't blow them so much as fail on the follow-through."

"Why didn't you call me?"

"I thought about it, but your silence sort of sent a message, and I wanted to respect that."

"My silence didn't send the right message. Night after night after night, I was wide awake, staring at the ceiling, calling myself every kind of fool for letting a woman like you get away. I lived in total dread of Mia telling me you'd met someone else."

"Did you?"

"God, yes. I was a mess over you, and I had no idea what to do about it because I'm like this emotionally stunted forty-seven-year-old who has stayed so far away from anything like this for so long, I can't remember how to do it."

"You're doing great so far."

"Am I?"

"Uh-huh."

"Will you tell me if I'm not?"

"You really want me to?"

"Yes, I do. The last thing I want to do is mess this up now that I'm finally here with you." He reached over to caress her face and run his fingers through her long hair. "That night in Boston last October, all I wanted to do was kiss you and hold you and sleep with you and everything else with you."

"I wanted that, too, but I just couldn't tell if you were on the same page, which was weird for me. I don't usually have that kind of trouble figuring out men. Your type tends to be rather easy to read. You were an exception in more ways than one."

"That's me, an exception to every rule," he said in a teasing tone.

"You are. I thought about you so much and how strange it was that I felt like you were as into me as I was with you, and yet… Nothing."

"Thank you for giving me a third chance."

"You didn't give me much choice," she said, smiling. "Showing up like you did in the hospital."

"The whole time I was driving there, like a madman, I might add, I was afraid you'd tell me to get lost. I wouldn't have been surprised if you had."

"I was so happy to see you."

He went up on his elbow and leaned in to kiss her. "That makes me a very lucky guy. I have a feeling that a woman like you doesn't give third chances very often."

"You're the first to get a third chance, but I knew you'd be worth it."

"I'm going to try really hard to be worth it, Iz. But you have to set me straight if I screw up. It's been a long time since I did something like this. I'm a little rusty on how it all works."

"I'll set you straight if you mess up."

"Please do. I don't want to mess this up. I haven't felt this good in so long that I'd forgotten it was possible to feel this good."

"I want that for you. So badly. I want you to feel good."

"You make me feel good. Being with you makes me feel better than I ever have."

Izzy had wanted to hear him say that for so long that she almost couldn't believe what she was hearing now.

"I'm sorry if I hurt you in any way. That was never my intention. I was just so freaking confused after we met. All I wanted was to see you again, but I was paralyzed by it all, emotional cripple that I am."

"You're not an emotional cripple."

"Yes, I really am."

"I don't believe it. I see you building a warm, loving rapport with your daughter, throwing her and her husband the most beautiful wedding, learning to cook vegan for them. She looks at you like you hung the moon. You see that, don't you?"

"I do, and I live in constant fear of disappointing her in some way."

"You won't disappoint her as long as you continue to show up for her. That's the secret, you know. Show up. Be present. Take it from someone who has an absent father. You're doing everything right with her, and she adores you."

"That's nice to hear." He curled a strand of her hair around his index finger. "You never said much about your visit with your dad."

"That's because he didn't come here to see me."

"What did he want?"

"For me to ask my mom to sign their divorce papers so he can get remarried."

"Stop it. He did not."

"Yes, he did."

"Oh, damn, Izzy. I'm so sorry he continues to hurt you like that."

"By now, I should know better than to hope for something more where he's concerned. I thought maybe a near-fatal illness might've changed him, but he's the same old selfish bastard he's always been. If you want to know how to be a good father—don't do what he does."

"It's unreal that he would come here after you've been so badly injured and ask that of you."

"It's par for the course where he's concerned. Imagine him coming back after years of silence to ask the eight children he abandoned if they'd mind donating bone marrow to him."

"The guy has some kind of nerve. It's amazing the way people who are supposed to love us the best end up hurting us."

"Yes, it is. Amazing and disappointing all at once. I'm so mad at myself because I dared to hope his brush with death would've changed him. But it was the same shit, different day."

"Are you going to tell your mom?"

"I don't know. I've been thinking about that all day. On the one hand, I hate to tell her anything that'll upset her, especially when she's been so happy with Ray lately. But I also don't want her to be blindsided when she hears from him."

"I can't believe they're still married after all this time."

"We didn't know where he was for most of it, and after my uncle Linc sicced a lawyer on him to get minimal child support, my mom had no desire to have any further dealings with him. She was too busy trying to keep eight kids fed and clothed and to pay the mortgage on one salary. All of us had jobs to help out at very young ages."

"She should go after him for back child support before she signs those divorce papers."

"You think she could still get it?"

"Hell yes. There's probably not a statute of limitations on being a deadbeat father. Grayson could help her with that. Why should he get off scot-free on neglecting his children?"

"He shouldn't." Izzy felt a fire spark inside her. "We do need to go after him. Why haven't we gone after him before now? Why should he get to have his comfortable little life after what he put my mother through?"

"Not to mention what he put the rest of you through, especially you, Gray and Noah."

"And Ness. She was babysitting every weekend from the time she was twelve because we needed the money."

"It's obscene."

"Yes, it is, and I'll talk to my mom about this. He wants something from her. She should get something from him."

"Makes sense to me."

"I saw this thing once about girls whose fathers break their hearts before any boy can do it, and sometimes I think that's why my sisters and I have never really come close to a true commitment with a man. Our hearts were broken early. We learned to expect so little of men, and it's just easier to stay single."

"You know how you said you want me to know what it's like to be in a safe, loving relationship?"

"Yes."

"I want that for you, too. I want you to have someone who has your back all the time and who'll do his best never to disappoint you."

"Know anyone who might want to apply for the job?" she asked, smiling.

"I have a candidate in mind. He's a rakishly handsome devil with some baggage that may or may not make him a bit risky when it comes to love and all the stuff that goes with it, but he's willing to give it his all, as long as he's giving it to you, that is."

"And who is this unicorn you speak of?"

"He's right here, sweetheart, and he's very much looking forward to the future for the first time in longer than he can remember."

IZZY'S MOTHER CAME WITH LUNCH THE NEXT DAY. KNOWING SHE needed to talk to her mom about some heavy stuff, Cabot, who'd spent most of the morning digging them out of the snow that fell overnight, had left to do some errands.

"How's the recovery progressing?" Hannah asked Izzy over grilled cheese sandwiches and more of Cam and Lucy's tomato soup.

"A little better every day, thankfully. I'll be glad to lose the sling and be able to use my left arm again. It's getting so stiff and achy from lack of movement."

"They said the immobilization was critical for the bones to set."

"I know, but it's driving me crazy to not be able to move it. And the cast is starting to itch."

"Two more weeks, and then you should be able to move it."

"I'll go mad before then."

"How are things with Cabot?"

"Really good. I think we've decided, you know, to give it a shot."

"Give what a shot?"

"*It.* A relationship."

"Oh, well, I sort of figured that was already happening based on the way he showed up at the hospital and wouldn't hear of anyone else caring for you at home."

"It wasn't happening. Not then, anyway. He's been through a lot, and it took him a while to come around to the idea of this being more than friendship."

"Don't take this the wrong way, but I hope you're being careful. The stuff that happened to him... It changes a person, makes them hard."

It wasn't lost on Izzy that her mother was talking from her own experience. "Maybe so, but that doesn't mean they lose the capacity for love. Look at you and Ray. You took a big chance on him, and that seems to have worked out well."

"It has." She sat back and tucked her shoulder-length gray hair behind her ears, almost as if she needed something to do with her hands. "I mean... It is, but not everyone can come back from the kind of thing that happened to Cabot. Sometimes that ruins a person."

"I hear you, but Cabot is definitely not ruined. I've seen that with my own eyes, and I know he has real feelings for me. And vice versa."

"Don't you want to have kids at some point? He's quite a bit older than you."

"We're talking about all of it."

"I want you to be happy, Iz. You deserve that as much as the rest of us do."

"Thank you. Everyone deserves happiness, and when you find it, you need to hold on to it with everything you've got."

"As long as you don't have to give up too much to make someone else happy. Don't do that. I made that mistake once, and I'll never do it again." Hannah dipped the corner of her sandwich into her soup and took a bite. "Speaking of my mistakes, I heard your father was here yesterday. How did that go?"

"Not surprisingly, he came with an agenda."

Hannah froze, her blue-gray eyes widening. "What now?"

"He wants you to sign the divorce papers so he can get remarried."

"Are you kidding me? He came *here*, to your home, after you've been so seriously injured, and dumped that bullshit on you?"

"He did, and I'm sorry to have to tell you."

"Don't you dare be sorry on his behalf. I guess his brush with death didn't make him a better person."

"Nope."

"That son of a bitch. Just when I think I've seen how low he can go, he tops himself."

"I was thinking last night that before you give him what he wants and sign those papers, you need to do something about the fact that he owes you a ton of money."

"Like what?"

"Sue him for it?"

"Ugh, the thought of dealing with him in any way makes me sick."

"And I get that, but letting him get away with what he did makes me sick for you."

"He probably doesn't have anything to sue for. He never was very good at holding down a job."

"If nothing else, you can make his life almost as difficult as he once made yours. At least he's not struggling to feed, clothe and house eight children."

"I need to think about this. Everything is so good now. I hate the idea of dredging up that negative energy."

"I hear you, and if you decide to let it go, that's completely up to you. But you have some leverage. He wants something from you. It's a good time to ask for what you want from him."

"I want *nothing* from him."

"He owes you hundreds of thousands of dollars, Mom."

"We did all right. We got by without him."

"We did, thanks to you, and while you scraped and struggled, he was off living his life with no consideration for you or us. Talk to Ray and Grayson. See what they say about it. You don't have to do anything you don't want to do, but this might be your only chance to go after him."

"I'll think about it." She waved her hand. "Enough about him. What else is new?"

Izzy took a deep breath and released it, trying to let go of anxiety that came with talking about her father. "Ness was here yesterday when Cameron, Lucy and their friend Troy were here for lunch."

"Oh yeah? And?"

"I think I detected a little spark of something between her and Troy."

"Is that right? Well, good for her. She needs a pick-me-up after the mess at work."

"I think I talked her into getting with Gray about that."

"I hope so. What happened to her is outrageous."

"What happened to you is, too."

Hannah gave Izzy her patented mom glare. "You've made your point, Isabella."

Izzy laughed and held up her good hand. "I'm just sayin'…"

"I heard you, and I promise I'll talk to Ray and Grayson and see what we can do. But I'm not going to let my very contented present be upset by past hurts and dramas, even if there's a million dollars in it for me."

"I understand, and I agree."

"If I've learned anything since your father left, it's that I need to take care of myself first and foremost, or I'm no good to anyone else. I wasn't good at that when I was married. I didn't speak up for myself or address things I knew were bothering him because I was so afraid of rocking the boat. Look where that got me."

Izzy was truly shocked by this unprecedented insight from her mother, who tended to keep such thoughts mostly to herself. "I certainly hope you don't blame yourself for him leaving."

"No, I don't blame myself for that, but a marriage takes two people giving it their best every day, and on many a day, I didn't have a thing to give him after dealing with work and kids and house stuff. He was always second-to-last on my list of priorities, with my own needs being dead last."

"You had *eight* children, Mom. I'm sure every day was more about survival than anything else."

"It was, but I loved being a mother. You kids were never a burden to me, but I neglected my husband during those years. I knew I was doing it, and I felt bad about it. However, I never did anything to try to change it. I figured he'd still be there when we eventually came up for air. That was on me."

"I want you to listen to me—really listen—okay?"

"I'm listening."

"Him leaving was not your fault."

"It was partially my fault, Izzy. If I don't own my role in it and learn from it, how can I expect to do better with Ray?"

"Fine, okay, so him not being happy in your marriage might've been partially your fault, but him walking away from you and his children and leaving us high and dry—that part was most definitely not your fault."

"No, that's all on him, for sure. I'll never understand how he could do that to you kids, who he claimed to love so much."

"Or to you, the woman he married and had eight children with. He owes you, Mom. We all want to see you get what you deserve from him."

"And you want to see him get what he deserves, too, right?"

"Well, that wouldn't break our hearts."

"Do me a favor and don't let your bitterness toward him take any more of your energy than it already has. Ray has really helped me see how damaging it is to allow that anger to continue festering. Me holding on to that isn't going to change the past, but it can hurt the present and the future."

"Ray is a very wise man."

"You have no idea."

"I'm so glad you have him in your life and that he makes you so happy."

"I feel like a teenager again when he's around, and if you'd tried to tell me even a year ago that I'd ever feel that way again, I would've said you were crazy."

"No one in this entire world deserves that more than you do."

"We all deserve it, Iz. I want it for you and the others, too. Look at how happy Noah is again since he let himself have feelings for Brianna."

"He's smiling like he used to."

"I know! It's incredible to have him back among us again, rather than off licking his wounds and being bitter." Hannah glanced at the clock on the stove. "I'd better get back to the office before someone complains that I'm taking a long lunch." She'd been the Butler town clerk for as long as Izzy could remember and worked out of an office that adjoined her home. That was how she'd managed to successfully juggle a job and the raising of eight kids as a single mom.

Izzy got up slowly and winced when stiff muscles objected to the movement. She followed her mother to the mudroom. "Hey, Mom?"

Hannah was wrapping a scarf around her neck when she turned to Izzy. "Yes?"

"I just want you to know that I admire you more than just about anyone. I know you don't want to hear it, but we all think you're Wonder Woman for the way you carried on after he left."

"I appreciate those kind words, but I certainly wasn't Wonder Woman on the inside. I was afraid all the time of losing everything."

"We never would've known that."

"I went to enormous lengths to make sure you kids didn't have anything more to worry about than you already did. And while we're being sappy, I'd like to thank you for not dying in that accident. That would've ruined my life, too."

"I'm very glad not to have ruined both our lives."

Hannah came toward her and gently hugged her. "Love you, sweet girl."

"Love you, too, Mama. Always."

"Let me know if you need anything."

"You do the same."

Hannah looked back over her shoulder. "As long as I have you kids and Ray, I have everything I'll ever need."

CHAPTER TWELVE

"Pain makes you stronger. Tears make you braver. Heartbreak makes you wiser." —Marc & Angel Chernoff

*A*s Hannah drove back to her house after the delightful visit with Izzy, she gave thanks to God for sparing her daughter's life in a crash that certainly could've gone the other way. In the hospital, she'd overheard her nephew Landon, a lieutenant with the Butler Volunteer Fire Department, telling Gray that it'd been a bad one and that Izzy was lucky to have survived it.

She shuddered at the thought of life without her Isabella, who'd been a joy to her since the day she was born and who had stepped up so incredibly to help with her younger siblings after their father left. Hannah would've been lost without her, Gray and Noah, in particular, all of whom had to grow up far too soon thanks to the selfishness of the man who should've been their rock.

Did she want vengeance where he was concerned? Hell yes. Was she willing to put herself through what it would take to get it? That was the part she wasn't sure of. She would never again have any kind of leverage over him, and hearing he wanted to marry again added a level of urgency that hadn't been there before.

Hannah wondered if the woman who was planning to marry him knew the full story of why he didn't see his eight children. She'd bet everything she had that Mike had made her out to be the monster who'd kept a devoted father from his children.

Mike Coleman had always had an issue with the truth. Too bad she hadn't realized that until it was far too late. Not that she regretted her marriage to him, because her greatest joy in life had come from the children they'd had together. But, oh, how he'd burned her and them in the end. And now he wanted her to do him a favor and sign the divorce papers she'd received months ago and set aside to be dealt with "later"? Not even Ray knew those papers were sitting in a pile on her desk.

When she pulled into her driveway, she parked next to Ray's big silver truck and shut off the engine. She sat there for two minutes, collecting herself, before she went inside. He was taking the cookies he baked daily for Simone's after-school snack out of the oven when she stepped into the kitchen. He spoiled that child crazy, but since Simone was the most delightful little girl, Hannah didn't say anything to ruin his fun.

"Hi, honey, you're home," he said with a wink and a smile.

"Yes, I am."

"How's Izzy?"

"So much better than she was, thank goodness."

"Thank goodness is right." He put three of the cookies on a small plate and placed it on the table for her.

"I owe five new pounds to you and these damned cookies," she said when she popped one of them into her mouth.

"Fifteen cookies a week never hurt anyone."

"Maybe not, but they make jeans fit tight."

"I think your jeans fit just right." He came over to her, put both hands on her ass and gave it a squeeze. "Yep, just right indeed."

It never failed to amaze her that she could feel like a teenager again when he touched her or smiled at her or winked at her or laughed with her. Everything was like brand-new with him, and as a result, she knew she needed to tell him about the papers in her office and the message Izzy had conveyed. "Can you sit for a minute?"

"Sure. I've got two hours before I need to get Simone off the bus. I'm all yours."

"I have about ten minutes before I need to open the office."

Ray looked out the window. "No one is waiting, so you're good."

"Mike went to see Izzy yesterday."

"What did he want?"

"He pretended like he wanted to see her and make sure she was all right, but what he really wanted was for her to ask me to sign the divorce papers he sent a while ago, because apparently he wants to get remarried."

Ray's genial expression turned stormy, the way it always did when Mike's name came up. He'd never understand how a man could abandon his wife and children. It was impossible for him to understand because he couldn't have been any more different from Mike. Ray was loyal and true and steady and solid. He was everything Mike Coleman would never be. "He sent you divorce papers... So, you're not already divorced, then."

"For a very long time after he left, we had no idea where he was. And since I had zero desire to get remarried, it didn't really matter to me that I was still married to him. Even after Linc's lawyer tracked him down for child support, I had zero desire to deal with him—and I would've had to if I'd filed for divorce then."

"So why didn't you sign the papers when he sent them?"

"Because I still don't want to deal with it or him."

"I understand that, but you do want to be free of him, don't you?"

"I'm already free of him. He's nothing to me but the father of my children. I haven't seen or spoken to him in years. None of us had until he resurfaced a while back to ask the kids to be tested for a bone marrow transplant, and don't even get me started on the audacity of that request."

"It was the very definition of the word audacious."

"Yes, it was. I still can't even think about it without my blood boiling, which is why I try very hard not to think about that or him or anything to do with him, including those damned divorce papers."

"Maybe if you just sign them and be done with it, you can stop thinking about it."

"I hadn't given them a single thought since the day they arrived, until Izzy brought it up today and also pointed out that if I'm ever going to go after him for the hundreds of thousands of dollars he owes me and the kids, this is the only chance I'm probably going to get."

"Huh," Ray said. "She does have a point."

"Yes, she does," Hannah said, sighing, "as much as I'd like to pretend otherwise."

"What do you mean?"

"I want to sign those papers and remove him from my life permanently. For so many years, I festered in bitterness, and I don't want to go back to that place. Ever. I'm afraid if I go after him, that's what'll happen."

"I won't let it. I'll be here to remind you of how bright the future looks these days. And we're doing all right for money between my pension and your income and future pension. We don't need anything from him, but maybe you could do it for the kids, to give them a nest egg."

"And make him the hero?" Hannah asked, brow raised.

"He will *never* be the hero of this story to them. Not ever. The money would come from you, not him, and that's if you even get anything."

"True. This may be a moot point. Who knows if he has a pot to piss in or a window to throw it out?"

"There's only one way to find out."

"And you'd be okay with me doing this?"

"I'd support you all the way, honey. What he did to you and the kids was criminal. Why should he get away with it?"

"He shouldn't." Hannah felt more determined by the minute to do something about it. She got up and retrieved the portable phone before returning to the table to punch in the numbers to Gray's house.

"Hey, Mom, how's it going?"

"It's going," she said, as she always did. "I need some legal advice."

"What can I do for you?"

"Your father served me with divorce papers quite some time ago."

"It's about fucking time."

"Yes, but I put them aside and didn't do anything with them because I didn't feel like dealing with him. But get this… When he went to see Izzy, supposedly to check on her, what he really wanted was for her to tell me to sign the papers so he can get remarried."

Grayson let out a sound that expressed his anger without him having to say a word.

"Izzy and I talked about it, and I talked to Ray about it, too, and I think I want to go after him for the rest of the back child support before I sign those papers. He wants something, and so do I."

"I think that's a brilliant idea."

"It's not too late?"

"It's never too late to sue someone for money they rightfully owe you."

"Would you be willing to sue your father on my behalf?"

"It would be my pleasure."

Hannah laughed at the way he said that.

"We've been wanting you to do this for years, Mom. You know that."

"Yes, I do." She reached for Ray's hand and locked her gaze with his. "I haven't felt strong enough to do it before, but everything is different now."

Ray squeezed her hand as he smiled.

"I'll get it started in the morning. We're going to have to sit down and figure out a number that makes sense, knowing you might never see a dime of it."

"That's okay. It's not about the money. It's about the principle."

"Agreed. I'll come by to talk to you about it tomorrow."

"Sounds good. Thank you, son."

"Very happy to help with this."

"I almost feel a little sorry for your father. He has no idea what a fantastic attorney his son grew up to be."

"How about we show him?"

"Hell yes," she said, laughing. "Love you."

"Love you, too. Talk to you tomorrow."

Hannah ended the call and put down the phone. "Well, I guess that's that, then."

"I guess so, but point of order on one thing you said to him."

"What's that?"

"You were *always* strong enough to go after him. Anyone who can suddenly become a single mom to eight children aged sixteen and under and do such a brilliant job of raising those kids into magnificent adults while also providing for them is probably the strongest person I'll ever meet. You lacked the *will* before now. Not the strength."

"I sure do like the way I look to you."

"So do I," he said, waggling his brows suggestively.

"Stop it." Her face heated like it did when he looked at her that way. Hannah hadn't blushed in years until Ray came along and made it a daily occurrence. "I have to go back to work, and you've got a bus to meet."

"Can I take a rain check for later?" he asked, kissing the back of her hand.

"We'll see."

"Yes, we will."

She tugged her hand free of his, but only because she was far too tempted to call in sick for the afternoon. "See you in a bit. Give Simone a smooch from me."

"Will do."

Hannah walked toward the breezeway that connected her home to her office.

"Hey, Han?"

She turned back to him. "Yes?"

"After you sign those divorce papers, you and I ought to talk about maybe getting married, huh?"

Though she loved Ray with all her heart, the thought of ever being married again made her feel panicky.

Of course he knew that. He came over to her, wrapped his strong arms around her and hugged her tightly. "It'd be nothing like the first time. Nothing at all. It'd be you and me and our kids and grandkids for the rest of our lives." He pulled back and kissed her forehead. "Go to work, and don't worry about stuff you don't need to worry about, you got me?"

"Yes, dear." She smiled up at him because how could she resist a man who knew just what she needed to hear?

"I love you, sweetheart."

She went up on tiptoes to kiss him. "I love you, too."

IZZY WOKE TO TOTAL DARKNESS AFTER A NAP THAT HAD INCLUDED more weird dreams, this time about her father, in which she and her mother and siblings were on a desperate search to find him. But like in real life, he'd been nowhere to be found. The search had exhausted her. She chalked up the weird dreams to the pain meds and vowed to quit taking them. The last thing she needed was to be dreaming about him.

She still couldn't believe he'd come to her home, where she was recovering from serious injuries, only to advance his own agenda. Nothing should surprise her when it came to him, but that did. How could he care so little about his own daughter that he'd treat her that way? The question was one she'd never get a satisfactory answer to, she realized as she got up slowly and painfully from the bed, adjusting her broken arm in the sling and giving herself a second to get her bearings before shuffling out of the bedroom to a house bathed in candlelight.

What the heck?

"Cabot?"

"I'm here," he said from the kitchen.

"What's all this?"

"Dinner for my girlfriend."

"You cooked?"

"I did."

"Wow, it smells amazing. What did you make?"

"Tenderloin, au jus, baby red potatoes and asparagus."

"My mouth is watering."

"Are you ready to eat?"

"I just need one minute, and then I will be." Izzy walked slowly across the room and surprised him with a kiss. "Thank you for this." She noticed the dozen red roses in a vase on the counter. "And for those."

"You're welcome. I figured just because you're still recovering doesn't mean we need to put the romance on hold."

Oh, hello. "I like how you think."

He kissed her gently. "I like how you do everything."

"I'm very much looking forward to my lip being completely healed."

"As am I."

Holy Moses. He'd really brought out the big guns with candles, dinner, roses and romance. She went into the bathroom to brush her hair and freshen up, wishing her face wasn't still covered in yellow bruises. She wanted to be beautiful for him, not bruised, so she dabbed on some cover-up, even if it didn't entirely hide the bruises. Thankfully, he'd seen how she really looked on two previous occasions.

When she returned to the kitchen, he'd put dinner on the table.

"How about a little wine?" He held up a bottle of red. "You haven't had painkillers since last night, right?"

"Nope, and wine sounds good."

He poured half a glass for each of them and put the bottle on the table before moving to hold her chair.

"This is very nice," she said as she sat. "Thank you."

"My pleasure. It's been such a long time since I had a girlfriend that I'm worried I've forgotten how it's done. But I figured candles, wine, roses, dinner and chocolate were a good place to start."

"There's chocolate?" she asked, eyes wide.

Laughing, he said, "Eat your dinner first."

"Hey, Cabot?"

"Yes, Izzy?"

"You're a wonderful boyfriend so far. I just thought you ought to know that."

"I'm very glad you think so. Your opinion is the only one that matters."

"I'm sure you were also a very good husband once upon a time."

"I tried to be," he said between bites of delicious tenderloin. "But I probably made a lot of mistakes."

"We all make mistakes. No one is perfect, even if we're perfect for each other."

"I suppose that's true. I'm such a perfectionist in my professional life that some of that spills over into my personal life, which can lead to unreasonable expectations for people. My sister is always reminding me that people are human and they screw up, even if—as she says—I never do."

"I'm looking forward to spending more time with your sister so I can gain even more insight into you."

"She'll be happy to tell you anything you want to know."

"Anything?"

"Yep. She's so thrilled that I'm here with you. Perhaps even more thrilled than I am."

"You're thrilled, huh? When I'm black and blue, wrapped in plaster with a fat lip and can barely move?"

"Yes, I'm thrilled, and you're gorgeous even when you're black and blue and wrapped in plaster with the cutest fat lip ever. And you're moving much better than you were, so let's celebrate your progress, shall we?" He raised his glass. "To my darling Izzy, who is on her way back to full health."

"And to my sweet Cabot, who's taking such great care of me."

"To us and to lots of good times to come."

"I'll drink to that."

As they touched glasses, he held her gaze, looking at her with so much affection.

Izzy had waited her whole life for a man who looked at her the way Cabot did. The more time they spent together, the harder she was falling for him, even if she wondered what would happen when he inevitably had to return to Boston. He couldn't hibernate in the woods of Vermont forever with his work and city council commitments to consider.

So while she was loving where this was going, she couldn't help but worry about what was around the next bend.

CHAPTER THIRTEEN

"Throw your dreams into space like a kite, and you do not know what it will bring back, a new life, a new friend, a new love..." —Anais Nin

*W*hen she found out Ally and Henry had gone back to Boston for the time being, and she would have Noah's place to herself for the night, Vanessa decided to cook dinner for Troy rather than go out. Good restaurants were a bit of a drive, and with the recent snow dump and the temperature dipping into single digits, Vanessa would rather not be driving on mountain roads.

She'd always been afraid of driving in winter weather, but her anxiety had been seriously triggered by Izzy's accident. Her older sister was a badass who was out and about in all sorts of crazy Vermont weather. If she could drive off a mountain road, anyone could.

Vanessa had made the huge mistake of driving by Nolan's garage in town, where what was left of Izzy's Jeep had been brought after the accident. Her sister's survival was truly a miracle. The vision of that smashed hunk of metal had haunted Vanessa since she realized it was Izzy's. She wished she hadn't looked.

Troy had called right at two o'clock on the dot, which had

earned him more points. They'd made plans for him to pick her up at Noah's around six thirty.

As she stirred the beef stew she'd made from her late grandmother Sarah's recipe, Noah and Brianna came into the mudroom, knocking snow off their boots and bringing an icy blast of cold air into the house.

"Wow, that smells delicious," Brianna said as she came over to see what Vanessa had made. "Yum."

"It's my grandmother's recipe if you'd like to try it."

Brianna was an incredible cook. Her lasagna had been a highlight of the dreadful week of Izzy's crash.

"I'd love to try it."

"I'll email it to you."

"Thanks."

"How's it going, Ness?" Noah asked.

She hadn't seen him in days. "All good here. How about you?"

"We had an excellent week at the inn. Made huge progress."

"Glad to hear it."

"Bri and I are also about to close on our first joint project, a farm in Lyndonville that needs a complete restoration."

"Congratulations. That's awesome."

"I'm already working on the plans," Brianna said.

"She was up half the night last night," Noah said, smiling at her. "I had to force her to go to bed at two a.m."

"It's never a hardship to go to bed with you."

"Ew," Vanessa said, cringing. "Young ears."

Noah's bark of laughter was one of the best things she'd ever heard. For a long time after he split with his ex-wife, they'd wondered if he'd ever laugh or smile again. Falling for Brianna had made him happier than Vanessa had ever seen him.

Her brother looked in the pot. "That's a lot of stew for one person."

"It's not for one person."

"Ohhh, do tell."

"I'm having a friend over for dinner."

"What friend?"

"No one you know."

"Do I need to stick around to meet this young man and make sure he's up to snuff for my baby sister?"

"You absolutely do *not* need to stick around. He's a friend of Emma's, Lucy's and Cam's, so he comes highly recommended."

"Very interesting. How'd you run into him?"

"He was with Cam and Lucy at Izzy's the other day. We got to talking, and now he's coming for dinner. But don't make it into a big deal, because it isn't. He's only here for this week."

"Here from where?"

"New York."

"Ah, gotcha. Well, I hope you have a nice evening. I'm just here to grab my ski stuff. I'm going with Will, Colton, Lucas and Landon tomorrow."

"That'll be fun," Vanessa said. "Just don't try to keep up with them, or we'll have another sibling in the hospital."

"Believe me, keeping up with them is not in the plans. The last thing I need right now is to get injured." He put his arm around Brianna and kissed her cheek. "Too many other things to do."

"Again, I say ew."

"I was talking about the inn. Get your head out of the gutter."

"Whatever you say."

"So, um, Elliott is coming for another visit on Sunday, and I thought you guys might want to meet him this time." Noah had recently learned that his ex-wife had been pregnant when she left him and had kept his son from him for nearly three years.

"I'd love to, and I know everyone else would, too."

"I'm trying to think of a way I can have everyone meet him without overwhelming him."

"Why don't we play in the snow, build a snowman or something like that? That'll get him comfortable with us, and then we can come inside to play and make hot chocolate."

"That'd be perfect. Thanks, Ness."

"No problem. We're so excited to meet him."

"I can't wait to see him again. Now that I know he's out there, it's torture not to see him every day."

"Would you consider moving closer to him?" Elliott, his

mother, and Miguel, the man she'd cheated on Noah with, lived in Burlington, which was ninety minutes from them.

"I would if my entire life and business wasn't based here."

"She could move closer to you." Vanessa failed to keep a bitter edge out of her tone. She wanted to bitch-slap the sister-in-law she'd once liked. "That'd be the least she could do."

"Not sure that's going to happen with *him* having a big job in Burlington."

Miguel was Noah's former best friend and foreman. Noah had caught them together in his own bed, ending a friendship and a marriage in one explosive moment. Since recently hearing the full story, Vanessa had been enraged for her brother.

"I'm going to run upstairs to grab my stuff," Noah said to Brianna. "Be right back."

After hearing him go up the stairs, Vanessa turned to Brianna. "How is he coping with all this? Really?"

"He's doing all right. He's trying to keep his focus on Elliott. That helps. He's such a delightful little guy."

"The whole thing makes me so angry. I can't imagine how he must feel."

"He has his moments, but for the most part, he's coping. What else can he do at this point?"

Noah had decided that suing for full custody wouldn't be in the child's best interest, as a "win" would take him from the only home he'd ever known. As a result, Noah had to suck it up and deal with the ex-wife who'd betrayed him so totally.

"I don't know how he can stand to be anywhere near her and not want to murder her."

"I'm there to make sure he doesn't do that."

"Thank goodness for you," Vanessa said. "We all feel that way."

"That's so sweet of you to say. We both feel lucky to have found each other."

Noah came pounding down the stairs, sounding like ten men rather than one.

"Is he always so loud?" Brianna asked.

"Afraid so."

"I thought you might say that."

"Say what?" Noah asked when he entered the kitchen carrying skis, boots and ski pants.

"Nothing, dear."

"Was she talking about me?" Noah asked Vanessa.

"I'll never tell."

He dropped his stuff on the floor with a loud crash and put his arms around Brianna, backing her up to the counter to kiss her. "Are you trash-talking me?"

"Would I do that?" Brianna asked, her dark eyes sparkling with mischief.

"Yes, I believe you would, and you'd enjoy it."

Brianna cracked up. "I was asking your sister if you're always the loudest person around, and she confirmed that you are."

"Blame it on my upbringing. If I wasn't loud, I wasn't heard."

"Oh, you were heard all right," Vanessa said.

Noah gave her a look that brothers had been giving sisters—and vice versa—since the beginning of time. "When's your friend coming?"

"None of your business."

"I want to meet him."

"Another time. Now move along."

"Does she remember this is my house?" Noah asked Brianna, who giggled.

"I remember, and I'm kicking you out."

"This is the thanks I get for letting my siblings squat at my house."

"We're very thankful. Now, get out."

"I'm getting the feeling I'm not wanted, and I'm hurt," Noah said to Brianna.

"Oh, please," Vanessa said, rolling her eyes.

"It's okay, baby," Brianna said. "I'll make you feel *very* wanted when we get back to my place."

Noah's dirty grin made Vanessa groan. "Now we're talking. Have a nice evening, Ness, and don't do anything I wouldn't do, which gives you a ton of latitude."

"Gee, thanks. I'll see if I can control myself."

Naturally, Troy had to be right on time and knocked on the door in time for Noah to answer it.

"Hey," Noah said. "Come in."

"How's it going?" Troy extended his hand to Noah as he wiped his feet on the mat. "Troy Kennedy."

The two men shook hands. "Noah Coleman, older brother to Vanessa."

"Knock it off, Noah," Vanessa said. "Let him in."

"I *am* letting him in."

"This is my girlfriend, Brianna," Noah said.

"Good to meet you," Troy said.

"You, too," Brianna said.

"Are you a Kennedy like in *the* Kennedys?" Noah asked.

"Nope. No relation, but I do get asked that just about every day."

"Noah and Brianna were just leaving," Vanessa said, giving her brother a pointed look.

"She's kicking me out of my own house," Noah grumbled. "Watch out for her."

"For God's sake," Vanessa said with an apologetic look for Troy.

He seemed amused by it all.

"You remember the number to Bri's if you need me for anything, right?" Noah asked.

"Brianna, will you please take him out of here before I'm tempted to stab him?" Vanessa asked.

"Let's go, dear. Your sister is feeling murderous."

"She's no fun."

"Yes, she is, but she's not interested in having fun with you tonight."

"Fine." Noah picked up his skis and boots while Brianna took the ski pants. He gave Vanessa a kiss on the cheek. "Have a nice evening, sis. It was nice to meet you, Troy."

"You as well."

"If you're not nice to my sister, I'll kill you."

"Duly noted," Troy said, chuckling.

"*Get out, Noah!*" Vanessa said.

"I'm going. Sheesh."

Troy rocked with silent laughter as the door slammed shut.

"I'm so sorry about him. He's such a pain in my ass." In truth, Vanessa was so relieved to see the old Noah that she didn't mind at all that he'd been a pain in her ass.

"Older brothers are like that."

"Mine drive me crazy, but I love them."

"Did you cook?"

"I did," she said, feeling shy for some odd reason. "I thought it would be easier than going out."

"It smells fantastic."

"Thanks."

He took off his coat and boots and left them in the mudroom. "What can I do to help?"

"Not a thing. It's all ready. What would you like to drink? I have wine, beer, soda, water."

"A beer would be great. Thanks."

She opened a bottle of Sam Adams for him.

"Thanks. I hope you didn't go to any trouble."

"It was fun. I haven't cooked in a while, and this recipe is one of my favorites. My grandma Sarah used to make it for us when we were kids. She's been gone awhile now, so it's like a visit with her to make it." And she was talking way too much. *Shut up, Vanessa.*

"That's so sweet."

She shrugged. "I miss her. I was very close to her."

"Sorry you lost her."

"I am, too, but my grandfather is still very much a part of our lives."

"Elmer, right?"

"Yes."

"I've met him several times. He's delightful."

"Yes, he is. He's the absolute best. He and my uncle Linc are like extra fathers to us Colemans." She poured herself a small glass of Cabernet. Alcohol tended to trigger her anxiety, so she avoided it except for special occasions. A date with this particular man felt like a special occasion.

Troy sat at the kitchen table and took a sip of his beer. "Your family is quite something."

"I suppose it would seem that way from the outside looking in." She glanced at him. "I'm sure you know about us."

"I did hear about your dad, and I'm sorry that happened to you and your siblings. I'm here for you if you want to talk about it."

"Thank you, but that's the last thing I ever want to talk about."

"I get it. Well, I don't really get it, but I get why you don't want to talk about it."

"I'm sick of talking about it after more than twenty years. I hate how it's still such a big part of my story, if that makes sense."

"It does. We all carry stuff with us from our childhoods. Some worse than others."

Vanessa brought her glass of wine to the table to sit with him. "What stuff are you carrying around?"

"Hm, well, my brother who overdosed was gay and put up with a lot of bullying and shit when he was younger—some of it right in our own family. I got myself into trouble defending him with my fists until I learned that words can be every bit as effective. That experience has influenced my entire life. My practice focuses mostly on disenfranchised communities, those who are harassed and bullied for being exactly who and what they are."

The thudding sound that echoed through her ears was Vanessa falling madly in love. Nothing turned her on more than someone who stood up to bullies, not that she could let him see that on this, their third meeting. "That's an amazing way to spend your life."

"It's been rewarding, if not always lucrative. But whatever. I'd rather be doing this kind of work than helping wealthy corporations get richer."

"What're you working on right now?"

"A case involving a transgender woman who was fired from

her job for not informing her employer that she was transitioning."

"Wow. Was she obligated to do that?"

"Absolutely not, and she's going to get a nice settlement from them as a result of their bigotry. The case is getting a lot of attention in New York, which is part of the strategy. I court the attention to put other companies on notice that they can't get away with discrimination."

His obvious passion for his important work was another reason to be attracted, not that she needed more reasons.

"I also do a lot of work in the area of drugs and overdoses and helping families go after dealers who sold their loved ones laced substances."

"Your career sounds amazing. I'm so impressed."

"Aw, thanks, it's satisfying work most of the time. But it can also be depressing and demoralizing when things don't go our way when they absolutely should. I get a close-up view of how effed-up our society is on a regular basis. Thus, the need for a week off to take out my frustrations on the ski slope."

Vanessa swallowed hard as thoughts of other ways he might work off his frustrations flashed through her mind like an X-rated movie.

"Enough about me. What do you do?"

"I'm between jobs at the moment after being sexually harassed out of my last one."

His face lost all expression. "What're you doing about that?"

"Funny you should ask. I just talked to Gray about my options, and he's got a plan that involves sending a letter to my former employer to let them know we're planning to sue unless they see their way clear to a significant severance package for me as well as firing the problem employee."

"Good," Troy said emphatically. "That's exactly what should happen. I'm sorry you had to deal with that bullshit at work."

"Thank you. It was an ordeal, to say the least. He's one of their top salesmen and brings in a ton of money every year, while I was a lowly admin assistant. When I complained to HR, they didn't do a damned thing."

"I really want you to sue them."

"Gray does, too, but we're starting with the letter."

"If I can do anything to help, let me know. Pro bono, of course."

"That's very kind of you."

"I freaking hate bullies and men who prey on women and subordinates just because they can."

His passionate words went straight to her heart and sent a zing of awareness through her entire body. She'd never met a man like him, who thought of others before himself. Well, that wasn't exactly true. Her grandfather, uncle, brothers and cousins were like that, but they didn't count. They were family.

Troy... He was special.

"What else do you like to do when you're not skiing or righting terrible wrongs?"

Smiling, he said, "I play in two basketball leagues in the city and a softball league in the spring and summer. Despite my closest friends falling in love with dudes who live in Vermont, I have a few other friends I enjoy spending time with. I also like to read."

"What kind of books do you like?"

"Mostly historical fiction where I learn something."

"I love historical spy thrillers and movies."

"Oh yeah, me, too."

Over dinner, they discussed their favorite authors, many of whom were on both their lists, movies and TV shows.

"Have you seen *The Crown*?"

"Uh, I might've watched the whole thing twice," he said with a sheepish grin.

"I loved it so much. I think I've watched it three times. And *Downton Abbey*."

"*Loved* it."

"I think I might love *you*," Vanessa said before recoiling in horror. "Did I say that out loud or just think it?"

He laughed so hard, he had tears in his eyes. "You can't take it back."

"I'm not sure I want to."

"I'm sure I don't want you to." He raised his beer bottle in a toast to her. "Best beef stew I've ever had on the best first date I've ever had."

Vanessa felt giddy and silly and happy as she touched her glass to his bottle. "Cheers."

CHAPTER FOURTEEN

"There are all kinds of love in this world but never the same love twice."
—F. Scott Fitzgerald

*C*abot wondered how something that felt this good could possibly be real. And he worried how they would make it work. His entire life was in Boston. Hers was in Vermont. She'd made a name for herself photographing the unique majesty that was Vermont. The state was not only her home, but it was also her muse.

As he spent a second night in her bed, holding her hand while she slept, his mind raced with scenarios and plans. He loved that they were having this time together with no chance of their relationship becoming physical. It gave them the opportunity to get to know each other while looking forward to more after she recovered from her injuries. When he met Deb, they'd been all about the sex to the detriment of the more important parts of any relationship. They'd failed to set the foundation and had paid for that later.

He'd waited his whole life to find someone who made him feel the way Izzy did, and he was determined to make this work, even if it meant giving up things that had sustained him during the long years he'd spent searching for his daughter. That seemed like a bad dream now that Mia was back in his daily life, but he still mourned for all the time they'd lost when she was growing up. He'd missed everything with her and was determined to spend as much time with her and her family as he possibly could going forward.

He looked forward to her having children so he could watch them grow up.

And now that he had Izzy, maybe he'd have a second chance to be a father, a thought that had never occurred to him before she came along. They hadn't talked about that subject again since the other day, but the topic had weighed heavily on his mind as he considered the pros and cons like he would a business opportunity.

Did he really want to start all over again with a new family at forty-eight? Was it fair to his future children to have a father who was already middle-aged when they were born? Would he be able to give them what they needed as a fifty- and sixty-year-old? Did he want to spend the next two decades raising children?

If it meant he'd get to be with Izzy, he'd be willing to do just about anything.

But fatherhood?

He just wasn't sure. That door had closed to him such a long time ago and had reopened only recently, even if he'd considered himself a father the whole time Mia had been missing. When people he met through business asked if he had children, he'd always answered that question the same way: *I have a daughter.* He left out the part about having not seen her in however many years it had been by that point. She'd always been present in his heart and mind, even when he'd had no idea where she was.

If he had more children, would he ever again know another minute of peace? Would he worry all the time about something happening to them, or God forbid, one of them going missing? One thing he was certain of was that he wouldn't survive that nightmare a second time. Not that he worried about Izzy doing what Deb had done to him. Even if he and Izzy ended up in the worst kind of breakup, which he simply couldn't imagine with her, he knew for certain she'd never take off with their children and keep them from him the way Deb had.

"What's wrong?"

Izzy's sleepy voice pulled him out of the weird spiral his thoughts had drawn him into.

"Nothing at all."

She shifted to find a more comfortable position and winced from the pain. "Are you going to start lying to me so soon?"

Her directness was one of the things he'd liked best about Izzy from the first time he met her, except for when that directness forced him to share thoughts he'd normally keep private. That wasn't going to work with her. "I'm thinking about a lot of things, such as how we'll make a Boston-to-Vermont relationship work. I'm pondering the idea of being a father again at my advanced age and whether it would be fair to our potential children to have an old man who's truly old."

"You are *not* old, Cabot."

"I'd be close to seventy when it's time to send them off to college."

"So? Seventy is the new fifty."

"Haha, so they say. But the reality is that seventy is seventy, and would it be fair to them?"

"Can I say something without appearing to be self-serving?"

"You're supposed to be sleeping."

"I'm hurting, and so are you, even if it's in a different way. And what I want to say is that you, Cabot, would be a wonderful, hands-on, down-on-the-floor-to-play father who would make sure his children knew they were deeply loved every day of their lives. As someone who didn't have that, I can assure you, it's the only thing they'll ever need from you."

"Well, when you put it like that, seems easy enough."

"They'd just need you to love them."

"I already do, and we've barely started dating."

Izzy laughed and then winced again.

"What's hurting you, sweetheart?"

"The bruises on my back are aching something awful."

"Didn't your uncle Linc bring you something from the store for that?"

"Yeah, but I can't reach them."

"That's what I'm here for. Where's the stuff?"

"In the bathroom cabinet."

"Stand by." He got out of bed and went to put another log on the woodstove before ducking into the bathroom to get the tub of balm.

When he returned to the bedroom, Izzy had turned on the bedside light and was sitting on the edge of the bed. Her face was pale, her expression pinched with pain. "Do you need one of the pills, too?"

"Maybe an Advil, but no more of the prescription pills. That stuff freaks me out."

"I'm glad to hear you say that. It freaks me out, too. A guy who worked for us hurt his back playing rugby and got hooked on opioids. It was horrible."

"Is he okay now?"

"He's clean, but it's been a hellish process. You're wise to take a cautious approach."

"Addiction is such a big issue everywhere, but it's been really bad in Vermont."

"I've read about that." He got on the bed behind her. "Do you want me to lift your shirt, or do you want to do that?"

"You'd better do it. I can't really twist the way I'd need to."

"No problem. I've got it." He carefully raised her shirt and gasped at the ugly bruises on her back. "Aw, Iz," he said, sighing. "That's got to hurt so much."

"Doesn't feel great."

"I'm afraid to touch you. I don't want to hurt you even more."

"The balm felt really good on the bruises I could reach. It's worth a shot."

"Okay, but let me know if it hurts too much."

"You'll be the first to know."

"I love how you can make me laugh even when we're talking about your evil bruises."

"Laughter is always the best medicine."

"I suppose so. Are you ready?"

"As I'll ever be."

"Okay, here goes." He made sure to barely touch her as he applied the balm, noting how rigidly she held herself, as if anticipating pain. Even with the colorful bruises marring her otherwise flawless skin, Cabot couldn't help but notice the elegant shape of her. He saw perfection under the bruises. When he was finished, he placed a gentle kiss between her shoulder blades, one of the few areas that had escaped the bruising.

His kiss made her shiver. "I can't wait to do that again sometime."

"I can't wait for that either. I've got a few more places that could use that kind of attention."

Cabot drew her shirt down to cover her back. "I'm here for that. For all of it." He offered her his arm to hold as she got herself settled in bed. By the time she was somewhat comfortable, her face had gone completely pale, and she'd broken into a sweat. "Be right back."

Moving carefully to get off the bed without jostling her, he went to the kitchen to get the Advil and stopped in the bathroom to wet a cool cloth that he used to wipe her face.

Her eyes were closed as she took shallow breaths. "Feels good. Thank you."

He kissed her forehead. "I hate to see you in pain."

"It's way better than it was at first."

"Still…"

"Yeah, not there yet," she said.

"But getting there. A little closer every day."

She opened her eyes. "I wish it would happen faster. I've got a life to get back to and a new boyfriend to have fun with."

He brushed the hair back from her face and kissed her unbruised cheek. "Your new boyfriend isn't going anywhere until you can go with him."

"That's a promise you might not be able to keep. I'm worried about you neglecting your own life to take care of me."

"Everything is under control. For now, anyway."

"Will you tell me if it isn't?"

"If you want me to."

"I do, Cabot. I don't want you to sacrifice your own well-being for mine."

"I would, you know. Sacrifice my own well-being for yours. I realized on the interminable ride from New Jersey to Vermont that I'd give up anything, anything at all, except Mia, of course, if only you would survive and give me another chance."

"You don't have to give up anything to have another chance with me."

"I would've, though. That's when I really knew that something had happened with you, as much as I'd tried to deny it."

Izzy's smile was a thing of beauty, especially when it was directed at him. She crooked her finger, telling him to come closer, which he was more than happy to do.

"Kiss me."

"Your lip hurts."

"That's one thing that seems to be healing quickly, thank goodness, because I really want to kiss my new boyfriend."

"Your new boyfriend would like very much to kiss you, even though he's not sure how he feels about being a 'boyfriend' at his advanced age."

"Quit acting like you're ancient. I need a young, vital man to keep up with me, in bed and out."

"Gulp."

Her laughter was every bit as magnificent as her smile, until she grimaced from the pain. "Don't make me laugh."

"Sorry, I'll try not to."

"Don't try too hard."

"I'm going to try *so* hard with you, sweet Isabella." He kissed her as gently as he possibly could. "I want to give you everything you've ever wanted and things you never dared to dream for yourself."

"A girl could fall madly in love with a man who says something like that to her."

"Don't let me stop that girl from falling in love."

"Is she falling all by herself?"

He shook his head. "Not at all. There's a whole lot of falling going on around here."

"Even when I'm black and blue and gross all over?"

"There's nothing gross about you. Even with bruises, you're still the most beautiful woman in any room you're in."

"Not when my sister Ness is there. She's the smoke show of the Coleman family."

"I beg to differ, my love. The Coleman family has more than one smoke show, whatever that is."

Izzy giggled at his baffled expression. "I can see I have a lot of work to do making you hip."

"Good luck with that. My niece Caroline has been trying for years to make me hip. She says I'm hopeless."

"Nothing is ever hopeless."

"You make me feel that more than I ever have. That I can do anything as long as you're there with me to make it all good."

"It's going to be so good," she said, reaching for him to bring him in for another kiss.

This time, he lingered, longer than he had yet, and the longer he kissed her, the more of her he wanted. He wanted all of her—heart, body and soul—and for a guy who'd avoided even the most rudimentary of commitments with women over the years, that was a very big deal indeed.

Izzy and Cabot were awakened early the next morning by the phone. Seeing a 617 phone number on the caller ID, she handed the extension to him.

"Coleman residence, Cabot speaking."

He was silent for several minutes other than an occasional "Uh-huh," "I see" and "No, no, I agree. I need to be there."

Izzy ached as she realized he was going to leave long before she was ready to let him go.

"I'll let you know," Cabot said. "I'll call you back in a couple of hours." He pressed the Off button to end the call. "I have to go back to Boston today. I need to be there for an emergency council meeting tonight."

She forced a smile for him. "That's fine. I knew you couldn't stay forever."

"I don't want to go. Not yet. Well, not ever."

"Your whole life is there, Cabot."

"Not anymore."

"Mia will understand."

"What about you?"

"I'll understand, too, and I'll be very happy to see you when we're next able to be together."

"Why don't you come with me?"

Izzy thought about that for a second. Her next doctor's appointment wasn't for two more weeks. Technically, there was no reason she couldn't go. But did she feel up to three hours in the car?

"We could stop as often as needed so you could move around."

"Are you sure I wouldn't be in the way?"

"No more so than I've been here."

"You haven't been in the way at all."

"There you have it," he said, smiling. "I'd love to have you come to my home, but only if you feel up to it. No pressure."

"I look horrible."

"No, you don't."

"My face is still bruised."

"You look beautiful."

"Have you had your eyes checked lately?"

"My vision is perfect, and I know beautiful when I see it." He twirled a length of her hair around his finger. "What do you think? You want to come? I can make you very comfortable on the main floor where my room is, with an adjoining bathroom. No stairs required, except to get inside. Other than a meeting here and there, I'll be with you like I am here."

"A change of scenery sounds fun as long as I won't have to see anyone looking like this."

"I'll tell you again that you look gorgeous as always, and the only person you might see is my sister, Emily, but you've already met her."

"In that case, I'd love to go."

He kissed her longer than he had yet. "Thank goodness, because I didn't want to go if I had to go without you."

"What time do we need to leave?"

"By one at the latest?"

"Okay, I'll be ready."

"I'll help you pack."

Izzy slowly and painfully showered, which was easier said than done with one arm wrapped in a plastic bag to keep her cast dry. She did what she could with her one good arm and hand.

"Ready for a blow-dry?" Cabot asked from outside the door.

"Come in."

"I am at your service, madam. I have done the hair of stars and celebrities the world over."

As she sat in the chair they'd brought in from the kitchen, Izzy giggled at the ridiculous accent he applied to that statement. In fact, he'd never used a blow dryer before she showed him how after returning home from the hospital.

As he expertly applied the styling products, she caught his gaze in the mirror and smiled. "Way above and beyond the call of duty."

Smiling, he moved her hair to the side and kissed her neck. "'Tis indeed my pleasure, ma'am."

"What nationality is that accent? You sound like Franck from *Father of the Bride*."

"Franck is my cousin!"

"No way!"

"Yes way, and that was a navy blue tuxedo."

Izzy couldn't stop laughing. "If you say so."

"I do."

He dried her hair with a kind of reverence that touched her heart, which was completely lost to him after this special time together.

"Will it be the same, you think?" she asked.

"What?"

"This, if we take it out into the world."

Cabot shut off the hair dryer, but continued to run his fingers through her hair. "This is incredibly portable. What we have can go anywhere, do anything."

"You sound very sure for a man who wasn't sure at all not that long ago."

He put down the blow dryer and placed his hands gently on her shoulders, propping his chin on top of her head. "I was always sure about you and that I wanted you. You've shown me what it might be like to be with you all the time, and now I want you more than I ever did before. You've shown me that I can trust you with my heart and my affection. You're making a believer out of me. If you hadn't agreed to go with me, I'm not sure I could've made myself leave."

Incredibly touched by his sweet words and the courage it had taken to say them, Izzy said, "Thank you for taking such a big chance on me. I know it wasn't easy for you."

"It doesn't feel like a gamble with you. It just feels right."

Even with one arm encased in plaster, healing bruises on her face and everywhere else, and more aches and pains than she could count, Izzy had never felt better than she did hearing him say those words. "It feels right to me, too."

He kissed her neck again and hugged her gently from behind. "I need to make a few calls, and then I'll help you pack."

"I can do it. Take care of your calls."

"I'll make some coffee, too."

"Yes, please."

While she packed for a few days in Boston, Izzy heard Cabot on the phone with Emily, telling her he was bringing Izzy with him. "Sure," he said. "That'd be great. No, we just need my room." After a pause. "None of your business."

Izzy laughed to herself at how he shut down his sister's apparent questions about why they needed only one room. She was looking forward to seeing Emily again and to gaining more insight into Cabot and his life in Boston.

When he was done with the phone, she called her mom.

"Morning," Hannah said. "How'd you sleep?"

"Pretty well, all things considered. I wanted to tell you that

Cabot has to go to Boston for a couple of days, and I'm going to tag along with him for a change of scenery."

"Are you sure you feel up to that?"

"It's only about three hours in the car, and then I'll be chilling at his place. I'll be okay."

"All right. Just take it easy. We don't need any setbacks."

"I'll be fine. I promise."

"I talked to Gramps this morning, and he was hoping to pop over to see you today."

"We'll stop to see him on the way out of town."

"He'd love that. Will you call to let me know you got there okay?"

It'd been years since her mother asked her for that, but she understood why she wanted it now. "Of course."

"Thank you. Oh, and you'll be glad to know I talked to Ray and to Grayson about the back child support thing, and they both agree with you."

"I had a feeling they would. What are you thinking about it?"

"That I ought to at least try, as much as I want nothing to do with him."

"It's about what's right, Mom, and he owes you that and so much more. It's the least he can do."

"I'm probably trying to get blood from a stone. He never was good about holding down jobs. He moved from one thing to the next and couldn't find anything that held his attention for very long."

"We have no idea what he's been up to since he left. It's possible he has resources now that he didn't have then."

"I guess we'll find out."

"I'm proud of you for doing this, Mom. I know how much you want to leave the past where it belongs, but this is a matter of fairness."

"I know, and my plan is to let Grayson handle it and stay somewhat removed from it. I don't need your father's negative energy messing with my happy life."

"No, you don't."

"Did you hear how things went with Ness and Troy last night?"

"Not yet. I need to call her."

"Don't tell her I told you, but when I went out to get the paper, I noticed an SUV with New York plates was still parked outside Noah's."

"No way. Go, Ness!"

"Let me know what you hear from her."

"I may or may not do that."

"Whatever, Isabella. We're all adults here."

Izzy laughed. "And you're still our mother. Gotta run."

"Be safe, and don't forget to let me know you got there."

"Will do. Love you, Mom."

"Love you, too, sweetheart. Have fun with Cabot and tell him I said to take good care of my daughter."

"He's taking very good care of me."

"Then tell him I said thank you—again."

"I will. Talk to you later."

Izzy hung up with her mom and immediately called Noah's house.

CHAPTER FIFTEEN

"It is difficult to know at what moment love begins; it is less difficult to know that it has begun." —Henry Wadsworth Longfellow

I don't do things like this, Vanessa thought as she looked over at Troy sleeping facedown on the other side of the bed. *But, oh my goodness, I'm so glad I did this.*

She wanted to giggle madly at her own thoughts and the complete lack of the usual regrets that followed an impulsive decision like the one she'd made last night when she'd asked Troy to stay. His car was parked outside, announcing to her mother and the rest of the world that he'd spent the night, and Vanessa couldn't care less.

That, too, was not like her.

After the best sex of her life, she couldn't spare the brain cells to worry about the implications or work up the usual level of concern about potential family teasing/ridicule over her stepping so wildly out of character.

Maybe it was time for such a thing, since playing it safe hadn't worked out so well for her. She was still single at thirty-two after expecting to be married with children by now. Her "career," such as it was, had flamed out, and she had no idea what was next for her. Most interesting of all was that the ever-present anxiety that kept her wired so tightly all the time was nowhere to be found this morning.

She stretched her arms over her head, took a deep breath and released it slowly, jolting when a warm hand landed on her belly.

"Morning," he muttered.

"Morning."

"What time is it?"

"Who cares? You're on vacation, and I'm unemployed."

He moved closer to her, put his arm around her and rested his head on her chest. "Thank you for the reminder that I have nowhere to be and nothing to do except this." His tongue found her sore nipple and gently stroked it until it stood up, ready for more of his special brand of magic.

Vanessa gasped as she ran her fingers through his thick dark hair, wanting to hold him in place even as she wondered if she could take any more than she'd already gotten. Never in her life had she been so uninhibited with a man, and as the memories of the night before came flooding back, she still couldn't find it in her to be embarrassed, shocked or anxious.

Who had time for such concerns when a hot, sexy, sweet, caring man was firing her up for the fourth—or was it fifth—time?

"We're out of condoms," she reminded him, and yes, she'd robbed her brother's stash, which was yet another indication of just how crazy last night had gotten.

"We can be creative," he said as he kissed a path from her breasts to her belly and below.

"If we'd been any more creative, someone would be dead."

His low rumble of laughter had goose bumps erupting on the surface of her skin. He looked up at her with brown eyes ablaze with desire. "Best night ever."

"Really?"

Nodding, he said, "So far in first place as to have no competition whatsoever."

"Me, too," she said softly, overwhelmed by emotions she'd never experienced quite so intensely before.

"Now, as I was saying..." He spread her legs and buried his

tongue inside her for like the hundredth time, or so it seemed, and like every other time, he had her on the verge of orgasm in a matter of seconds. How did he do that so easily?

"Troy."

"Yes, Vanessa?"

"I'm on birth control."

He stopped what he was doing to look up at her. "Are you saying what I think you're saying?"

"I'm clean."

"I am, too. Had a full physical a month ago, and this is the first time I've been with anyone since."

"So, um, we don't need condoms, then, I guess."

His eyes lit up with something that went beyond desire. "Are you sure?"

"One thousand percent positive."

Laughing, he moved so he was above her, looking down at her with things she'd waited a lifetime to find in a man. "This might be quick."

"It can't be. I'm sore."

"Oh, we'll go easy, but it'll still be quick."

He kissed her with lips and a tongue that tasted of her as he pressed carefully into her sore and swollen channel.

This was utter madness. The best kind of madness, and she couldn't get enough. But damn, it really hurt for a second.

He froze. "Want me to stop?"

"Absolutely not."

After another few seconds, the pain eased, and the pleasure took over. Soon they were moving together like they'd been doing this for years rather than hours, and Vanessa came with a shout that surprised them both. Everything about this surprised her, but in the best possible way.

"Damn," he muttered after he'd collapsed on top of her. "I didn't think we could top ourselves from last night…"

"Mmmm." She'd pay for her sexual gymnastics later, but couldn't bring herself to care about anything other than how good it felt to be held by him. "Noah has one of those big cast-iron bathtubs. You want to check it out?"

"I'd love to."

"Do you need to tell Cam where you are?"

"She knows."

"The whole town and my entire family is going to know, too."

"Do you care?" he asked.

"Not even kinda."

"Is it like you not to care about what your family says about you?"

"Not even kinda."

That made him laugh.

"We're touching off a scandal the likes of which Butler hasn't seen since Cam crashed into Fred. Just so you're aware of what you're getting yourself into."

"Do I get to be with you in the midst of this epic scandal?"

"Yep."

"Then it's worth whatever sacrifices must be made."

Vanessa affected a grave expression. "A Butler scandal can be all-consuming, with fire and brimstone and moose and other things you'll never see coming."

"I'm here for it all, especially the moose, but only if you're there to protect me."

"I gotcha."

"Then how about that bath?"

"First coffee and then the bath."

"Best vacation day ever," he said as he kissed her.

The phone rang, interrupting the kiss. "So it begins," Vanessa said as she picked up the extension on the bedside table and saw Izzy's number on the caller ID. "Morning."

"Did I wake you?"

"Nope, I was up."

Troy, who was still on top of her, pressed his hips against hers and nearly made her laugh out loud.

"Anything you want to tell me?" Izzy asked with a telltale tone to her voice that indicated she already knew Troy had spent the night.

"Not at the moment."

"Oh, come on, Ness! Spill it!"

"I'm busy."

"Yes, I heard."

"Gotta run, but I'll call you later?"

"I'm going to Boston with Cabot. I'll call you later, and you'd better answer the phone."

"I will if I don't have anything better to do, and with the way things are going lately, I'm apt to be quite busy." Vanessa was loving this all-new morning-after version of herself.

"This is the best thing ever," Izzy said with a squeal of laughter.

"Sure is."

"Ness..."

"Knock it off, and go to Boston. I'll talk to you later."

"You certainly will."

"Thanks for the warning. See ya."

She ended the call just as the phone rang again with a call from Cameron. "For you," she said to Troy.

He withdrew from Vanessa and flopped on his back next to her before pressing the button to answer the phone. "Yes, Mom?" Reaching for Vanessa's hand, he held on tight as he listened to Cameron. "I'm fully aware that I didn't come home last night and missed curfew. Am I grounded?" Glancing at her, he smiled and waggled his brows. "I'm fine. More than fine, actually."

Vanessa could hear Cameron screaming.

Troy held the phone away from his ear. "Will you please get yourself together, woman?" After another pause, he said, "I agree it's the best thing ever, so go away and let me enjoy it, will you? No, I don't know when I'll see you. Later, probably, since my clothes are at your place. For now, anyway."

Vanessa was excited by the thought of him getting his stuff from Cameron's so he could spend the rest of his vacation with her.

"I'll see you later, and butt out." Another pause. "No, it's not your business. Fine, tell Lucy and Emma whatever you want. I don't care. I've got better things to do, and you're bothering me."

More screaming.

"*Goodbye*, Cameron." He ended the call. "As you could probably hear, she's lost her mind."

"I tried to warn you about how scandals work in this town."

"I can handle it. No worries." He cupped her face and looked at her with tenderness and amusement. "You're well worth any scandals that may arise."

"You say that now..."

He kissed her. "I say that indefinitely. Where can we get a good breakfast around here?"

"That's easy. Megan's diner."

"Coffee, bath and breakfast. Then I want to see that moose who's so famous around here. After that, it's back to bed for an afternoon nap. How does that sound as an agenda for our day?"

"That sounds perfect."

CHAPTER SIXTEEN

"Some people come into our lives and quickly go. Some people stay for a while and move our souls to dance. They awaken us to a new understanding, leave footprints on our hearts, and we are never, ever the same." —Flavia Weedn

By the time Cabot and Izzy pulled away from her house in his rental car, it was nearly noon.

"What time is your meeting?"

"Not until seven, so we have plenty of time."

"Can we swing by to see my Gramps on the way out?"

"Absolutely."

They pulled up to Elmer Stillman's home ten minutes later, and Cabot laughed at the sign hanging from Elmer's mailbox that advertised JUSTICE OF THE PEACE, NOTARY PUBLIC, FREE ADVICE. "That's the best thing I've ever seen."

"That's Gramps for you. A jack-of-all-trades and the sweetest guy you'll ever meet."

"I remember that from the wedding."

Cabot parked the rental car behind Elmer's pickup truck and then came around to help Izzy out of the car.

She hated that she needed the help, but with the abdominal incision still healing, every movement caused her pain.

As they made their way up the walk, the front door opened,

and Elmer greeted them with a warm smile. "Well, if this isn't the nicest surprise I've had in days."

"Hi, Gramps."

"Hi, honey. Cabot. Come in, come in."

A million memories assailed Izzy as she walked into the familiar warmth of her grandfather's home, which still smelled like the candles her grandmother had loved. She recalled many a Saturday spent baking in the kitchen or learning to crochet in the living room. Sarah had been a wonderful grandmother to all eighteen of her grandchildren, but she and Izzy had shared a special bond. Izzy had never stopped missing her.

She hugged Elmer with her good arm and kissed his cheek, breathing in the familiar scent of aftershave that would forever remind her of him.

He shook Cabot's hand. "Take your coats?"

"I'm going to keep mine on," Izzy said, unzipping the top part. "It took ten minutes to get the sling on over the coat. We don't need to go through that again."

Cabot handed his coat to Elmer.

"How you feeling, sweetie?"

"Much better than I was, but not quite back to full steam."

He led them to the cozy kitchen, where they sat at the table. "Your mom tells me you're heading for Boston for a few days."

"Cabot has a meeting he needs to attend, and I decided to tag along for a change of scenery."

"Where are you going to find scenery better than what we've got right here?" Elmer asked with a twinkle in his eye.

"Nowhere," Izzy said, smiling. "But the scenery seems a little better when he's around, so I decided to go with him."

"Ah," Elmer said, "I see how it is. I was hoping something would come of him wanting to help care for you at home."

"I'm in the room and can hear you guys," Cabot said with a laugh.

"This is how we roll, young man," Elmer said, grinning. "You'll get used to us."

"I haven't been called 'young man' in a while," Cabot said.

"Compared to me, you're an infant," Elmer replied as he put

mugs of steaming hot chocolate in front of them, along with the whipped cream Izzy loved. "Watch out for this one with whipped cream. She was famous for squirting full cans into her mouth as a kid."

"Good to know," Cabot said with a meaningful look for Izzy.

Her face flushed with heat. "Not in front of my grandfather."

The two men cracked up.

"I like him," Elmer said.

"So do I." Izzy kept her gaze focused on Cabot. "Most of the time, anyway."

"What are your intentions toward my granddaughter, young man?"

"Oh my God, Gramps. What the hell?"

"Haven't you learned from recent events, sweet Isabella, that there's no time to waste in this life?"

"Well, when you put it that way..."

"About those intentions," Elmer said, zeroing in on Cabot.

"I would like to spend as much time as I possibly can making your granddaughter happier than she's ever been," Cabot said. "Beyond that, I'm not entirely sure yet. It's mostly up to her." He shifted his gaze from Elmer to her. "Whatever she wants is what I want."

Izzy fanned her face. "I suppose I should thank you, Gramps, for helping to clarify things."

"That's what I'm here for. I've been thinking of adding CLAR-IFIER OF THINGS to my sign outside."

"You should." Cabot took Izzy's hand and gave it an affectionate squeeze. "You're good at it."

"Cutting through bullshit is one of my special skills. Another is seeing potential obstacles that stand in the way of us getting what we want. For instance, a man like you, Cabot, having been through the ordeal that doesn't need to be rehashed, might have some unresolved *matters* that might... How should I say this? Cause heartache for my granddaughter."

"You're not wrong about the unresolved matters, but I'm working through them and focusing on the present rather than dwelling on the past. Izzy has been helpful in that regard by giving me a present well worth focusing on."

"I'd imagine she's quite exceptional that way. She's always been exceptional. Smartest little kid you've ever met. My Sarah and I used to say that we needed to be at the top of our game when she would come by to bake or sew with her grandmother. She kept us on our toes, asking questions about things a thirty-year-old wouldn't know yet."

Cabot's warm smile made his eyes sparkle as he studied her. "I can so picture that. Little Izzy must've been so cute."

"Got some pictures around here somewhere. Give me a minute. I know just where they are."

While they were alone in the kitchen, Izzy said, "Sorry about the inquisition."

"I think he's fabulous, and I love how he puts it right out there."

"He's the absolute best. Thank you for letting him move things along for us by six months in the span of a ten-minute conversation."

Laughing, Cabot said, "He did do that, didn't he? But he's right. There's no time to waste. Your accident was a wakeup call in that regard."

"Yes, it was, but we need to be realistic, too."

"I've never been more realistic in my life than I've been since I arrived in your hospital room. You're my reality now, Isabella. It's that simple."

She fanned her face. "Am I swooning?"

"Must be the blood loss."

She made a fist to playfully punch his shoulder. "It's not that at all, and you know it."

Cabot glanced at the doorway to the hall where Elmer had gone in search of photos before he leaned in to kiss her.

He was still kissing her when Elmer came back into the room, clearing his throat. "Get your lips off my granddaughter."

Izzy slid a hand around the back of Cabot's neck to keep him there. "I don't want him to, Gramps," she said while sliding her lips over his.

"Whimper," Cabot said.

Elmer returned to his seat at the table and put the pictures he'd found in front of Cabot.

"Not that one!" Izzy said. "That was before I had braces."

"You're beyond adorable," Cabot said as he gazed at the photo of her, with her hair parted down the middle and captured in pigtails that fell almost to her waist. "Your hair was so long!"

"She refused to have it cut for years," Elmer said. "She wanted it to be as long as Rapunzel's."

"I wish I still had that sweater." The red sweater with the white snowflake in the center had been a favorite. "Ally lost it at a skating party. I remind her once in a while that she owes me a replacement."

"Awww, look at you in your Girl Scout uniform and your front teeth missing," Cabot said.

"That was Brownies, and it took a year for my permanent teeth to come in. My mom took me to three different dentists asking where the hell my teeth were."

Elmer chuckled. "Hannah was so afraid you were going to be toothless forever. Remember how you could spit water six feet through the gap?"

"Yes! And my mom got mad when I'd do that, so I started doing it when her back was turned. Of course my siblings always told on me."

"That's what siblings are for." Cabot flipped through photos of junior high cheerleading and high school lacrosse, prom and graduation. "You look exactly the same as you did the day you graduated from high school."

"That is just not true. I have crow's-feet now."

Cabot looked up from the photos to study her face. "I can't see where the crows have been anywhere near you."

"I like this young man very much, Isabella," Elmer said. "Very much indeed."

"And, of course, that's all that matters, right, Gramps?"

"Absolutely. If I didn't like him, he wouldn't stand a chance with my girl."

"Nope. Remember how you couldn't stand Connor?" For Cabot's sake, she added, "He was my high school boyfriend."

"I had that one's number from the second he first started sniffing around. I hate to say I told you so, but…"

"You love to say, 'I told you so'!"

"Not in that case, I didn't. I keep an eye out for him around town. If I happen to nudge him with the front of my truck on Elm Street, I'll make sure it looks like an accident."

"Don't you dare, Gramps! I don't want to have to bail you out of jail."

"It'd be worth it. That fella doesn't deserve to be running around doing what he does. I heard he left his pregnant wife for his assistant, meaning he hasn't changed one bit."

"Where'd you hear that?" Izzy asked, stunned by the info.

"I have my sources, and they're reliable."

They spent another half hour with Elmer before they left to continue on their way to Boston, taking freshly baked cookies with them for the ride.

"If there's a more delightful man on this earth than that one, I've yet to meet him," Cabot said as they headed into town on the way to the interstate.

"He's my favorite person in the whole wide world, second only to my grandmother."

"How old were you when she passed?"

"Thirteen. She was truly my best friend. I was inconsolable for weeks. Took me a long time to bounce back from losing her."

"And it was around the time your dad left, too, right?"

"Yep. That was a rough couple of years, to say the least."

"I'm so sorry you went through that. If she was anything like her husband, they must've been quite a pair."

"Oh, they were. Cute as can be, dancing in the kitchen, laughing all the time. I'm very thankful I spent so much time with them and my aunt and uncle so I know what a happy marriage looks like. There was none of that with my parents. I never remember them being happy together. Were yours?"

"I think they were, mostly," Cabot said. "I don't recall any dancing in the kitchen, though."

"That ought to be the goal, you know? Dancing and laughing and being happy just to be together."

"Sounds perfect to me. We need a road-trip playlist. What've you got handy?"

Izzy had charged the cell phone she used when she traveled outside of Butler. "Since I spend half my life on the road, or at least I did until I totaled my Jeep, I've got an awesome road-trip playlist." She paired her phone to the car's Bluetooth and hit Play on *Viva La Vida*.

"Ah, I love Coldplay. Have you seen them live?"

"Not yet."

"We'll have to do that. Their show is amazing."

"I'd love to see them."

"Almost everyone comes through Boston or the local area at some time or another. I saw the Eagles at the Garden a couple of months ago. That was one hell of a show."

"My dad loved them. Had all their albums on vinyl."

"Does that ruin the band for you?" he asked, looking over at her.

"Nah, I love them in spite of him."

"Good for you."

They were singing at the top of their lungs to Coldplay when Cabot rounded a curve and had to slam on his brakes to avoid hitting Fred the moose. The car spun in a full circle before coming to a stop facing the nonplussed moose.

Johnson, Analisa

33400

Thursday, May 19, 2022

31183206723998   Rosie's curl and weave

CHAPTER SEVENTEEN

"Love is a fire. But whether it is going to warm your hearth or burn down your house, you can never tell." —Joan Crawford

"Holy shit," Cabot said on a deep exhale.

Izzy was shaking so hard, she couldn't breathe. Her chest felt tight and constricted as dots danced before her eyes.

"Izzy! Breathe!" He gave her shoulder a gentle shake. "Izzy!"

All at once, the panic subsided enough for her to take a breath. Tears spilled down her cheeks as she gulped for air.

"I'm so sorry, honey. But we're okay. Everything is fine."

She clung to the comforting sound of his voice as he wiped away her tears.

When Fred let out a loud *moo*, they couldn't help but laugh.

"He doesn't have a care in the world after he scared the crap out of us," Cabot said.

"That's Fred for you."

"I've heard the stories about him, but I had no idea he was so freaking huge."

"He's the sweetest guy, but he has a bad habit of standing in the middle of the road."

"Are you all right?"

"I think so. Are you?"

"As long as you are, I'm good. Do you want to turn back? I'd totally understand if this was too much for you after your accident."

"No, no. It's fine. Let's keep going."

"Are there others like him I need to be watching for?"

"He's the only one who likes to stand in the road."

Cabot laid on the horn, hoping Fred would get the hint to move out of the way, but nothing was that simple when it came to the Butler town moose.

"Sometimes it helps if you put the window down and ask him nicely to move along," Izzy said.

Cabot gave her an arch look. "Seriously?"

"Uh-huh."

He put down the window. "What do I say to him?"

"Try just asking him to please move. He seems to appreciate good manners."

"Do you understand how crazy that sounds?"

"I don't make the moose rules. I just follow them like everyone else around here."

"Okay, here goes. Hey, Fred, would you *please* move your ass? We've got somewhere to be."

"Moo."

Izzy dissolved into giggles that only intensified when Fred remained stubbornly positioned smack in the middle of the road.

"Is there another way out of this crazy town?"

"There is, but it's much longer."

Cabot tried beeping the horn again.

Fred gave him an "are you serious?" look.

"Try saying please again, but leave out the 'move your ass' this time," Izzy said.

"Hi, Fred. I hear you're a nice guy, and if you wouldn't mind please moving, Izzy and I need to get to Boston."

With another loud moo, he finally took a few steps forward, stopping once more before he disappeared into the woods.

"See?" Izzy said. "All you have to do is ask nicely."

"The funniest part is you don't even realize how insane that is," Cabot said as he pressed the accelerator to get them moving again.

"I realize it, but that's how we roll in Butler. There's nowhere else like it in the whole world."

"No, there isn't."

"Can you see the charm along with the crazy?"

"Absolutely. It's one of the prettiest places I've ever been, even if it's one of the last towns on earth that doesn't have cell service."

"That also makes us special. There's talk from time to time about putting up a cell tower. One of the companies offered my uncle Linc seven figures to put a tower on the back field behind the store, but he declined. The townspeople don't want it. We like being the last place on earth without cell service."

She'd no sooner said that than both their phones came alive with beeps and chimes and other notifications that indicated they'd found service.

"Back to civilization." Cabot glanced at her. "Although I have to say, I did enjoy life off the grid for a while. I can't recall the last time I was untethered."

"You're welcome to come visit any time you wish to be untethered."

"Are we back to visiting now? I was sort of hoping we might, you know, figure out a way to spend most of our time together."

"How's that going to work with your life and business being headquartered in Boston and mine in Vermont?"

"I figure where there's a will, there's a way. I have the will. Do you?"

"I do, but I'm also realistic. One of us is going to have to make some fairly major changes to their life in order for us to be together almost every day. It would be hard for me to do that with my work focused primarily in Vermont. That's not to say I couldn't work somewhere else, but it's taken me a while to become established in that niche. It'd be like starting over for me if I did something else."

As she spoke, Cabot listened as he kept his eyes on the road while trying not to feel despondent over the significant challenges that stood between them and happily ever after. In addition to the emotional baggage that was so much a part of who he was, they had a rather serious geography problem. After spending the last two weeks with her, all he wanted was more of her, of the peace he found in her presence, of the feelings for her that were growing and multiplying by the day and the promise of a future filled with things he'd never imagined for himself, including more children.

It wasn't lost on him that if they were going to get that future, he was the one who would have to give up a big chunk of the life he'd been leading before. Was he prepared to do that? There was so much to consider that it made his brain tired even thinking about it. Disengaging from the big life he led in Boston wouldn't be simple, but it could be done.

The simplest part of this equation was his growing feelings for Izzy. It hadn't been so long that he didn't know love when he saw it. Holding on to that feeling—and to her—had become increasingly more important to him with every day he spent with her. He couldn't conceive of her going home to Vermont and him staying in Boston to carry on with the life he'd been leading before her.

Even with his frantically busy schedule, there would be a hole in the center of his life that only she could fill. Nothing would be the same without her. So either he could live with that gaping hole, or he could make some changes to accommodate a whole new life. Living most of the year in Vermont appealed to him for other reasons, too, with his daughter now permanently settled there.

"You're thinking awfully hard over there," Izzy said, breaking a long silence between them that'd been filled by music.

"I'm trying to make this work."

"How's it going so far?"

"Well, I'm seeing that there will have to be some significant concessions, but on the plus side, I get you and Mia and Wade and the family they're going to have together. I get the possibility of more children and a happy, sweet life with you."

"What's the downside?"

"There isn't one as far as I can see, other than the crazy moose that stands in the middle of the road and no cell service."

"Don't forget the humungous family that's always around and in your business."

"That's not a downside."

"Your life would be much quieter in Vermont."

"Would it, though?"

"Well, you wouldn't be able to catch as many concerts and ball games and art shows and other such things."

"I've been there, done that. I'm okay with less of it if it means spending every night snuggled up to you."

"There would be significant snuggling."

"I can't imagine anything better than that."

IT WAS AFTERNOON BY THE TIME TROY AND VANESSA MADE IT TO the diner for breakfast. All conversation came to a halt as everyone stared at them, or so it seemed to her. "Nothing to see here, people," Vanessa said.

"Now that's just a damned lie," Lucy said, waving them over to join her and Colton.

"You want to sit with them or by ourselves?" Troy asked Vanessa.

"I'm not afraid of them if you're not."

"I'm good." He squeezed her hand and led her to the booth.

Vanessa's cousin moved to sit next to Lucy, which left the other side open for her and Troy.

Troy.

Back in middle school, she would've been drawing hearts around his name on the covers of her notebooks and dreaming about their fairy-tale wedding when she was supposed to be paying attention in class. Her romantic heart had been broken so many times since then that she'd all but given up on ever finding *him.*

Until Troy Kennedy had walked into her sister's house the other day and changed everything that quickly.

"So, kids," Lucy said, beaming at her friend. "Do tell."

"Nothing to tell," Troy said as he stirred cream into the coffee Butch had delivered with a grunt along with two menus.

The cranky cook was filling in for Megan, who was out on maternity leave after giving birth to baby Carson. Everyone was looking forward to having her back soon.

"Don't lie to me," Lucy said. "I've already talked to Cam and gotten the scoop."

"There's no scoop, so chill."

"I know scoop when I see it, and I see scoop."

"Will you please do something about your wife?" Vanessa asked Colton.

"Uh, well, there's not much I can do about her. She's like a dog with a bone since Cameron called her earlier."

"Woof," Lucy said. "So, kids… How's it going?"

"Shut up, Luce," Troy said, perusing the menu, "and tell me what's good here."

"I like the BLT," Vanessa said, "and the fries are so good. Best fries I've ever had."

"I remember that from when I was here before. I'm going to make the BLT a turkey club and call it lunch."

Vanessa giggled at how he said that.

"Oh Lord," Lucy said. "This is worse than I thought."

Troy put his arm around Vanessa and kissed the top of her head. "So much worse."

Again, Lucy squealed and clapped and generally made a scene.

"Did you act like this when she started seeing me?" Colton asked Troy.

He rolled his eyes. "Hardly. I was already sick of this place by the time you entered the picture. And don't even get me started about Grayson coming for Emma and Simone—and then even Ray left me. You all suck."

"So much I could say to that," Lucy said with a low dirty laugh.

"But you won't," Colton said with a grin for his wife.

Butch approached their table, pad in hand and a tray trapped under his arm. "Whaddya have?"

After they ordered—quickly, so as not to annoy him—Butch took off without another word.

"Was it something we said?" Troy asked.

"Oh no," Colton said. "That's him being charming. Have you met our sister-in-law Megan, who runs this place?"

"She's Hunter's wife, right?"

"Yep," Colton said. "She's on maternity leave, and Butch refused to hire someone to cover for her because he 'doesn't do change.' So now he's trapped doing her job and his, and thus, his extra charm."

"Ah, I see."

"The food is still great, though," Colton said. "It just takes a minute or two longer than it does when Megan is here."

"We're not in any rush, are we?" Troy asked Vanessa, who smiled up at him.

"Not at all. We've got all day to do whatever we want. After this, we're going to Hannah's to see Fred and Dexter."

"Wait, who's Dexter?" Troy asked.

"I didn't tell you that Fred brought home a baby moose named Dexter?" Vanessa asked.

"Ah, no. I think I would've remembered that. So is Fred actually a girl moose?"

"Nope. He's all man, and we have no idea how he came upon Dexter, but one day he showed up with him."

"And my sister, the moose whisperer, made it her mission to raise Dexter, who's now more of a family pet than a wild animal and even has a bed by the fireplace in Hannah's house," Colton said.

"What'll they do when he's fully grown?" Troy asked, sounding amazed.

"Isn't that the question of the year?" Colton asked with a laugh. "Hannah's poor husband, Nolan, has been saying all along that they're going to end up with a fully grown bull moose in bed with them."

"I love this place so much," Troy said, laughing.

"I thought you hated it because it took all your best friends from you," Lucy said.

"I have a love-hate relationship with Butler," Troy said, glancing at Vanessa. "With much more love than hate, especially recently."

Vanessa wondered if her face turned as bright red as the heat inside her indicated, and then she realized she didn't care. Today was shaping up to be one of the best days of her life, and nothing, not even the whole town knowing she was sleeping with Troy, could bring her down.

CHAPTER EIGHTEEN

"A hundred hearts would be too few to carry all my love for you."
—Bangambiki Habyarimana

"*I* can't believe it's snowing—again," Lucy said to Colton as he drove her back up to their mountaintop for an after-lunch nap.

"You can't? Really? This is your second winter here, Luce. I'd think by now you wouldn't be surprised by snow."

"I'm still surprised by how much of it falls on Vermont."

"That's part of our charm."

"If you say so." Lucy shifted to try to find a more comfortable position, although at this point in a pregnancy seemingly without end, no position was comfortable. "How much are we supposed to get this time?"

"I heard between twenty-seven and thirty-six inches on the mountain."

"Sweet Jesus. Does it ever end?"

"Yep, but not for a couple of months yet." He looked over at her. "Are you okay?"

"Yeah, just some heartburn and the usual feeling like I'm being stretched to the point of bursting. Other than that, all is well."

"Three more weeks, honey, and Bruiser will be here."

"I'm not sure I can stand three more weeks of being pregnant."

"I'll rub your back when we get home."

They had to take it slowly going up the steep road to their mountaintop home with the snow coming down fast and furious all of a sudden.

"Are we going to be able to get there?" Lucy asked, wondering how he knew where the road was in the complete whiteout.

"Of course we are. Don't worry, my sweet."

"What? Me worry?"

She was so bloody uncomfortable. The skin across her extended abdomen felt so tight, and her back ached like crazy. She couldn't wait to get home to lie down, with her head raised, of course, lest she die from heartburn. How had her mother-in-law, Molly, done this *eight* times and had *two* sets of twins? The woman was a marvel, but Lucy had known that from the start. Not to mention Molly's sister, Hannah, who'd also done it *eight* times.

With that kind of maternal royalty in her midst, Lucy didn't feel right complaining about the misery of pregnancy. And she sure as hell couldn't whine about fearing the actual birth. No, that wouldn't be happening, even if it was all she thought about.

They'd done the classes and the tour of the cozy birthing suites at the local hospital and were as prepared as anyone could be to have their baby. But she was still scared shitless and had stopped reading the books and watching the videos, because they only made her more anxious than she already was.

True to his word, Colton got them up the steep incline that led to their home, but not without some serious shifting, down-shifting and four-wheel driving. Their yellow Labs, Sarah and Elmer, came racing out to meet them, seeming relieved to see them with the storm raging even more intensely up here than it was below. Visibility had shrunk to about five feet, and the pathway Colton had carved out of the sidewalk that led to their cabin was already piled high with new snow.

"Wait for me. I'll come get you."

As he trudged around the front of the truck, a pain in the center of her pregnant belly had her gasping. "Ugh, what the hell?" The damned Braxton-Hicks contractions were the worst. She shook off the pain before Colton opened the door so he wouldn't hover over her all afternoon when he had work to do.

She took his outstretched hand and let him lead the way toward their warm, cozy home. If you'd told her a couple of years ago she'd live such a rustic life, the city girl in her would've laughed her ass off. But that was before she'd met Colton, who'd changed everything. She wouldn't trade anything about their life for the fanciest of en suite bathrooms. Although, he had promised her indoor plumbing in the next year. She wouldn't say no to that.

"Are we stopping at the potty before we go in?"

"Probably ought to," she said.

"Right this way, ma'am."

After she'd used the facilities, she washed her hands and face and grimaced through another of those damned Braxton-Hicks contractions. Cameron was right. They were no joke.

Colton extended his arm for her walk to their cabin while the dogs followed, hot on their heels. Inside, she removed her coat and went to the kitchen to start the kettle to make some of the decaf tea that had become a mainstay during the frigid winter months.

Another pain nearly brought her to her knees, and she couldn't help but cry out from the sheer shock of it.

Colton, who'd been adding logs to the woodstove, raced to her side. "What?"

"Braxton-Hicks contractions."

"Are you sure that's what they are?"

"What else would they be three weeks before my due date?"

"Uh, well, didn't the book say any time after thirty-six weeks is in the window?"

"It's not labor, Colton. I'd know if it was."

Lucy had no sooner said those words than a gush of fluid between her legs made a liar out of her. She looked down at the

169

puddle on the floor and then up at him, her mouth hanging open. "We, ah, should get back to town."

Colton rubbed the back of his neck. "Don't freak out, but I don't think we can."

"*What?*"

"We barely made it up the hill. It wouldn't be safe to try to go back down, even if I plow the driveway. There's a layer of ice under the snow from the last storm, and I'd be afraid of losing control of the truck with you in labor."

"Then call EMS! Get your brothers here!"

"I'm not sure they could get up the hill either. We just have to remain calm."

"Calm." She said the word quietly, but her blood pressure spiked as another contraction ripped through her, this one even more intense than the one before. "How am I supposed to stay calm when I'm having a baby on top of a mountain with only my husband with me? *I want a doctor, Colton!*"

"Let's get you out of the wet clothes, and then we'll figure out what to do."

"You have to get us off this mountain, Colton."

"I'm going to try, sweetheart."

IZZY DOZED OFF AS THEY LEFT THE SNOWSTORM BEHIND AND crossed the state line into Massachusetts. Cabot's thoughts wandered as he enjoyed her eclectic playlist, which included everything from Poison to Ariana Grande to Taylor Swift, Adele and Creedence. The music and the time with Izzy's wonderful grandfather had given him further insight into the magnificent Isabella Coleman. Not only was she an extraordinarily talented photographer and artist, but she was a devoted daughter, granddaughter, sister, cousin and friend.

She was someone he wanted on his side and by his side because he already knew she was loyal, trustworthy, patient, loving and sweet.

So why did he still have a feeling of dread he couldn't shake no matter how hard he tried? Was the fear of disaster so deeply ingrained in him that he didn't know how to function without it?

His former therapist would've had a field day with that thought. She'd tell him to stop anticipating trouble where there was none. Everything was as perfect as it'd ever been for him, so why did he have to dwell in a place of negativity? Why couldn't he relax and enjoy the moment? Probably because life had taught him not to get too comfortable, especially in a situation in which he wasn't in control of the outcome.

That was why he thrived in his business. He was in charge. He said yes or no or maybe. There were few surprises he didn't see coming and hardly anything he couldn't handle. He went out of his way to anticipate every possible outcome so he was ready for whatever might happen.

He couldn't do that with Izzy. He couldn't look into the future to see that everything would work out great with them, and without that assurance, he couldn't shake the dread. It was unrealistic, he knew, to need that kind of guarantee, because there was no such thing. No one could promise that everything would work out the way he wanted it to. But without that guarantee, he couldn't fully relax and allow himself to fall the rest of the way in love with her.

Cabot was already way more than halfway in love. It was the second half that concerned him. Izzy wasn't the kind of woman who'd settle for halfway or who'd tolerate a man who only gave her part of himself. That wouldn't fly with her, nor should it. She was a woman who deserved to be loved without reservation, and he wanted so badly to be the one who loved her that way.

He just didn't know how to do it.

Yes, he loved Mia without reservation or hesitation, but she was his daughter. It was easy for him to give her all of himself, because she was as relieved to be back with him as he was to be with her. She wasn't going anywhere.

Izzy had options. She could have any man she wanted, for one thing.

She wants you, you idiot. Cabot could hear his sister's voice as clear as if she were sitting next to him. *Why do you have to do this stupid shit to yourself? Why would you want to sabotage something so perfect by dwelling on negativity?*

A man couldn't change the way he was wired overnight. That wiring had saved his sanity during the endless search for his missing daughter. He'd become the master of control in all corners of his life. No one was ever going to hurt him like that again, not if he had anything to say about it.

And wasn't that the crux of his dilemma? By loving Izzy, by envisioning a future with her, he was giving her the power to hurt him. In reality, she already had the power to decimate him. If she walked away now, for whatever reason, he wasn't sure he'd survive it. Which was why he needed to get this negativity under control before he sabotaged himself—and her.

He'd tried to tell her he was a mess on the inside, but she'd refused to believe that, choosing to see only the parts of him he'd shown her so far. It was only fair that she be aware of the dark side before she made any big decisions. If only the thought of opening that part of himself to her didn't make him feel sick.

She was all sunshine and light, peace and happiness.

It would kill him if he somehow caused that light to dim.

Later, he would have almost no memory of the hours on the Mass Pike, but his hands ached from gripping the wheel so tightly. He'd promised Izzy they'd stop to stretch, but he didn't want to disturb her rest, so he let her sleep.

After navigating through the traffic that was part of life in Boston, he pulled up to his home on Acorn Street right around five o'clock. He had just enough time to get Izzy settled and grab something to eat before he was due at City Hall for a vote on a major downtown development that he opposed for a variety of economic and environmental reasons. Without his vote, the project would've been approved.

"Hey, Iz." He touched her hand. "We're here."

Her eyes fluttered open, and she took a look around. "Did I sleep the whole way?"

"Most of it."

"Sorry."

"Don't be. Your playlist kept me company."

She shifted in the seat and winced from the pain.

"Wait for me to help you."

He got out of the car and went around to open her door. "Take your time," he said, offering her a hand.

"You might have to pull," she said, grimacing.

He was as careful as he could be helping her to stand and then waiting for her to get her bearings.

"This totally sucks," she said, her face pale and pinched.

Cabot kissed her cheek. "Not totally."

Her small smile made her look much more like herself.

He offered her his arm. "Right this way, madam."

"I need my purse and bags."

"I'll come back for them."

They walked through a gate and up the stone stairs to his four-story brick-fronted townhouse. He'd asked Emily to come by and get it ready for Izzy's arrival, so Cabot wasn't surprised when his sister opened the door for them.

"You made it," she said.

He could tell with one look at her that she was elated to see him with Izzy. Of course she was, after what he'd put her and the rest of his family through after Mia went missing. "We did."

"How was the traffic?"

"Brutal as always."

"Welcome to Boston, Izzy," Emily said. "It's so nice to see you again."

"Thank you. Nice to see you, too."

Cabot walked Izzy through the foyer into the open-concept kitchen, dining and living area.

"You didn't tell me your place was a mansion," Izzy said in a softer-than-usual tone that told him she was in pain as she looked around at his home.

"It's not a mansion," he said, feeling slightly embarrassed. "Not exactly."

"Oh, hush, Cabot," Emily said, laughing. "It is, too, and you know it."

"Fine. Whatever. Call it what you will. I just call it home."

"It's beautiful, Cabot," Izzy said.

He helped her to sit on the sofa and waited for her to catch her breath. "What can I get you?"

"A glass of water and three Advil? Oh and my phone so I can let my mom know we got here."

"Coming right up."

While he went into the kitchen, Emily took a seat on a chair across from Izzy. "We were so glad to hear you were well enough to go home and then to come here with Cabot."

"Thank you. I definitely got lucky, even if the recovery sucks."

"You're doing great," Cabot said when he returned with the water and pills.

Izzy took them from him, swallowed the pills with a drink of the cold water and put her head back against the sofa, seeming completely drained from the small effort it had taken to walk inside.

Cabot put the glass on a coaster and covered Izzy with a throw blanket before leaning in to kiss her forehead. "I'll grab your purse and phone."

A few minutes later, he returned with the phone, and she made a quick call to her mom to let her know they'd arrived safely in Boston.

"Rest, sweetheart," Cabot said after she ended the call, giving her another kiss on the cheek.

"Don't let me sleep too long or I'll be up all night."

"I won't."

Emily followed him to the kitchen.

"Is she all right?" Em asked in a whisper.

"She's a thousand times better than she was, but still has a ways to go."

"Poor thing." She came over to hug him. "And how are you?"

"I'm good. Things are good."

"So it seems." With a gleam in her eye, she said, "Dare I get excited for you?"

Cabot shrugged. "If you'd like."

Her smile faltered. "What is it?"

He tipped his head toward his office off the dining room.

After closing the door, he leaned against it. "I think I'm in love with her. No, wait. That's not true."

"It isn't?"

"I *know* I'm in love with her."

"Oh, Cabot," Emily said on a long exhale. "That's wonderful."

"It's pretty great."

"But?"

"You know... The usual stuff. The demons. They're reminding me that someone like Izzy deserves a man who isn't a disaster on the inside."

"You're not a disaster. You've been through some rough years that'll always be part of who you are, but you're *not* a disaster."

"I'm worried I'm going to hurt her somehow. She's... She's everything, Em. Absolutely *everything*."

"How does she feel about you?"

"The same as I do about her. I think."

"If she didn't, she wouldn't be here. Not feeling the way she does. She came because she didn't want to be separated from you."

"I'm afraid I'm going to screw this up. I may not be a complete disaster, but I'm so out of practice with things like this that I have no idea—"

"Stop, Cabot. Just stop and take a breath."

He did as she directed, but his chest ached when he tried to take a deep breath.

"You're feeling this way because it's the first time you've truly cared for someone since... Well, you know. You're flexing muscles you haven't used in years, so of course you're a bit out of shape and uncertain. What matters is that you *care* about her, and she knows that. Just keep doing what you're doing."

"Other than finding Mia, I've never wanted anything the way I want her. I have from the first time I met her, and I made a bloody mess of it until she got hurt and then..." He couldn't even think about getting those calls from Mia and then Linc without the sick feeling of dread returning. Neither of them had been able to assure him that she'd be all right. They hadn't known that for sure yet.

175

"And then everything came into focus for you," Emily said, "and you acted accordingly. You're doing all the right things. You've been there for her when she needed you, and that'll matter to her. You're building a solid foundation. Now you just have to have faith in it."

"Faith is tough for me."

"And for good reason, but Izzy is nothing like *her*. You can't compare who and what you were with her to who and what you are with Izzy. You've lived a lifetime since then, learned a million lessons. You've been preparing for this all that time, and now it's within your reach. Everything you've ever wanted is right there." She gestured to the living room. "She's right there."

"I was doing pretty well with it all until we left Vermont."

"Then go back to Vermont and stay there. Stay as long as it takes for you to believe this is different. You lived a nightmare here. It's no wonder coming back triggers you."

"What about everything here?"

"Screw it, Cabot. You've worked like a *dog* for years. You have everything you need to live comfortably for the rest of your life —and to leave your daughter set for life. Don't use your work to hide from your life."

The thought of walking away from his commitments in Boston to be with Izzy in Vermont made him feel happier than anything had in longer than he could remember. If only the reality of *doing it* weren't so daunting.

Emily put her hands on his shoulders, forcing him to look at her. "One thing I know for certain… If you let her get away, you'll regret it forever. And just so you know, I've thought that since the wedding last June. You were different with her from the beginning. I saw it. We all saw it."

"I almost screwed it up." He ran his fingers through his hair. "Well, I did screw it up. I couldn't bring myself to take the next step because I knew if I did…"

"That you'd be taking a chance you've refused to take for decades because of what that evil witch did. If you miss out on this chance to be happy, she wins, Cabot. And she *cannot* win, do you hear me?"

Cabot couldn't help but smile at the vehemence in her words. "I hear you, and I appreciate you more than you know."

"Likewise. I want so badly to see you happy."

"I haven't been *un*happy…"

"You have no idea what you've missed out on, but I think you're about to find out, if you haven't already."

"I'm starting to get a clue." He kissed his sister's cheek. "Thanks for the pep talk, for getting the house ready for Izzy and for a million other things I'll never have the words to thank you for."

"You can thank me by going out there with her and being happy. Just be happy."

"I'm working on it."

He walked Emily to the door when she left and then went to check on Izzy, who was still asleep. Since he had an hour before he had to leave, he sat next to her.

She opened her eyes a few minutes later and turned to him, smiling. "Sorry to be such a 'good time had by all' today."

"No worries. You must've needed the rest."

"I didn't mean to conk out again ten seconds after we got here. Is Emily still here?"

"She had to get home, but she said to tell you she'll come by to see us tomorrow."

"She seems very sweet."

"She's my best friend. I never would've survived… well, everything… without her and her husband and daughter."

"How old is their daughter?"

"Caroline is twenty-three."

"Wait… Is she the one my cousin Max was hanging out with at the wedding?"

"Yep."

"Ah, okay. I remember her. Was it hard for you… watching her grow up while you were looking for Mia?"

"I tried to keep the two things separate."

"How'd that go?"

"Good days. Bad days. She was a constant reminder of what I

was missing out on with my own daughter, but I adore her. She was and is a ray of sunshine in the darkness."

"You seem tense. Is everything all right?"

"You want the truth?"

"Always."

"Everything was fine in Vermont. I'm not as sure of myself or anything else here."

"Why is that?"

"Emily says it's because I lived a nightmare here, and coming back triggers me."

"What do you think of that theory?"

"It's very possible. I used to stick pretty close to home in case… well… I wanted Mia to be able to find me. I've never been away from here as long as I just was."

"Not even on a vacation?"

"I haven't been on a vacation in more than twenty-five years. My life was about work, my family and finding my daughter. There was no room for anything else."

"You have a lot of living to make up for, Cabot."

"So I'm told. I'm working on trying to break old habits, but it probably won't happen overnight. There're fixer-uppers, and then there's me."

"I'm not going anywhere."

"You promise?"

"I promise, and you're not a fixer-upper. You're a man who's faced struggles that the rest of us can only imagine. Anyone who would judge you or how you've lived needs to walk a mile in your shoes to understand the nightmare you endured. I give you credit for the things you accomplished while Mia was missing, including building an incredibly successful business."

"Thank you for that. I appreciate that you seem to understand how hard it was."

"I can never fully understand that and hope I never do, but I can empathize with how terribly difficult and awful it had to be."

"It was, and work became my salvation during those years. Building my company gave me something other than despair to focus on."

"I'm glad you had that."

He kissed the back of her hand and then her lips. "I'm glad I have you now to give me something new and exciting to think about."

"Because I'm super exciting lately."

"You, Isabella, are the most exciting thing to happen to me since my daughter was born."

CHAPTER NINETEEN

"A joyful heart is the inevitable result of a heart burning with love."
—Mother Teresa

Moose playtime at Vanessa's cousin Hannah's house was about the coolest thing Troy had ever experienced. Fred was clearly the "alpha dog" of the pack that included Dexter, Hannah's dog, Homer Junior, and her little girl, Callie, who ran around with the animals as if playing with bull moose was the most natural thing in the world.

For her, it probably was, because she'd been exposed to the moose her entire life.

"Nolan would kill me if he could see her playing with them like that." Hannah sipped from a thermal cup. "Playtime is a little more restrained on the weekends when Daddy is home."

"You're not afraid of them hurting her?" Troy asked warily.

"They would die for her," Hannah said. "She's as much their baby as she is mine."

"Don't try to make sense of it," Vanessa said to Troy. "There's no sense to be made."

"It just is," Hannah said with a sigh of happy contentment.

She never looked away from the activities of child, dog and moose, and Troy couldn't deny the moose were exceptionally gentle if Callie was anywhere near them. The dog seemed to keep himself positioned between the moose and the little girl as an added layer of security.

Callie kept running back to show her mother treasures she found in the yard, including acorns left from the fall, an icicle that fell from a tree and a snowball she made.

"Thank you, my darling girl," Hannah said after every treasure was delivered.

Troy noticed that the moose got much rougher with each other when Callie was near her mother, and poor Homer ran back and forth, keeping a watchful eye on the little one.

"So, you two... Way to stir up a sleepy town in the dead of winter." Hannah eyed her cousin over the top of her cup.

"Who, us?" Vanessa said. "What did we do?"

"Don't make me say it in front of the child," Hannah said.

"I'm sure the child has seen her share of crazy in this household," Vanessa said.

"Don't turn it around on me. I've done my time in the spotlight. Twice. It's your turn now." Hannah raised a brow in Vanessa's direction. "So..."

"We're hanging out. Having fun. Everyone else is making a bigger deal of it than we are, right, Troy?"

"I'm not sure that's true. It's a really big deal to me."

Vanessa whipped her head around to look at him, must've seen the amusement dancing in his gorgeous eyes and laughed. "Well played, my friend."

"I like this," Hannah declared. "You two would be very good for each other."

"I agree," Troy said, this time without the amusement. He'd already decided that the gorgeous, funny, smart, sexy Vanessa Coleman could be *very* good for him. And vice versa. He could be good for her, too. For the first time in longer than he could remember, he wanted that for himself, but only because he might be able to have it with her.

"Stop." Vanessa nudged him with her shoulder. "The scandal is already bad enough without you making it worse."

"We have so little to entertain us this time of year," Hannah said. "We appreciate you giving us something to chew on."

"We're happy to oblige, aren't we, Vanessa?"

"Absolutely thrilled," she said, seeming mortified again.

Mortification was adorable on her.

"You knew what would happen the minute you let his car stay parked outside Noah's overnight," Hannah said.

"I couldn't find the wherewithal to care—at the time."

Hannah laughed hard. "I'll bet. I remember when I was first officially with Caleb. We were in high school, so sneaking around was in our DNA. But we thought we were fooling everyone. Turns out the whole town knew. Apparently, we weren't as smart as we thought we were."

"You two were 'a couple' long before it was official," Vanessa said. "I can't believe you thought anyone was fooled."

"Ah, young love," Hannah said with a sigh. "Everything is so big and dramatic and ridiculous with hindsight."

"I'm really sorry you lost him," Troy said. He'd heard about Hannah's first husband being killed in Iraq, but had never gotten the chance to express his condolences before now.

"Thank you. It was a long time ago. Sometimes it seems like another lifetime, which makes me feel guilty, so I tend not to think that way too often."

"I'm sure there are a lot of complicated emotions, even now that you have Nolan and Callie," Vanessa said.

"And baby number two on the way," Hannah said, patting her abdomen.

"Oh! I hadn't heard!" Vanessa hugged her cousin. "Congratulations, Han."

"Thanks. We're excited. Callie will be a wonderful big sister."

Troy gave Hannah so much credit for rebuilding her life after she lost her young husband so tragically. He'd suffered through his own tragedies, albeit different from what she'd been through, but no less heartbreaking. Ten years ago, he might not have recognized how special his connection with Vanessa was. Now he was older, wiser, ready for something lasting, especially after seeing how happy his closest friends were with their partners.

But damned if there wasn't something in the water in this crazy little town. Whatever it was, he was thankful it had led him to Vanessa, and he couldn't wait to see what happened next with her.

AFTER SHARING THE DELICIOUS PORK TENDERLOIN, MASHED potatoes, green beans and apple sauce dinner Emily had left for him and Izzy, Cabot sat through the tedious city council meeting, wishing he was home watching a movie with Izzy. His usually dependable concentration was shot to hell as the lawyers for the company requesting the variance droned on for hours. Usually, the minutiae interested him.

Tonight, he couldn't be bothered to care, and if he was being honest, he hadn't truly cared about city business the way he ought to for quite some time. Now that Mia and Izzy were in his life, he wanted to spend more time in Vermont, and he simply couldn't do that if he remained on the council.

He couldn't do this for another year, even as he knew he probably shouldn't make a decision that important while bored out of his mind.

One of his fellow councilmembers saved him when he called for a vote.

"But we have more information to share," one of the lawyers said.

"I think we've heard more than enough," the mayor said.

Cabot wanted to stand up and cheer.

"All in favor, please say aye," the mayor said.

Four members said aye.

"All opposed, please say nay."

Five members said nay.

"The request for a zoning variance is denied." The mayor banged the gavel and moved the agenda along at a rapid clip after that.

They were about to wrap up when Cabot requested a short executive session.

"So moved," another member said.

"Seconded."

"All in favor?"

Everyone said aye.

The mayor adjourned the public meeting, asked for the room to be cleared of everyone but the city clerk and solicitor and then gave the floor to Cabot.

He wished he'd given this more thought ahead of time, but now that the moment was upon him, he tried to speak from his heart. "I want to thank you all for your patience and kind thoughts when I was with my friend in Vermont these last couple of weeks. I'm happy to report she's on track to make a full recovery, and in the time we've spent together, we've decided to, well, give romance a whirl."

The others offered their congratulations as he tried not to be embarrassed to be sharing such personal information with his fellow councilmembers. But he wanted them to know why he was stepping away.

"As you know, my daughter also lives there, and I find myself wanting to spend more time three hours from here. I'd intended to stick out this year on the council and not run for reelection in the fall, but the changes to my personal life have made it so I'm unable to give my council duties the time and attention they deserve. As such, I'm offering my resignation, effective immediately. I'll make it official tomorrow with a letter and will release a statement to the media as well."

He took a moment to contend with an unexpected surge of emotion. "I want to thank you all for the kindness and latitude you've given me since my daughter came back into my life. I'm not one to leave a commitment unfulfilled, but if I've learned anything, it's that life is short, and time with our loved ones is the thing that matters the most. It's been the honor of my life to serve the city of Boston and to have the opportunity to work with all of you."

His colleagues offered him their best wishes for the future and thanked him for his service.

"I wish you all good things, Cabot," the young mayor said when she shook his hand. "We all know how much your daughter means to you."

"She's everything." He smiled as he thought of Izzy, too. "Well, *almost* everything."

After he spent a few minutes shaking hands and speaking one-on-one with the others, he walked out of City Hall for the last time as a member of the Boston City Council. Walking to the navy blue Mercedes sedan he hadn't driven in weeks, he already felt lighter, having shed a considerable responsibility that he hadn't had time for lately.

His father used to tell him and his siblings that if they couldn't give something a hundred percent, then they shouldn't do it at all. The council hadn't gotten a hundred percent from him since the day Mia came back into his life. In truth, he probably should've resigned before now.

As he drove through the congested streets of the city he'd called home all his life, he felt less at home there than he ever had before. How was it that a few weeks in a crazy little mountain town with no cell service and a rogue moose had begun to feel more like home to him than Boston?

He recalled something his late mother had once said, when the family was about to move to a bigger house, leaving their childhood home behind. Cabot had worried about whether the new house would feel like home. "A home is not a roof over your head," his mother had said. "It's the people who live under that roof. As long as we're all together, we're home."

His home was now wherever Mia was, not that he expected to live under the same roof. He'd missed those years, but he wasn't going to miss anything else with her. She lived in Vermont, and he would, too, most of the time, anyway. He couldn't wait to get home to see Izzy, to make plans, to tell her what he'd done.

She was curled up on the sofa watching a movie when he came in from the garage under his house. Tomorrow, he needed to return the car he'd rented in New Jersey after getting the call about Izzy's accident.

"How was the meeting?"

"Eventful," he said when he sat next to her and kissed her cheek.

"How so?"

"Well, it seems I resigned, effective immediately."

Her mouth fell open. "You did what?"

"It was kind of like this... As I listened to lawyers try to convince us to approve a zoning variance to allow for yet another development we don't need, I found myself thinking about things such as a moose that stands in the middle of the road, a town without cell service, freshly made maple syrup available at a moment's notice, and my daughter, son-in-law and girlfriend, all of whom live in this place that must be experienced to be believed. And then I asked myself where I wanted to be—where I *really* want to be—and it's there where you and Mia and Wade and your extended families are. And before you worry that I'm rushing you into things you're not ready for, I was thinking about this before I met you in June. Well, not the part about leaving the council, but about spending more time in Vermont to be with Mia. And now," he said, smoothing a strand of her silky reddish-blonde hair back from her face, "where you are."

"You're moving to Vermont," she said, sounding astounded.

"I believe I might be."

Izzy shocked him when she threw her good arm around him and hugged him as tightly as she could. "That's the best news ever!"

"Is it?"

She pulled back so he could see her nod. "You know what I was thinking about the whole time you were gone?"

"Tell me."

"How we were ever going to make this work with three hours between us."

"I'm glad you're happy about my news."

"I'm thrilled! You can live with me and see Mia any time you want."

"I wasn't asking to live with you, Izzy. Not yet, anyway."

Her brows furrowed adorably. "Why not? We had fun the last week, didn't we?"

"So much fun, but I don't expect you to—"

She surprised him again when she kissed him. "I want you to live with me. Is it fast? Maybe, but neither of us is a child, and we both know what we want, so why postpone the inevitable?"

"I want you to think about this before you commit to anything."

"It's already decided. You're going to live with me in Vermont, and we're going to make this work."

"What if we can't? What if a month from now, you decide this isn't what you want?"

"That's not going to happen."

"You can't know that."

"Yes, I actually can know that, and I do know that. I've wanted this," she said, gesturing between them, "since the minute we met, and I've wanted it every minute of every day since then, and I've never wanted *this* with anyone else."

"Why me, sweet Isabella?"

"I'll never forget your joy at the wedding. It was palpable."

He groaned. "I was a fucking mess that entire day. It was mortifying."

Laughing at the face he made, she said, "It was beautiful. Everyone knew your story, yours and Mia's, and it was an honor and a tremendous joy to be part of that celebration. I remember thinking to myself, 'This man is special. He loves big, and he doesn't care who knows it.'"

"That was the best day of my life, second only to the day she was born. Not only did I get to celebrate my beautiful daughter, but I met you, too, and then proceeded to mess that up in spectacular fashion."

"That's ancient history now. The only thing that matters is where we go from here."

"How does bed sound?"

He loved the way her cheeks flushed with heat. "That sounds really good. I can't wait until I can do more than snuggle with you."

His body responded immediately to that statement with all the blood in his body heading to one central location. "I can't wait either, but there's no rush."

"I'm in a big rush."

Groaning, Cabot got up and then helped her up.

She wrapped her arms around him. "Are you really moving to Vermont?"

"I believe I am."

"That makes me so happy."

At some point over the last few weeks, making her happy had become as important to him as making himself and Mia happy.

"Mia will be thrilled."

He shut off the TV, took her hand and led her to the main bedroom, which was on that same floor. "I hope so."

"She will. I'm sure of it." They were halfway there when she stopped to catch her breath. "We'll need to add on at some point. You'll want your own office, and we need room for babies."

Cabot wondered if it was normal to have heart palpitations when she talked about having babies.

"Why do you look like you're going to pass out or puke or something when I mention babies?"

"Do I?"

Smiling, she flattened her hand on his chest. "Uh-huh. And your heart is racing."

"I'm working on coming around to that. I swear I am."

Her smile faded ever so slightly. "But you're not there yet."

"I'm getting there."

"I don't want you to do it just for me."

"Who else would I do it for?"

"Yourself."

"If it wasn't for you, I'd never consider having more children. That's just the truth of the matter."

Izzy sat on the end of the bed. "If it's not what you really want, Cabot—"

He sat next to her and put an arm around her while being careful not to hurt her. "I want you, Isabella. You want children. That makes it a rather simple proposition."

"It's hardly simple, as you know all too well."

Cabot took a minute to think about what he wanted to say —and how he wanted to say it. "A year ago today, I had a sixteen-hour workday between my regular job and a political fundraiser at night. I came home completely exhausted and fell into bed, with another long day ahead of me. That was my life —work, sleep, eat, repeat. A year ago tomorrow, I found my daughter, and everything changed. Just that quickly, I had something that mattered more to me than working myself into an early grave. And then I met you and discovered there could be even more, if I could find the courage to reach out for what I wanted."

He ran his fingers through her gorgeous hair, the color a cross between copper and gold. "If you'd asked me a year ago if I'd ever consider having more children, I would've laughed at the absurdity of it. But now... Everything is different, and I'm working on opening myself to all the possibilities, including more children. I just need you to be patient with me when you've already been so incredibly patient."

"Thank you for sharing that with me. It helps to know what you're thinking and how you're feeling about all this. I don't want you to feel obligated—"

He kissed her. "I don't. I swear I don't. You know that saying about how hard it was to turn the *Titanic*?"

"What about it?"

"I'm like that. Set in my ways. A creature of habit so deeply ingrained in me that redirecting me is like trying to turn the *Titanic*. It's not going to happen overnight, but it *is* happening. Slowly but surely."

"You said something before about not having had a vacation in decades."

"Work kept me sane. I couldn't imagine not having that to occupy my time. A vacation would've sent me over the edge."

"What about now?"

"What do you mean?"

"It occurred to me that I'll never again have this much free time. Like you, I'm usually booked solid, but for the next month or so, I'm free as a bird. What do you say we go somewhere warm and sunny?"

"Are you sure you feel up to something like that?"

"It'll be mostly downtime in the sand and sun, right? I can handle that."

"Then I say yes. One thousand percent yes. When do you want to go?"

"Tomorrow?"

Laughing, he said, "We might need a day or two to set something up. And you'll need clothes."

"I'll borrow from my sisters who live locally. We all wear the same size in everything."

"My sister will die from me doing something spontaneous. She says I don't have a spontaneous bone in my body."

"That's because you needed to be hyper-scheduled to survive what you were going through. Letting go of that habit also won't happen overnight."

"Maybe not, but a vacation would be an excellent first step." He kissed the top of her head. "Hold that thought."

CHAPTER TWENTY

"Butterflies can't see their wings. They can't see how truly beautiful they are, but everyone else can." —Unknown

When he got up and left the room, Izzy stayed seated at the end of the bed and watched him go, thinking about what he'd said about who he'd been a year ago. In some ways, he was like a chrysalis, emerging from his cocoon to take a look at the world around him for the first time in decades. She couldn't wait to watch him spread his wings and experience things he hadn't allowed himself during the desperate years he'd spent searching for his daughter.

Cabot returned with his iPad. "Let's get comfy and figure out where we want to go." He helped her up and led her into the walk-in closet, where he'd put her suitcase earlier. "The bathroom is through there, and I put towels on the counter for you. What else can I get you?"

"I think I'm all set. Thank you."

"Take your time. I'll meet you in bed."

"I'll be right there."

Izzy wanted more than anything to feel like herself again because she wanted to be with Cabot for more than hand-holding, kissing and sweet cuddling. The parts of her that were uninjured in the accident were wide awake and letting her know she was still a woman, even if other parts of her weren't ready for the next level with him.

She'd experienced desire many times in the past, but it'd never been coupled with the overwhelming feelings she had for Cabot. Of course, that had to happen when she could barely move, but hopefully it wouldn't be long before she could act on the feelings and the desire.

After she changed into pajama pants and a T-shirt, she brushed her hair and teeth, which was easier said than done with only one working arm. She was sick to death of the cast that extended past her elbow, which ached all the time from being immobilized. But it was the abdominal incision that was still giving her the most grief. Until this, she'd never realized that every movement included core muscles that'd been cut during the emergency surgery to remove her ruptured spleen.

The whole thing sucked, but she was damned thankful to still be alive and refused to complain about anything. It wasn't lost on her that if she hadn't been nearly killed in an accident, she wouldn't be in Cabot's bathroom in Boston. She might never have seen him again, except in passing with Wade and Mia, and that would've been a damned shame.

She walked slowly from the bathroom to the bed where Cabot waited for her, propped up on pillows, his chest bare, putting broad shoulders on full display. He had black-framed reading glasses propped on the end of his nose as he messed around with the iPad.

"Glasses, huh?" Izzy asked when she sat on the bed and eased herself back against the pillows, breathing through the pain that subsided faster than it had at first.

"Only after I remove the contacts." He looked over at her. "Are you okay?"

"Just the usual any time I move."

"Do you need pain pills?"

"Nope. I just needed a second, which is better than when I needed five minutes."

"You're doing so much better than you were. I hope you can see that."

"I do, but I'm annoyed by the things I still *can't* do."

"Like what?"

"Um, well… Like, you want a list?"

"Sure, that'd be good."

"Work, drive, have sex…"

Cabot's lips quivered with amusement. "Which of those three are you most eager to do?"

"The last one. For sure."

His low groan indicated his feelings on the matter. "Don't talk about it."

"Why not? If we can't do it, we can at least talk about it."

"Do we hafta?"

"Nah, that's okay," she said, laughing. "But just so you know that it's at the top of my agenda for when I feel better."

"Thank you for the warning. I need to prepare myself for that."

"How so?"

He fell back against the pillows, laughing. "I can't even think about it without feeling like it's going to be over before it starts."

"It hasn't been that long for you, has it?"

"No, but it's been a very long time since it mattered as much as it will with you, and I'm going to want it to be perfect and—"

"It'll already be perfect because it's you and me."

He removed the glasses, put them and the iPad on the bedside table and turned on his side to face her. "I look at you every day, without a doubt the loveliest woman I've ever met, and wonder what I did to get so lucky as to be even talking about these things with you."

"Flattery will get you everywhere, my friend."

"Are you that easy?"

"Only with you."

He raised himself up on one elbow and leaned in to kiss her. "I should hope so. I'd be extremely sad if you were easy with anyone but me."

"You have nothing to worry about."

When he would've pulled back from the kiss, Izzy curled her hand around his neck to keep him from getting away. She ran her tongue over his bottom lip, which brought him in even closer to her as the kiss quickly became urgent. When his tongue rubbed against hers, she wanted to weep from the sweet relief of finally getting to this moment with him.

"Iz." He sounded as undone as she felt. "I don't want to hurt you."

"I'm okay." She ran her fingers through his hair. "Don't stop yet."

The next kiss made the last one seem like nothing, and by the time they came up for air, Cabot was partially on top of her.

"This can't feel good."

"I feel better than I have since before the accident." She squirmed restlessly. "I just wish…"

"What, sweetheart? What do you wish for?" He placed soft kisses on her face and neck. "I'd give you anything."

"How about a nice easy orgasm?" She'd never asked any man for that but felt entirely comfortable asking this man.

"How easy are we talking?"

"I'll leave that up to you."

"And you'll tell me if something hurts?"

"I promise."

"Am I allowed to warm you up a little first?"

"Yes, please."

He eased her T-shirt up until her breasts were exposed.

Her nipples were already tight and tingling before he lowered his head to suck gently on the left one.

Izzy wrapped her good arm around his head to anchor him to her chest. She had to force herself to remain still to keep the pain from intruding.

"Feel good?" he asked after he'd moved to the other side.

"*So* good. That might be enough to get the job done."

He kissed down to her abdomen, making a wide circle around the incision. "Still good?"

"Mmm."

"Can we remove these?" he asked, giving a gentle tug to her pajama pants.

She started to help him.

"Let me. I've got it." He went up on his knees to gently remove the pants and bikini underwear.

She'd lost weight since the accident, and her hip bones were more prominent than they'd ever been, which made her feel self-conscious.

He dropped his head to kiss a line across her lower abdomen. "You're so beautiful, Iz. Every part of you is lovely." As he settled between her legs, he moved slowly and carefully to ensure her comfort before he began kissing her inner thighs. "Still okay?"

"*Yes.*" She kept her eyes closed and focused on breathing when he pressed his tongue to her core and slipped two fingers into her. The combination made her gasp from the pleasure while trying to stay as still as she possibly could, which wasn't easy.

Cabot put an arm across her hips to anchor her to the bed while he used his tongue and fingers to give her the orgasm she'd requested.

It rolled through her in easy waves that left her panting in the aftermath and wishing she felt well enough for more.

"Are you okay?" he asked after a moment of silence.

"So much better than okay. Thank you."

His gruff rumble of laughter made her smile. "My pleasure."

"Speaking of your pleasure…" She gave his hair an easy pull. "Come to where I can reach you."

"That's okay, love. I'm fine."

"Please?"

He moved up and settled next to her.

Izzy shifted her broken arm out of the way so she could put her other hand on his chest. "When do you have time to work out?" she asked, marveling at the defined muscles of his chest and abdomen.

"We have a gym at the office. I usually work out every day, but I've fallen off the last couple of weeks. That was another big part of my daily stay-busy routine."

"It was time very well spent."

"I'm glad you think so."

"I definitely think so. When we danced at the wedding, I

could tell you were ripped under your tux. I was hoping for a closer look."

"I came this close to asking you to come home with me that night."

"Why didn't you?"

"I've asked myself that a million times since then, and I honestly don't know why I didn't. Part of it might've been that you were Wade's cousin, and I was still getting to know him then and wasn't sure what he'd think of me being with you. I thought maybe he'd think I was way too old for you, which I am."

"You are not. You're perfect for me."

"Whatever I did in whatever lifetime that made it so you feel that way was worth it."

"I wish I could do everything I want to," she said, laughing when he groaned as her hand moved down to cup his erection through his pajama pants.

He closed his eyes and arched his back to press harder against her hand. "Izzy... You don't have to..."

She slid her hand inside his pants to stroke him.

"Okay, then..."

Laughing, she tightened her hand around the long, thick length of him. Her mouth watered when she thought of taking him inside her and hoped it wouldn't be long before she could do that.

"Iz... Isabella... Christ have mercy. I'm gonna... Iz..." He flooded her hand and covered his abdomen with his release. "Ah, shit, we made a mess."

"It was worth it," she said, smiling at him.

"Sure was." He kissed her and said, "Let me get a towel." She heard water running in the bathroom, and when he came back to the bedroom, he sat on the edge of the mattress and used a towel to clean up her hand. Tossing the towel aside, he got into bed and helped her rest her broken arm on his abdomen and her head on his chest as he put his arm around her. "There. That's perfect."

"Mmm, sure is. I knew it would be good... with us... Even when I was still wondering if we'd ever get the chance."

"I spent a ridiculous amount of time after both our prior meetings beating myself up for letting you get away. I knew it would be good, too. I just didn't think I'd be good for you in other ways."

"You've been very good for me—and to me."

"I'm still afraid I'm going to disappoint you in some way."

"You won't."

"How do you know that?"

"I don't know. I just do. When I met you at the wedding, it was just the strangest feeling of, oh, there he is, finally. I can't explain it, but I knew it. I just knew."

"And I totally blew it—twice."

"You've more than made up for it in recent weeks. Now, about that vacation I want to take you on..."

"You made me forget all about that, and PS, I'm taking *you* on vacation."

"It was my idea!"

"You're out of work, and I'm not."

"That doesn't mean I'm destitute."

"Never said you were, but this vacation is on me. You can pay for the next one."

"Can I get that in writing?"

Chuckling, he said, "If you must."

"I must. I make very decent money with my photography. Not like what you make with your business, but it's a nice living, and I can afford to pay for a vacation."

"We'll fight about the next vacation when the time comes."

"No fight. I'm paying, and that's it."

"You're very sexy when you're bossy, but then, you're sexy all the time."

"I'm just a walking sex goddess lately," she said with a snort of laughter.

"The bruises mean you're alive, which is all that matters." He reached for his iPad and glasses from the bedside table. "Now, where would you like to go?"

"Somewhere warm. Palm trees, umbrella drinks, sandy beaches and sunny days."

"I've got a good friend who works in travel. How about I send her your list and see what she can find?"

"Works for me."

While she remained snuggled up to him, he used voice commands to compose and send the email. Then he put the iPad back on the table. He'd told his friend to let him know what was available ASAP.

"Will that cause you trouble with work?"

"A little. Nothing I can't handle or delegate to others. Don't worry about it. They'll be more shocked that I'm actually taking a vacation than annoyed by the timing."

Izzy yawned. "That's good. I don't want them to be upset with you because of me."

"They won't be. Everyone in my life has been trying to find me a girlfriend for years. They'll be thrilled to hear I finally have one."

"Did you ever go out with any of the women they fixed you up with?"

"A few here and there, mostly just to shut everyone up."

"I hate to think about how lonely your life was for so long."

"It wasn't all bad. I had Em and her family nearby and my brothers and lots of good friends. I give them credit for sticking it out with me during all the years I was obsessed with finding Mia. I wasn't easy to be around."

"I'm glad you had them to support you."

That was her last thought before sleep claimed her.

CHAPTER TWENTY-ONE

"We loved with a love that was more than love." —Edgar Allan Poe

"Is it healthy to have this much sex in one twenty-four-hour period?" Vanessa asked Troy after yet another sexual marathon. Her entire body buzzed with aftershocks that she felt from her scalp to the soles of her feet and everywhere in between. The man was a god in bed—and out of bed.

"I think I might be dehydrated from fluid loss."

Vanessa snorted with laughter. "That's gross."

"But true." His hand slid from her belly to her breast, and just that quickly, she wanted him again. "This is the best vacation I've ever had."

"Even though you haven't gotten more than one day on the slopes?"

He gave her breast a gentle squeeze. "I've had lots of time on the slopes."

She rocked with laughter. He was funny, handsome, sexy as all hell and just an overall good guy. "Where've you been all my life, Troy Kennedy?"

"Waiting to find you, Vanessa Coleman."

"You don't mean that. Come on..."

"I do mean it. I've never done anything like this with anyone but you."

"I haven't either. I mean, I've done *this*, but it wasn't like it is with you."

"Exactly my point, and I'd say we're both old enough and wise enough to know when something is special."

"Who you calling old?"

His smile was the sexiest thing about him. Wait, no, that wasn't entirely true… But it was definitely in the top five things. Vanessa was thinking about making an actual list when the phone rang. She reached across Troy to grab the phone off the bedside table and saw Grayson's number on the caller ID.

"Hey," she said. "What's up?"

"I just got a call from the general counsel at Smith Corp."

"And?"

"How would two hundred fifty in severance sound?"

"As in two hundred fifty *thousand*?"

"Yep."

Troy pumped a fist into the air.

"Holy shit, Gray. You're not messing with me, are you?"

"Would I do that to you?"

"Yes, you absolutely would."

"Not about this, Ness. It's too important."

"Oh my God. Is this for real?"

"Sure is. They know you have a case against them, so you'd have to sign away your right to sue now or in the future in exchange for the payout. They're also offering two years of medical and dental insurance."

Tears filled her eyes as relief flooded the rest of her. That kind of money would buy her the time to figure out what was next, rather than having to take some crap job just to stay afloat. "I can't believe this."

"There's one sticking point."

She was almost afraid to ask. "What's that?"

"They don't want to fire him. They're willing to severely discipline him, but not fire him."

Vanessa's reaction was swift and succinct. "Then no deal. It's not enough for them to refuse to pay his country club membership fee for a year. They need to send the message that his behavior is unacceptable."

Troy nodded and mouthed the word *yes* as he took hold of her free hand.

"You can go back and tell them either he gets the ax, or we'll see them in court." She swallowed hard as she said the words, trying not to think about how much she could use that money. But she wasn't willing to sell her soul to the devil to get it.

"For what it's worth, I'm proud of you, Ness."

"It's worth a lot, as you know." Grayson had been a rock to her and their other siblings. "But this is about more than just money. I don't want him to turn around and do the same thing to whomever they hired to replace me. He needs to suffer at least a fraction as much as he made me suffer."

"I'll go back to them and tell them no deal without his head on a platter."

"Say it just like that, will you?"

Grayson chuckled. "Will do."

"Thanks, Gray."

"My pleasure. I'll keep you posted."

After they said their goodbyes, Vanessa handed the phone to Troy, who returned it to the bedside table.

"How do you feel?" he asked.

"Powerful for once."

"Good for you. You're doing the right thing. Why should he get a free pass when he harassed you out of a job? The company's insurance will pay you off, and he'll go on with his life like nothing ever happened."

"Exactly. I want him to *pay* for what he did."

"I have to say I find this bad ass side of you incredibly sexy—as long as it's only directed at bullies."

"It's not really like me to do that. I... uh... I tend to avoid confrontation because of the anxiety, which has been pretty bad since all the shit with work. When I reported it to HR, and they didn't do anything, that's when I knew I had to leave before he found out I'd reported him. For like a month after I left, I stayed home out of fear that he was going to come after me. I could barely function. That's the worst anxiety I've ever had."

"I'm so sorry you went through that."

"It's one more reason why the money isn't enough."

"I completely agree. You're doing the right thing demanding he be fired."

"I could really use that money," she said with a grim smile.

"Hold out for the terms you want. You've got all the power here, and they know it. If you sue them, and that goes public, that'll seriously damage their reputation. They know that, too. What do they do?"

"The company sells advertising for a lot of the radio and TV stations in the city. All the partners care about is their image."

"Then the last thing they want is for this to end up on the front page of the *Globe*."

"They would hate that," she said with an evil little smile.

"I have a good feeling you're going to get everything you want."

"The money would be life-changing."

He propped his head on an upturned hand. "What would you do with it?"

"I'd take some time off to find something that really interests me. I've had a lot of 'jobs,' but I've never felt like I had a *career*."

"Do you know where you ought to do your thinking?"

"Where?"

"New York City, the land of opportunity."

"Hmm, well, technically, I live in Boston."

"Is that something you might be able to get out of?"

Her heart nearly stopped beating as the implications hit her all at once. "What're you asking me, Troy?"

"To come home with me."

"To…"

"Come home. With me. To continue this incredible thing we've started here."

"You… You're asking me…" She blew out a deep breath. "Wow." Looking over at him, she said, "Can we actually do that?"

"What's stopping us?"

"Nothing, I suppose. I sublet my apartment from a friend, and if I helped her find someone to take my place..." She looked at him again. "Are you serious about this?"

"I'm dead serious. I've never connected with anyone like this before. I don't want it to end when my vacation does."

"But what if... What if we're caught up in the moment, and that's all it is? A moment."

"I don't think that's all it is, and just so you know, I've never asked anyone to come home with me before. Especially not for forever, hopefully."

She fanned her face. "Am I going to suddenly wake up and find I've dreamed all this?"

"Nope. It's real. I'm right here, and I'm asking you to be with me."

Vanessa understood this was a moment of truth. When she asked herself what she really wanted, at the very top of her list was true love and a family of her own. She could have that with him. She knew that after only a few days together, and she wanted it with him as much as she'd ever wanted anything. As she was between jobs and didn't have anything holding her in Boston or Vermont now that Izzy was on the mend, she could think of no reason not to accept his offer.

The fact that Emma, Lucy and Cameron considered him among their closest friends helped to cement her resolve.

"Would it be okay if we tried it for a week or two to make sure we're not in some sort of sex-fueled fantasy that doesn't hold up in the real world?"

"Of course. Whatever you want to do is fine with me as long as I don't have to leave you on Sunday and not see you again for a long time."

Vanessa licked her lips that had suddenly gone dry while her heart beat wildly.

"Will you come home with me?" he asked again, head tilted, gorgeous brown eyes full of affection and maybe the start of much more than that.

"Yes, I believe I will."

. . .

As Lucy screamed her way through another contraction she could tell Colton was trying to take his earlier advice to stay calm. That was much easier said than done for both of them, as it turned out. With her midwife walking them through the steps on the phone, Colton waited for the contraction to subside before he again checked to gauge whether she was fully dilated. He'd said earlier that he never expected to learn the size or shape of a fully dilated cervix, but there he was, giving a reading of approximately eight centimeters.

"Still a little ways to go before you can push, Lucy," the midwife, Helen, said.

Lucy whimpered in distress and despair. This could not be happening. Not like this. She'd had that same thought a thousand times over the last five hours as the storm outside howled, and the contractions came faster and with more intensity. Not to mention, her husband had become her midwife and OB, two roles neither of them had ever expected him to perform.

In between contractions, Colton ran cool cloths over her face and helped her take sips of cold water. He'd found plastic to put down on the bed to protect their mattress and had gathered the various things they would need to deliver the baby at home.

What if something went wrong? That was the only thought in her head when she wasn't contending with another hellish contraction.

She wondered if the word was out with the family that they were having the baby—alone—on the mountaintop in a blizzard, which would have them in a panic. She'd give anything for some qualified help, but she couldn't share that thought with Colton, who was doing everything he could to assist her.

Another hour passed in a haze of pain and agony that got her only a little further along. Did it always take this long?

She was about to ask that question when the door to the cabin burst open, and two snow-covered bodies came in, dropping bags on the floor as the dogs howled in outrage at the invaders. Was she dreaming this, or did they have guests?

The removal of hats and other gear revealed two identical faces.

Colton's brothers Lucas and Landon, both of them EMTs.

They weren't doctors, but they were a hell of a lot closer to being doctors than Colton would ever be. *Thank you, Jesus.*

"How'd you get up here?" Colton asked them.

Landon raised his foot to reveal a snowshoe. "We walked."

"You walked two miles up a mountain in a blizzard?" Colton asked, incredulous.

"We heard you needed help," Lucas said.

At least she thought it was Lucas. Usually, it took a minute —or two—to be sure, especially since Lucas had shaved his beard for the prank they'd recently played on Dani and Amanda.

They removed snowshoes, boots, backpacks, coats and other gear.

"How's the baby mama?" Lucas asked.

"Trying not to freak the eff out," Lucy replied.

"Same with the baby daddy," Colton said. "I've never been happier to see you two idiots."

"Watch it, mister," Landon said. "You need us."

"Yes, we do," Colton said. "The midwife, Helen, is on the phone. Helen, my brothers the EMTs just showed up."

"Oh, that's great news," Helen said, sounding relieved.

"Luce, I know all of this is super weird and scary, but I need to check you to see where we're at." Lucas warmed his hands over the woodstove. "Is that okay?"

"Do whatever you have to in order to safely deliver this baby."

"Boys, I have to warn you first," Colton said gravely. "This isn't just any cooch. This is the *Rolls-Royce* of cooch, and seeing it could ruin you for all others."

"Oh my God, Colton," Lucy said as the boys laughed. "*Shut up!*"

"It's only fair to warn them," Colton said. "What if seeing you ruins them for Dani and Amanda?"

Lucy gritted her teeth. "I'm going to put you outside if you don't shut up *right now.*"

"Yes, dear."

"We stand warned." Lucas chuckled as he put on medical gloves. "Try not to worry."

"Colton, come here."

Her husband came to her and took the hand she held out to him. "Stay with me, and don't freak out about your brothers seeing things they shouldn't see."

"I'm so happy they're here, they can look at whatever they want," Colton said with a grin that made her laugh and then grimace. Lucas's exam was much more thorough than Colton's had been.

"I'd say you're fully dilated and effaced," Lucas said, "which means it's time to push, Luce."

That news sent a fresh wave of terror through her. She was going to deliver this baby with no drugs and only her husband and brothers-in-law standing between her and disaster.

"Take a breath, love," Colton said. "You've got this." He brushed the sweaty hair back from her forehead and kissed her. "You're the strongest person I know. If anyone can do this, you can."

Lucy didn't feel strong at the moment. She only felt afraid— for the baby and herself. What if something went wrong? Lucas and Landon were highly skilled, but they weren't doctors.

"Breathe, Luce," Colton said. "Just keep breathing. I know you can do this."

She clung to his certainty as the next contraction began to build.

Time ceased to exist as pain rolled into pain into nearly unbearable pressure. She had no idea how long she pushed or if this was normal or if the baby would ever come. Colton never left her side while Lucas and Landon worked together at the other end. That she didn't even care that her brothers-in-law were face-first in her vajayjay said a lot about her current priorities.

"Lucy, on the next contraction, I want you to push as hard as you can—harder than you think you can," Lucas said. "The hardest you've pushed yet. Let's get this baby delivered."

Was that concern she heard in his voice? Before she could

ask, another contraction required her full attention. She pushed so hard, she nearly blacked out.

"Yes," Landon said, "that's it, Lucy! The head is out. Shoulders are next. One more big push, and hold it for as long as you can."

The next thing she heard was the outraged cry of a baby.

"You have a son," Lucas said, sounding tearful now, "and he's absolutely perfect."

"We have a son, Luce," Colton said as tears streamed down his face. "We have a son!"

"What's his name?" Landon asked as he cut the cord and tended to Lucy.

Lucy glanced at Colton. "Do not say Bruiser."

"I wasn't gonna," Colton said, laughing as he accepted the swaddled baby from Landon. "Hey, buddy." He wiped the tears from his face with his sleeve.

Lucy had never loved him more than she did watching his emotional reaction to seeing their son for the first time.

"You need to meet your mom." Colton handed the baby over to her. "She's the hero of this day."

"Hi there," Lucy said on a long exhale. Every part of her hurt like it never had before, but who cared about that when she had a sweet baby face to gaze at?

"You want to tell them his name?" Colton asked her.

"Christian Raymond Abbott," Lucy said, obsessed with every detail of the baby's tiny face. He had reddish peach fuzz on his head and tiny little brows furrowed with confusion as he took in his new surroundings.

"Nice to meet you, Christian," Landon said. "We're your Funcles Landon and Lucas."

"Mom will love another C name," Lucas added.

"He's going to have his mommy's red hair," Colton said, seeming completely besotted with the baby.

"Two redheads, bro," Lucas said. "You're going to have your hands full."

After Landon helped her deliver the placenta, he glanced up at Lucy. "You need a couple of stitches, Luce. I can numb you up with some lidocaine, but that's not going to be particularly pleasant."

"Oh jeez, a shot to the cooch," she said, groaning. "Will the indignities never end?"

"They're almost done," Landon assured her. "Why don't you hand the baby to Luc to hold so Colton can hold you?"

She parted with the baby reluctantly and grabbed hold of Colton.

"Ready?" Landon asked.

"As I'll ever be."

Holy motherfucking pain in the...

"Almost done," Landon said. "Okay, that's it."

Lucy had broken into a sweat, and tears flooded her eyes. But other than some tugging, she didn't feel the stitches at all. She couldn't wait until the numbness wore off. Ugh.

When they had finished cleaning her up and getting her and the baby settled, Landon looked at his twin brother. "Our work here is finished, bro."

"I'd say so," Lucas said. "Congratulations, guys. He's a beaut!"

"Where're you going?" Lucy asked them. "There's a blizzard raging out there."

"We're going home," Landon said as if that was no big deal.

"Um, how's that happening?" Colton asked.

"We're borrowing your skis to get down the mountain," Landon added. "We've got four-wheel drive waiting for us down below."

"That's just crazy enough to make sense," Colton said. "I'll get you suited up."

"You guys," Lucy said.

Lucas and Landon turned back to face her.

"Your heroic efforts to get to us will never, *ever* be forgotten, but what will be forgotten is any memory you two have of my netherlands. Do we understand each other?"

"You got it, Luce," Landon said with a grin.

"What netherlands?" Lucas asked. "I've already forgotten."

"My wife's netherlands are *unforgettable*," Colton said.

"End it, Colton," Lucy said. "Be safe, boys. Let us know you made it home okay."

"Will do, Mama," Landon said, giving a jaunty wave as they headed out into the tundra with Colton to retrieve boots and skis from the shed.

Luckily, Colton had tons of both and could set his brothers up with what they needed while she cradled her son.

"I bet Daddy is giving them big bro hugs for what they did for us," she said. "I suppose we'll need to ask them both to be your godfathers since they hiked up a mountain in a blizzard to help us deliver you."

The baby looked up at her with big, wide eyes full of wonder, and despite the stressful, chaotic day, all Lucy could see or think about was him—and his daddy—and how blessed they were.

Colton came back inside a few minutes later, covered in snow and bringing a blast of cold air with him. "It's really coming down. Our Christian is going to be a mountain man after being born on one in a blizzard."

"I was just telling him how his uncles have to be his godfathers for what they did for us."

"Totally agree, even though I want to host a brain scrub to make them forget everything they saw here."

"Oh, who cares? You've seen one cooch, you've seen them all."

"I care! Those are my idiot little brothers."

"Who possibly saved the lives of your wife and son, so maybe we can forgive them for having to see the promised land in the process."

"I hate when you make sense." He came over and sat gingerly on the side of the bed. "In case I forget to tell you, I've never been more amazed by you, prouder of you or more in love with you than I was and am today."

"Thank you for being there for me."

"Cripes, I didn't do a freaking thing. That was all *you*, babe."

"It was all *us*. Aren't you glad I bought so much stuff ahead of time?"

"You were right about the diapers and stuff, dear."

"I'm right about everything. Isn't he incredible?"

"Most beautiful baby ever born."

"We need to call the parents and siblings and let them know he's here before Lucas and Landon steal our thunder."

"Yeah, that's true." Colton grabbed the portable phone from the bedside table. "Who first?"

"Your parents in case they talk to the boys."

Colton dialed the number at his parents' barn. "How cool is it that my mom and my aunt will be his grandmothers?" With his aunt Hannah now all but living with Lucy's dad, Ray, their baby would know her only as a grandmother.

"That's so cool." Lucy looked down at the sleeping baby. "You're one lucky boy, Christian."

"Hey, Mom, it's Colton and Lucy." He'd put the phone on speaker so she could hear, too.

"Hi, guys. We were just talking about you up on the mountain during this storm. Do you still have power?"

"Yep." Colton smiled at Lucy and waggled his brows. "And we have a baby."

"What did you just say?"

"Lucy had the baby."

"Oh my God! Linc! Lucy had the baby! Are they both okay?"

"They're great, thanks in large part to your sons Lucas and Landon, who *walked* up the mountain in a blizzard to help us."

"Oh Lord, did they really?"

"They did, and we're forever thankful."

"Those boys," she said, sighing. "I guess I should say *men*. They're incredible."

"They'll always be boys," Colton said, "and yes, they are. We couldn't have done it without them. I've never been so relieved to see their identical nitwit faces in my life."

"I'll bet! Wow, this is such big news. Congratulations, you guys. We're so happy for you!"

"Your mother is so excited, she forgot to ask if we have a new grandson or granddaughter," Linc said as Molly laughed.

"A boy, Christian Raymond."

"Aw, that's lovely," Molly said. "Ray will be thrilled. And we've got another C baby!"

"We thought that would make you happy," Colton said.

"I'll add Christian's hook to the mudroom first thing tomorrow," Linc said.

"With all these babies, you're going to need a bigger mudroom," Colton said.

"We've still got plenty of room," Molly said. "How're you feeling, Lucy?"

"Like I got run over by Fred and wondering how *in the hell* you did this eight times."

"You forget," Molly said.

"How long does that take?" Lucy asked, grimacing as she tried to find a comfortable position.

"Oh, a day or two. Maybe a week tops."

"I'll have to take your word for it. We're going to go call my dad and Emma. Will you spread the word among the Abbotts?"

"We'd be happy to," Molly said. "Congratulations again. We'll be up to see you all the minute this weather settles down."

"We'll be here," Colton said as the caller ID beeped with a call from Landon. "That'll be Landon telling me they successfully skied down the mountain."

"Those boys," Molly said, laughing.

"Our heroes," Colton said. "Talk to you tomorrow."

"Congratulations," Linc said.

"Love you guys."

"We love you, too," Molly said. "All three of you."

They took the call from Landon on the satellite phone he kept in his fire department vehicle and then left a message at Hannah's for Ray to call them and another for Emma. Then they settled in to figure out breastfeeding.

"Hey, Luce?"

"Yes, Colton?"

"I just love you so damned much. Thank you for giving me a son."

"I love you, too, and thank you for giving *me* a son."

"I had all the fun, and you did all the work, but I'm happy to provide stud service any time you'd like."

"Easy, big fella. I'm not going to be needing any stud services for a while."

"Um, how long exactly?"

"Six to eight weeks."

"That long?" He released a deep, dramatic breath. "It's gonna be a long, cold winter around here."

"At least we'll have the baby to keep us entertained."

"Thank God for him."

"You said it."

CHAPTER TWENTY-TWO

"It is hardly possible to build anything if frustration, bitterness and a mood of helplessness prevail." —Lech Walesa

For a long time after Izzy fell asleep, Cabot was awake, reliving the sexy encounter and thinking about how she brought vivid color to his black-and-white existence. Everything was more fun and exciting when she was there —even something as simple as eating dinner or watching TV.

Until she'd suggested taking a vacation, the idea wouldn't have occurred to him. He'd already seen how good she was going to be for him, but still he worried if he'd be as good for her.

When she talked of having babies, all he could think about was what would happen to their children if things didn't work out between him and Izzy. Even though everything about this relationship was already a million times better than his marriage had ever been, the thought of her leaving him and taking their children made him break out in a cold sweat.

Not that he honestly thought she'd ever deny him his children, especially after what she'd endured with her own father.

Ugh, he needed to stop torturing himself with this shit. Things were good, and he needed to take Emily's advice and fully enjoy it all.

While she slept, he gently disentangled himself from her so he could get up and book the vacation she'd described. His travel agent, who worked as much as he did, had already sent a few options. Cabot took a careful look at each of them before he told her to book the resort in Bermuda, mostly because it was the shortest flight. Izzy was doing better, but the drive had worn her out, and he didn't want her on an airplane for any longer than necessary. The direct flight from Boston to Bermuda was just over three hours.

He didn't think that was too bad, as they would do nothing but rest and relax once they arrived. Since they needed a day to prepare and pack, he asked the agent to book it for the day after tomorrow. That would also give Izzy another day to rest before they traveled.

Now wide awake, he took care of some pending work emails and told his coworkers about the vacation. *Sorry for the short notice*, he wrote, *but a window of opportunity arose, and I decided to take it. I'll be reachable while I'm gone, but I'm planning to take a real break and am very much looking forward to it. Thanks for all you do. Cabot*

His COO wrote back ten minutes later, which didn't surprise him, as she was always up crazy late. *Are you forgetting about the Hamilton meeting next Monday and the summit with the Kenworth partners on Tuesday?*

In truth, he had forgotten the two important meetings coming up, which was further proof that he was in bad need of a break. *I leave both meetings in your capable hands. CL*

Cabot was sure his response would shock the woman who'd been his right hand for more than a decade, but he refused to feel an ounce of guilt for taking some time for himself—and for Izzy. Even while he'd been in Vermont, he'd remained fully engaged with work, so that didn't count as a real break.

Bermuda would be a real break, and he couldn't wait to have that time away with Izzy.

. . .

Two days later, Emily dropped them at Logan at seven for a nine a.m. flight to Bermuda.

"Have a wonderful time, you two," she said as she helped take the suitcases out of the back of her SUV.

Cabot gave her a quick hug. "We will."

"Thanks for the ride, Emily," Izzy said.

"You're very welcome. I'll see you back here next Saturday night. Enjoy every moment."

Izzy was amused by how excited Emily was to see her brother being spontaneous and romantic. She gave Emily a one-armed hug.

"This makes me so, so happy," Emily whispered to her. "*So* happy."

"Thanks for all the support," Izzy replied while Cabot moved their bags to the sidewalk.

"So happy to support this lovely romance. I hope you have the best time."

"Ready, Iz?" Cabot asked.

"Yep."

They waved to Emily as she drove off, and then Izzy followed Cabot into the busy terminal. As he'd insisted on handling both their bags, she hung back while he went through the steps to get them checked in, stepping forward only to show her passport to the ticket agent. Cabot and her mother had conspired to have it couriered to her from Vermont the day before.

He helped her to remove her sling, coat and sneakers before they went through security and then helped her get resituated on the other side.

Her sister Sarah had come through with swimsuits, dresses and sandals for the trip and had dropped a bag for Izzy at Cabot's yesterday.

"Holy crap," Sarah had said when she'd gotten a look at his gorgeous home.

Her sister had been between classes when she came by, so they hadn't had time to talk more about Sarah's reservations about her nursing program. Once again, Izzy had advised her not to make any big decisions while she was in the middle of a semester. Izzy felt that Sarah needed some perspective and time to breathe before she decided anything.

And Vanessa! Going back to the city with Troy! Izzy had only gotten to talk to her for a few minutes, but Ness had sounded more excited than Izzy had heard her in a long time. What a thrilling development for her beloved sister.

Izzy was still thinking about Sarah and Vanessa when Cabot let out a gasp next to her. She looked over to find his gaze affixed to the face of a woman coming toward them, holding hands with a man. He stopped walking, so Izzy did, too.

"Hey," he said to the woman. "What're you doing here?"

The woman seemed as shocked to see him as he was to see her.

"I asked you a question. *What the hell are you doing here?*"

Izzy was stunned by his harsh tone. She'd never heard him speak to anyone that way.

The woman looked away from him and pushed past them, keeping her head down. The man with her glanced back over his shoulder at them before rushing to catch up to her.

For a full minute after they walked away, Cabot stood so still that Izzy wondered if he was breathing.

"Ah, Cabot…"

He glanced at her with eyes that looked right through her.

"Who was that?"

"Deb."

Oh God.

His gaze shifted in the direction Deb had gone, as if torn between going after her and making their flight.

"What do you want to do?" Izzy asked him.

"What?"

"Do you want to follow her?"

After another long pause, he said, "No, I don't want to follow her. We need to get to our gate."

His tone was so cold, so lacking in emotion, that Izzy couldn't help but fear that a ten-second encounter with his ex-wife had ruined everything.

. . .

WHAT THE FUCK IS SHE DOING IN BOSTON? FROM THE SECOND HE saw her coming toward him, Cabot felt like he'd been electrocuted. He'd recognized her even more than twenty-five years after the last time he saw her. He would've known her anywhere after spending so much time looking for her and Mia and having had numerous age-progressed photos created for both of them.

His stomach churned, and his chest ached the way it had when he'd had pneumonia a few years ago, like he couldn't get enough air no matter how hard he tried.

Mia.

He needed to tell her he'd spotted Deb in Boston. What other reason would she have for being anywhere near there but to see their daughter? He'd talked to Mia yesterday to tell her about their vacation, and she'd never mentioned plans with her mother. But would she tell him if she was seeing Deb? He didn't know.

"I need to make a call," he told Izzy when they'd reached their gate. "I'll be just a minute."

While she took a seat, he walked away to call his daughter, praying that she answered. He tried the home line first.

"Hey, Dad," she said, answering on the third ring. "Aren't you off to Bermuda today?"

His heart contracted the way it always did when she called him Dad. "Yes, we're at Logan now, and I wanted to tell you…" The words got stuck when his throat tightened, and the old familiar rage resurfaced to remind him it was always there, on simmer, waiting to boil over without warning.

"What? Is something wrong?"

He forced a deep breath past the ache in his chest. "I saw your mother. Just now."

"*What?* You saw her? Where?"

"In the airport, walking toward security, so arriving, I presume." He took another breath and released it. "Did you know she was coming?"

"No! I haven't talked to her in months."

He was relieved to hear that. They'd carefully avoided the subject of her mother, especially after Mia had made dropping all charges against Deb a condition of seeing him when they first reconnected a year ago. "It's possible she may be planning to surprise you."

"Oh God, Dad. Today's a year since everything came to light, and the last time we talked, she said she wasn't going to wait forever to work things out with me. You don't think she came here because of that?"

"I really hope not. Do you want me to come there? I will. We can go to Bermuda another time."

"No, Dad. No. That's not necessary. Wade is here, and I'll be fine if she shows up, but thank you for the warning."

"You're under no obligation to see her or have it out with her. You know that, right?"

"I do," she said with a sigh that he deeply resented.

How dare Deb show her face anywhere near either of them? She was goddamned lucky she wasn't in prison. You'd think she would leave their daughter alone until Mia was ready to mend fences—if she was ever ready for that.

Standing across the crowded concourse, he noticed people beginning to head toward the boarding area for their flight.

Izzy caught his gaze and tipped her head toward the doorway.

He'd sprung for first-class seats to ensure Izzy's comfort, so they could board at any time. "I've got to go, Mia. Will you please let me know if she shows up there?"

"No, I don't think I will, Dad. You need to go with Izzy and have a wonderful time and not worry about any of this crap."

"I'll worry more if I don't hear from you."

"I'll text you, but don't worry, okay? I can take care of myself, and I've got Wade. You've saved me from being blindsided if she does show up, so you've done what you could for me. Have a great trip, and try to relax, will you?"

"Yeah, sure." He told her what she wanted to hear while knowing there was no hope of relaxation for him now. Not after seeing *her*. He probably ought to turn around, go home and bury himself in the work that had sustained him through all his trials. He would have if it weren't for Izzy.

Suddenly, the last place he wanted to be was on a plane bound for Bermuda. The trip seemed ludicrous.

"Are you okay, Dad?" Mia sounded worried about him, and he couldn't have that.

For the first time since they'd reconnected, he lied to her. "Sure, honey. I'm fine. I'll text you from Bermuda."

"Safe travels."

"Thank you." He didn't want to end the call, but there was nothing left to say, so he pushed the red button and put the phone in his pocket. Then he headed across the concourse to where Izzy stood, waiting for him to board.

"Everything okay?"

Nothing was okay. The festering wound had reopened, spilling its poison on everyone and everything around him.

"We don't have to go," she said when he took too long to answer her. "I'd totally understand if you didn't want to."

He believed her. She would understand and wouldn't hold it against him. For a second, he thought about taking her up on the offer to cancel the trip. He was this close to saying, *Fuck it, let's go home*. But what would he do once he got there? At least in Bermuda, Izzy would have something to do while he dealt with the festering wound.

"It's okay." He reached out a hand to her. "Let's go."

She seemed hesitant as she took his hand.

Cabot didn't blame her. He'd be hesitant to go anywhere with him, too. She knew him well enough by now to realize he'd been knocked off his feet. What she didn't know was how bad things could get when that happened.

Maybe it was just as well she found out now how bleak the darkness could get, rather than a year or two and a couple of kids down the road. Even though the thought of losing her made him sadder than he'd been about anything in a long time, at the end of the day, he was a realist. Life had given him no choice but to face reality every time it punched him in the face.

. . .

Butler Town Clerk Hannah Coleman had just seen off one of her favorite town residents, her father's friend Cletus, when the home phone rang with a call from Grayson. "Hi, honey."

"Hey, Mom. How's your day going?"

"Pretty well so far. Cletus was just in and brought me doughnuts from the store. That always makes my day."

"That was nice of him. Listen, I wanted to tell you… I talked to Dad about the divorce and other matters."

All it took to ruin Hannah's good mood was a reference to Mike Coleman. "And?"

"He's broke."

"Why did I know you were going to say that?"

"I did a little digging and discovered it's true. However, the woman he's engaged to is wealthy."

"Of course she is. He's no fool." *No, I was the fool when it came to him.* "Who is she?"

"Her name is Lisa Duckworth. Her late husband was the CEO of a tech firm. He left her very well-off."

"So that's that, huh?"

"Not exactly."

"What do you mean? He's broke. He can't pay past child support."

"No, but his future wife can."

"Ugh, do I really want to make another woman pay for his past sins?"

"It's the principle of the matter, Mom. He wants something. You want something. Why should he be the only one who gets what they want out of this? He'll have a choice—ask her for the money or no divorce. Either way, it'll cause him considerable discomfort, and isn't that the least of what he owes us all?"

"I heard about Vanessa turning down the money her firm offered if they're not also willing to fire the guy who harassed her."

"Pretty ballsy move, if you ask me."

"Like you said, it's the principle of the matter."

"You don't have to do anything, Mom. You can sign the divorce decree and call it a day—a long overdue day."

"I'm going to be honest with you. Going after the money feels vindictive to me. It's not like I need it. Ray and I, we're in good shape between his pension and the one I'll have when I retire. We don't need his money—or I guess I should say his fiancée's money."

"I hear what you're saying, but that wasn't always the case, was it? You're looking at this in the present tense. Not the past tense, when every day was a struggle to feed, clothe and shelter eight children, not to mention trying to get us through college."

"I don't know what to do, Gray. I look at Vanessa, such a badass going after that guy who harassed her, and I don't have the same moxie to go after the man who left me with eight children to finish raising?"

"You have *all* the moxie, Mother. All of it. That's not what this is about."

"What would you do?"

"I'd stick it to him, but that's me. I can't tell you what to do, and I'll respect whatever you decide."

"You know what I think most about when I think of your father?"

"What's that?"

"How much he missed out on. He has no idea what a good man you are, what a fine lawyer, what a great brother, cousin and friend—and now a wonderful father and fiancé. He doesn't know how you and Izzy and Ness took care of your younger siblings or how you all still take care of each other. He missed the best part of parenthood—the payoff when your children become adults that you not only like, but respect. I think the fact that I have that, I have all of you, and he doesn't might be enough vindication for me, Gray."

"That's a really great way of looking at it. Do you want me to let him know you're going to sign the divorce papers?"

"Yes."

"Is it all right if I also tell him he owes you *everything*, and if he ever gets the chance to make it right with you financially, he ought to do that because it's the right thing to do?"

"I would have no objection to that. Thank you for handling this and for taking another one for the team by having to speak to him."

"Happy to do it for you, Mom. I'll let you know if he has anything else to say."

"Sounds good. Love you, son."

"Love you, too."

For a long time after she ended the call, Hannah held the portable extension to her chest, hoping she'd done the right thing. She turned it round and round in her mind, and twenty minutes later, she still felt the same way about what she'd decided.

She heard Ray's truck in the driveway and went to meet him when he came into the mudroom.

"There's my best girl." He greeted her with a big smile and a kiss on the cheek. "How's your day going?"

She put her arms around him. "It just got much, *much* better."

"Everything all right?" he asked in a wary tone.

Hannah filled him in on her conversation with Gray.

"You're damned right we have everything we need—and then some. We don't need anything from him, unless it's important to you that he pay up."

"I just can't make myself care anymore. I know I probably should, but I don't."

"I think you're doing the right thing. Dredging up crap from the past doesn't change what happened then." He slid his big hands down her back to cup her backside. "It only screws up what's happening now—and now is pretty damned sweet, if you ask me."

She gazed up at his rugged, handsome face. "It's the sweetest time of my entire life."

"You know what the good news is about you finally getting divorced?"

"What's that?"

"We can get married. If we want to, that is."

"I always said I'd never get married again. The first time didn't work out so well, as you've probably heard."

Grinning, he said, "The second time would be nothing like that, and you know it. I can be perfectly happy for the rest of my life just the way we are, but if you want more, I'm here for it."

She laughed. "Which one of the kids taught you that saying? 'I'm here for it.'"

"I think it was Simone, but that's beside the point."

"I suppose if you would be the husband, I might be convinced to take another spin around the marriage rodeo."

"Let's keep that in mind for when things are signed, sealed and delivered, shall we?"

Hannah went up on tiptoes to kiss him. "We shall."

CHAPTER TWENTY-THREE

"What hurts us is what heals us." —Paulo Coelho

*A*fter the phone call from her father, Mia spent the next few hours on edge, waiting to see if her mother had flown into Boston with plans to come to Vermont. She was so anxious that right after a lunch of soup that she couldn't quite stomach, she called Wade, who'd gone into the office for a few hours earlier to catch up on some work.

"Hey, baby, do you miss me?" he asked when he took the call.

"Always, but something sorta happened, and—"

"What?" he asked, all the playfulness gone.

"My dad called."

"I thought they were going to Bermuda?"

"They are, but he saw my mother coming into Logan."

"What? What's she doing in Boston?"

"I have no idea, but he thought—and I tend to agree—she might be coming here."

"Why now do you suppose?"

"Today is a year since Hunter told me my SSN was a fake. I've hardly spoken to her since that day."

"Ah, yes. That's probably it. She gave it a year, and now she's coming to you. I'll be home in fifteen minutes."

"I'm sorry to interrupt your work—"

"As you well know, nothing is more important to me than you are. I'm coming, love."

She breathed a sigh of relief. Not that she couldn't handle a confrontation with her mother on her own, but everything was better when he was with her. "Thank you."

"You don't have to thank me. I'll be right there."

The line went dead, so she put the portable phone back on the charger and went to the front window of the farmhouse they were renovating, while wondering if her mother would even know where to find her in Butler.

Her stomach ached, and her chest felt tight with the anxiety that had been such a part of life with her ex, Brody, who was now in prison, thanks in large part to her testimony. She'd escaped that nightmare, found a blissful new life with Wade and had reconnected with her long-lost father, too.

Mia had been shocked to learn that her mother had basically kidnapped her and kept her from her father. She'd worked hard over the last year to get to know Cabot, to spend as much time with him as she could and to try to make up for lost time that could never be recovered. And in the year since everything blew up, she'd mostly avoided her mother's calls, letters, emails and pleas for a chance to talk, to explain, to make sense of something that could never make sense to her—or her father.

She didn't want to see her mother.

She didn't want to hear her pathetic explanations.

She didn't want any of that to invade the happy space she and Wade had created together.

When he arrived home ten minutes later, skidding to a stop in the driveway with snow flying behind his SUV, she stepped outside to meet him on the porch.

He wrapped his arms around her. "I'm here."

"Thank you for coming."

"You never have to thank me for coming to wherever you are, because you're my favorite place in the world."

She slid her arms around his waist and held on tight to her love, her anchor, her everything. "I don't want to see her."

"Then you won't."

"I know I should, but—"

"You don't owe her *anything*, Mia. Not one fucking thing."

"She did give birth to me and raise me…"

"While keeping an awful secret from you that she never would've told you if Hunter hadn't figured it out. You owe her *nothing*."

She shivered from the cold as much as the anger she heard in his voice. Unlike in her last relationship, his anger was on her behalf, not directed toward her, and his support made all the difference.

"Let's get you inside before you catch cold," he said.

For the next two hours, they snuggled on the sofa and watched a movie, a rom-com she couldn't have named afterward if her life had depended on it. Though they had a hundred projects underway in the house, and weekend time was precious, neither of them could focus on anything else when her mother might be coming.

By the time they heard the crunch of tires in the driveway, Mia had begun to think her mother had come to New England for something other than seeing her. No such luck.

"Stay put. I've got this." Wade kissed the top of her head, got up and put on a coat to go out to greet their visitors.

Mia knew she shouldn't let him fight her battles for her, but this was one she was happy to cede to him. She cracked one of the windows so she could hear him, but kept the blinds drawn so she couldn't be seen.

"I'm Wade Abbott, Mia's husband."

She peeked around the blind to see he had his hands in his pockets as he stood before her mother and stepfather. Her mother had gone completely gray since Mia had seen her last.

"I'm Mia's mother, Deb, and this is my husband, Roger."

"Yes, I know who you are."

"Of course Cabot called to tell her he saw me," Deb said with a bitter edge to her voice.

"Yes, he saved her from being ambushed by a visit she doesn't want."

"I'm not ambushing her! She's my daughter!"

"Showing up uninvited to confront a daughter you know doesn't wish to see you is the very definition of an ambush."

"What else am I supposed to do? She doesn't take my calls or respond to my emails."

"Because she doesn't wish to speak to you or hear from you. She's told you that in so many words."

"We've never had a chance to talk... since everything happened."

"You mean since she found out that you kept her and the father who adored her apart for twenty-five years and never would've fixed it unless my brother had uncovered your deception? Is that what you want to talk to her about?"

Mia wanted to cheer as she listened to her wonderful husband go to bat for her. He would be richly rewarded for that later. Wade knew better than anyone how much Mia had suffered after finding out what her mother had done—and how hard she'd worked to forge a meaningful relationship with her father.

"I... There are things... Things she doesn't know."

"She knows everything she needs to know, and she doesn't want to see you. I'm sorry you came all this way for nothing, but if you'd have asked first, she would've told you not to come."

"Is this you speaking for her? Is this what you want or what she wants?" Deb asked with a hint of hostility in her tone now.

"She speaks for herself. She doesn't need me or anyone else to do it for her, except for when something might hurt her. I won't let you hurt her again."

Oh, how Mia loved him. Even more than she had a few minutes ago, and she wouldn't have thought that was possible.

"I need you to leave now. You're not welcome here, now or in the future. You made your choices, and now Mia has made hers. If she wants to speak to you at some point, she'll let you know. Otherwise, you need to respect her wishes and her privacy."

"Tell her... Tell her I love her, and I'm sorry. I'm so sorry."

Wade said nothing in response. He waited for them to get back in their car and stayed outside until they had driven off.

Mia opened the door for him and threw herself into his arms.

Thankfully, he was ready for her and wrapped her up in a tight hug.

"You were so perfect." She kissed his face and then his lips. "Thank you, thank you, thank you."

"You're very welcome, sweetheart. She has no right to show up here unannounced and try to force you into a showdown."

"No, she doesn't, but I appreciate you handling it for me so I didn't have to. I probably would've buckled and hated myself for that later."

"Like I said, if or when you talk to her, it should be on your schedule, not hers."

"I'll talk to her at some point," Mia said, sighing. "I'm just not ready yet, and I'm not sure when I will be."

Wade hugged her close again. "She did a terrible thing to you —and to Cabot. Both of you are still dealing with the fallout. I don't blame you for not being ready to deal with her yet."

"I feel the most sorry for him. I had no idea, for all that time, that someone was missing. What he went through..." She shuddered. "I can't even imagine."

"I know, honey. It's unbearable. Will you tell him she was here?"

"I suppose I'll have to, but I'll wait until they get back from Bermuda. I really hope he and Izzy have a wonderful time together."

"I do, too. How cool is it that they met because of us?"

"It's super cool, but I'm done talking about anyone except you."

"What about me?"

"You need to be rewarded for taking one for the team."

He pulled back to gaze down at her with eyes full of love and desire. "There're *rewards*?"

She took him by the hand and returned to the sofa, gesturing for him to sit so she could straddle his lap and kiss him. "Oh yes. The very best kind of rewards."

. . .

IZZY HAD NEVER SEEN CABOT LIKE THIS—CLOSED OFF, REMOTE, quiet, brooding. Of all the people to run into on their way out of town! *Ugh.* The poor guy. Just when he was starting to make a new life for himself, the past smacked him in the face, reminding him he'd never truly be free of it.

She didn't know what to do or say to help him, so she kept quiet and let him work through it in his own way and time. Anxiety pinged at her, making her wonder if this would derail him—and them. She'd gotten caught up in their talk about the future, about the babies they would have and the life they would share. It would totally suck to discover the foundation they'd built was made of sand and would crumble at the first sign of trouble.

Although she understood this wasn't your run-of-the-mill kind of trouble. This was the thermonuclear, asteroid-crashing-into-earth kind of trouble and was bound to set him back for a time. But would he come back from it? That was the question with no answer, not yet, anyway. As far as Izzy knew, that was the first time he'd laid eyes on the woman since she'd taken off with their child.

What would that be like, to see someone who'd betrayed you so completely, decades later? Izzy knew how it'd felt to find out her dad had only come to visit her because he wanted something from her mother. That'd hurt her, but it hadn't broken her. She'd learned to expect nothing from him, so it wasn't possible for him to break her.

But Cabot had no warning before seeing the woman who'd ruined his life, and it must've been like a baseball bat to the gut to realize it was her.

He didn't say a word for the entire three-hour flight. He declined drinks and food. His arms were crossed, his gaze set dead ahead. If he blinked, Izzy never saw it while she drank orange juice and coffee and enjoyed a hot breakfast, which then sat in her stomach like a brick.

They landed, disembarked into bright, warm sunshine and walked like zombies to the terminal, went through Customs and found the shuttle to their resort. All without exchanging a single word. Izzy told herself to look out the window, to take in the scenery, but how could she do that when the turmoil inside her demanded her full attention?

They were greeted at the resort, given cool, lemon-scented towels to freshen up and a fruity rum drink that hit the spot. A chatty young man escorted them and their luggage to a gorgeous waterfront suite. Cabot thanked him, handed him a twenty and closed the door behind the man after he left. He walked outside to the patio that overlooked the pool and the beach in the distance and lowered himself onto a lounge chair.

Izzy wasn't sure what to do, so she sat next to him. "What can I do?"

He looked at her as if he'd never seen her before, sending a chill down her spine even though the air was warm. "Nothing. It's fine. Don't worry about it."

"Right, okay. Don't worry about it when you haven't said a word to me in hours, and we're on vacation together for the next week. What do I have to worry about?"

"I'm sorry. Obviously, the last thing I expected today was to see her. I'm just… Well, I don't know what I am, but seeing her fucked me up."

"I'm sorry that happened to you."

He shrugged. "Every time I think I've moved on, I find out otherwise. That's how it's gone for all this time."

"You're not alone with it, Cabot. You have Mia and me and your family."

"This is what the setbacks look like, Isabella. I'd understand if it's too much for you. It's too much for me."

"It's not too much, as long as you keep talking to me."

"What's there to say? I saw my ex-wife today for the first time since she abducted my daughter and got away with it. She's probably with Mia now, having a grand reunion."

"You really think their reunion is going to be grand after what Mia knows about her now?"

He shrugged. "Who knows? She's still the person who raised her."

"Why don't we go home? We can go to Vermont and see Mia and make sure she's all right."

"She's fine. She has her husband. There's nothing we can do there. She doesn't need me."

Izzy didn't believe that for a second, but figured there was no point in arguing with him. "Do you want to take a walk and get something to eat?"

"Nah, I'm not hungry, but you go ahead."

The man who hadn't left her side in weeks was now willing to let her roam a resort by herself. She didn't know this version of him or how to respond to him. "If that's what you want."

He had no response to that, so she went inside.

His phone, which he'd left on the counter in the kitchen, rang with a call from Emily. Acting on impulse, Izzy grabbed the phone and took it with her into the bathroom.

"Hey, it's Izzy."

"Is everything all right? I texted Cabot to make sure you guys got there okay, but he didn't reply."

"He saw Deb at Logan."

"*What?* Oh my God! What the hell was she doing there?"

"He asked her that, but she didn't reply, just kept moving with the guy she was with."

"Did he call Mia?"

"He did. If she's headed to Vermont, Mia was unaware of it."

"Oh Lord."

"I don't know what to do with him, Emily. He's barely said a word to me since he saw her, and he's really..."

"Mean and nasty?"

"Yeah, I guess so."

"That's how he gets. I'm sorry you're having to see him that way. That bitch did some serious damage to him. I was hoping having Mia back in his life would repair it, but I realized a while ago that it's not going to be that simple, especially since Deb basically got away with what she did to him—and Mia."

"What should I expect?"

"When the dark moods hit, he sort of disappears into himself for a time."

"How long of a time?"

"It varies. It can last days, weeks, even a couple of months once."

Izzy felt her heart sink as gritty reality came swooping in, the way it always did when things were going well in her life. "I'm not sure what I should do."

"I don't know what to say," Emily said with a sigh. "He can be completely unreachable when he gets like this."

"I'm not one to cut and run at the first sign of trouble, but this might be bigger than I can handle."

"You should tell him that. It might make a difference to hear that from you."

"I'm not sure it would. He barely seems to know I'm even here."

Emily moaned with distress. "I'm so sorry, Izzy. As you well know, this isn't him. This isn't how he usually is."

"No, it isn't, but it also *is* him, part of him, anyway. He tried to warn me about it, but I didn't grasp the full extent."

"How could you? Until you experience it firsthand, it's sort of hard to understand." Emily made a sound of frustration. "God, I hate that this happened when he was so happy with you. It was such a big deal for him to go to Vermont after your accident and then to stay on with you after you got home. And the vacation... It was all so promising."

"Yes, it was."

"Izzy... I know it's a lot to ask, but would you consider just giving it a day or two and see how he is before you decide anything?"

"I'm not going to leave him because things got complicated."

"This goes beyond complicated, as you probably can see for yourself. Seeing her triggered all the bad stuff that he works so hard to keep at arm's length with his frantic schedule. Whenever something happens—like a lead in the search for Mia that didn't pan out, her birthday, the spring she would've graduated from high school—it just comes rushing back like a tsunami that overtakes him for a time before he finds the wherewithal to battle it back—again. It's been that way from the beginning of this nightmare."

"All those difficult things probably have nothing on seeing the person who caused all this for the first time since it happened," Izzy said, her heart sinking.

"I would imagine so. And he's probably worried about Mia having to deal with her."

"I suggested we go home to Vermont and be there for her, but he says she doesn't need him. She has her husband."

"It's probably best for him to be nowhere near there if Deb is around."

"Yes, I suppose you're right about that. The way he spoke to her... I couldn't believe he was the same man."

"I wouldn't have blamed him if he tried to murder her right there in public where anyone could see him."

"He sounded as if he could have."

"He never would, because she's Mia's mother, but God, he must want to."

"I'm not sure what I should do here, Emily."

"Just stay close to him. Be there, but give him space. When he's ready, he'll talk to you, but it might take a while."

"I can do that."

"I'm here if I can help. Give me your number so we can communicate directly."

Izzy recited her phone number.

"I'll text you so you have mine."

"Thank you, Emily."

"Oh gosh, thank *you*, Izzy. It's been so great to see Cabot moving toward something lovely with you. I just hope he can get back to that sooner rather than later."

"Me, too. I'll do what I can to get him there, and I'll keep you posted."

"Thank you. Give him my love if you get the chance."

"I will. Talk soon."

CHAPTER TWENTY-FOUR

"I don't know why they call it heartbreak. It feels like every other part of my body is broken, too." —Terri Guillemets

*I*zzy ended the call feeling like she understood what she was up against a little better than she had before she talked to Emily. If only she knew what to do about it. For now, she would take Emily's advice to stay close and to be there if he needed her while also staying focused on her own recovery.

After she returned Cabot's phone to the counter in the kitchen, she went to unpack her suitcase and take a shower. She applied some makeup to cover the last of the bruises on her face and emerged from the bathroom wearing one of her sister's cute dresses and flip-flops, her broken arm in the sling, determined to take a look around at the place she would call home for the next week.

She found Cabot right where she'd left him on the patio. "I'm going to take a walk."

"Okay."

Izzy wanted to ask him to come with her, but knew it would be pointless, so she went alone to explore the lush grounds. After walking for a short time, she began to tire, so she headed for the restaurant by the pool and took a seat at one of the tables. She ordered a piña colada and a salad, enjoying both as she watched the action at the pool.

After she'd sat for a long while, she withdrew her phone from her bag and called Noah's house, hoping to talk to Vanessa.

She answered on the third ring, sounding out of breath.

"I'm not interrupting anything important, am I?" Izzy asked.

"Not yet," Vanessa said with a laugh. "We just got back to Noah's."

"We did, did we?"

"Uh-huh. We got to meet Elliott today, and Mom made dinner for everyone."

"Oh! How was it?"

"It went really well. He's absolutely adorable, and Noah is so great with him."

"I can't wait to meet him."

"You'll love him."

"I have no doubt. So, things are going well?"

"Very well. If they were any better, I might spontaneously combust into a Disney movie with singing animals."

Izzy laughed at that. "I heard you're going back to New York with Troy."

"He asked me to, and I figured why not? He's the best thing to happen to me in like forever, and there's nothing keeping me here or in Boston. We're going to see what transpires."

"I'm glad it's going well for one of us."

"Uh-oh. Aren't you guys in paradise by now?"

"Yep, but paradise isn't turning out so great." She filled her sister in on what'd happened at the airport and how Cabot had reacted. "He's withdrawn into himself, and it's like he's a million miles away. His sister says this is how it goes when the past resurfaces, so I guess it's normal for him."

"But not for you."

"I have no idea how to handle it."

"Of all the freaking people for him to see in the airport."

"I know, right? What are the odds? But today's a year since Hunter uncovered the fake SSN, and we figure Mia's mother gave it a year."

"What are you going to do?"

"I don't know. Part of me wants to just go home. It's so weird to be away from both our homes dealing with something like this. I wish we hadn't come here, but I didn't realize right away that it was going to be this bad."

"I think you need to decide, Iz. Are you in this with him, for better or worse, come what may? Or is this too much for you to deal with? No one would blame you if it was. It's a lot. He's clearly dealing with deep-seated trauma that can resurface at any time, without warning, and derail his life and yours for who knows how long. Are you prepared to live like that?"

"I just don't know. A few days ago, we were talking about having kids together, and now…"

"Do you love him?"

"I do. I think I have since the day I met him. That was one of the most magical days of my entire life. He's been so great since the accident, barely leaving my side for days on end and insisting on caring for me at home. He's so sweet and funny and smart and handsome… He's everything I've ever wanted and thought I'd never find."

"Then you stick it out, and you wait him out. You let him do what he needs to in order to process this and hope that when he comes through the other side of it, he'll still want the same things he did before."

"And if he doesn't?"

"Then you'll know what you need to do. You're not so far into this that you can't get out if that's what's best for you."

The thought of leaving Cabot, of never seeing him again, of not having the life they'd dreamed about, brought tears to her eyes. "I hate this. Things were going so well."

"Honestly, Iz, I would've been shocked if you didn't discover some residual fallout from what he went through for all those years when Mia was missing. Finding her and having her back in his life doesn't mitigate the trauma of it all."

"Yeah, you're right, and he tried to warn me. He said there were things about him that might make me change my mind, but

I sort of blew it off because I didn't want to ruin such a good thing."

"He's a great guy. We can all see that. You're going to have to take this a day at a time and see if it's more than you can handle. Only you can decide that."

"Thanks for listening."

"Oh my God, Iz. I owe you a thousand hours of listening for all the times you've been there for me."

"I love being there for you. Always have."

"Same goes, sister. I'm here. Call me if I can help."

"You already have. Your guy is waiting for you. Go have a nice evening."

"I have a guy! And I found him in Butler, of all places. Can you believe it?"

"I believe it. He's a lucky man, and I'm sure he knows it."

"I think he's the one."

Izzy's eyes filled with tears. "Aw, Ness."

"Yeah, and you know me. I don't say stuff like that."

"No, you don't. I'm so happy for you."

"I'm pretty happy for me, too, even if I'm sending myself all sorts of messages to slow my roll and all that. I'm caught up. Can't seem to help it."

"As you're well aware of all the potential pitfalls, you don't need me to tell you to be careful."

"That's the thing. With him, I don't feel the need to be careful. Everything about this is different."

Izzy could hear the difference in her sister's voice. "How's the anxiety been?"

"What anxiety?"

"Really?"

"Yeah, it hasn't been an issue the last few days, which is miraculous in and of itself, as you surely know. I just feel... calm."

Izzy wanted to weep hearing that. Vanessa's debilitating anxiety had been a cause for major concern for their entire family at various times in her life.

"That's not to say it's gone or anything, because that's not how it works, but it's leaving me alone for once."

"Enjoy every minute of this time with Troy, and keep me posted."

"Oh, I will. Let me know what you decide to do about Cabot and Bermuda."

"Will do."

"Look out for yourself in this, Iz. As hard as that might be, do what's best for you."

"Thanks for listening. Love you."

"Love you, too."

Izzy ended the call and turned toward the gorgeous sunset unfolding over the beach, wishing Cabot was with her to enjoy it together. Vanessa's news had filled her with happiness for her sister, which helped to offset some of the despair over her own situation.

She needed to go back to their suite and figure out what to do. It pained her to realize she might have no choice but to leave him to work out his problems without her. What else could she do if he refused to share it with her? From the beginning, she'd understood that he'd endured a long, horrific ordeal at the hands of his ex-wife. After today, she also understood what he'd tried to tell her—that despite the reunion with his daughter a year ago, the damage was still an integral part of him—and always would be.

If she took her sister's advice and looked out for herself first, that might leave her with no choice but to walk away.

God, she hoped it didn't come to that.

CABOT WAS FULLY AWARE THAT HE WAS DESTROYING HIS LOVELY new relationship with Izzy, but he couldn't pull himself out of the spiral no matter how hard he tried or how much he wanted to. It'd been a while since the darkness had sucked him in this deep, but seeing his ex-wife for the first time without any warning or preparation had flattened him.

He fucking hated her.

He hated that she was off living a whole new life while he was trying to form a relationship with the daughter who hadn't known his name until a year ago.

He hated that he hated her, that he wished her the same agony she'd perpetrated on him, that he wanted her dead.

After years of therapy, he knew those feelings were only harming him. They had no effect whatsoever on *her*. She'd gotten to raise their daughter while he'd gone crazy looking for his child. And then he'd been forced to drop all pending charges against her in exchange for having his adult daughter in his life.

He'd done as Mia had asked, but it hadn't been easy to let go of any hope of justice. Yes, having Mia back had helped some, but every wonderful encounter with her also served as a stark reminder of everything he'd missed.

From his post on the patio, he heard the main door to the suite open and then close. A light went on inside before Izzy came to find him.

"I brought you a sandwich." She put the plate and a bottle of cold water on the table next to him. "You need to eat something."

Cabot could hear the confusion and dismay in every word she said. She hadn't signed on for this bullshit. He'd tried to warn her about his dark side, but she hadn't wanted to hear it. That was why he'd kept his distance after the wedding and the dinner in Boston. He hadn't wanted her to see him this way. While others in his life had remarked on how well he'd been doing since Mia returned, he'd been painfully aware that the darkness was still there, lurking, waiting to suck him back into its web at any time.

He'd seethed over the fact that Deb had gotten away with what she'd done, with no ramifications other than a deeply fractured relationship with her daughter. As far as he knew, Mia had spoken only sporadically to her mother since the deception had been uncovered, which had happened only because Hunter Abbott was thorough in his role as CFO of the Abbott family businesses.

Otherwise, Cabot might still be looking for his daughter.

The rage was so much a part of who he was that he didn't

remember himself before it had taken hold of him. It simmered on low burn most of the time, always there, but not keeping him from living his life. Until something threw gas on it, like seeing his ex-wife arriving in Boston as if she had a right to be there, and then the flames surged, incinerating everything around him until there was nothing left but a bleak, barren landscape.

He was used to it after all this time, but Izzy wasn't. She wouldn't stand for it, and who could blame her? Like he'd said before, she could have anyone she wanted. What did she need with a wreck of a man who couldn't control his emotions, who retreated into himself like a toddler having a tantrum?

As he picked at the turkey club and sipped from the water bottle, he tried as hard as he could to bring himself out of the death spiral he'd been in since he saw Deb's face earlier. He dusted off all the techniques his longtime therapist had taught him to cope with the dark spells—visualization, meditation, journaling, looking for the positives in any situation, exercise, writing down one or two "good" things that were happening at the same time as the bad thing. He'd tried them all at various times over the years, and sometimes the tactics had helped, and other times they hadn't.

The current darkness was tinged with a feeling that the universe was trying to tell him something by putting Deb in Logan that morning, right when he was heading for a vacation with his new love. How could he see the encounter with her as anything other than a sign that he had no right to a new life and a new love with Izzy while rage this potent still burned within him?

God, he loved Izzy. He loved her like he'd never loved any woman. The life they'd dreamed about together was right there, his for the taking if only he could find a way to put out the fire before it consumed her along with him. He couldn't let that happen, couldn't be responsible for doing anything to dim the light that burned so brightly in her.

While he burned with rage, she was incandescent with joy, light and serenity.

Rage was like the paper in a game of rock, paper, scissors, covering and smothering everything around it.

He forced himself to stand, get his bearings and walk inside to find her.

She was in bed, with her broken arm on a pillow, her gorgeous hair, the color of the finest whiskey, raining down around her shoulders as she eyed him with trepidation.

He hated Deb for that, too, for crushing this beautiful second chance for him. "I think we should go home tomorrow."

"Okay."

"And after that, you should go back to Vermont. I'll have a car service take you." He could see how his words hurt her and wished he didn't have to say them, but he couldn't leave her with any hope. That would just be cruel. "I'm sorry."

Unshed tears made her eyes shiny. "Me, too."

Turning, he left the bedroom, closing the door behind him while telling himself it was for the best. This was why he'd avoided her after the first two times they'd met, because he knew he'd hurt her eventually. He'd gotten carried away after the accident, but nothing in him had changed.

Today had proven that once and for all.

CHAPTER TWENTY-FIVE

"You flew off with the wings of my heart and left me flightless."
—Stelle Atwater

*I*zzy managed to hold it together during the long, sleepless night and the seemingly endless trip home the next day.

After they arrived at Logan and cleared Customs, Cabot summoned an Uber to take them back to his place, where Izzy packed up her belongings and waited for the car service to arrive.

They didn't exchange a single word until he told her the car had arrived for her.

She thought maybe he would hug her or kiss her or tell her again he was sorry, but he didn't do any of those things. He carried her bag down the stairs and out to the car, handing it over to the driver, and then held her door like the gentleman he was, waiting until she was settled to close it.

Then he turned and walked up the stairs and back into his house, rid of the problem she'd caused for him.

That's when she got mad.

How dare he dismiss her that way, as if what they'd shared hadn't meant a thing to him? For a second, she thought about getting out of the car and charging up the stairs to bang on the door to demand... what, exactly? Only pride and self-respect kept her from making a scene as the driver put the car in Drive and headed out of Beacon Hill.

Izzy composed a text to Emily. *We flew back to Boston this morning. Cabot sent me home to Vermont in a car service. Thought you should know.*

Before she sent the text, she tried to think of something else she could say, but what else was there? She and Cabot had shared something special that was over now. He'd made that perfectly clear with his surgical strike last night and his silence today.

She sent the text.

Emily replied when they were on Interstate 93, approaching Manchester, New Hampshire. *OMG, I just got out of a meeting and saw this. I'm heartbroken. I can't imagine how you must feel. I'm so sorry, Izzy. I don't know what else to say.*

There's nothing to say. It is what it is.

He's going to regret this.

Maybe so, but this is how he wants it.

He's a FOOL!

Thank you for your friendship. I wish you—and Cabot—all the best. Take care, Emily.

You, too. I'm sorry again.

Izzy didn't reply to that, but she didn't want Emily's apology. She hadn't done anything wrong. All Izzy wanted was to go home and be alone for as long as it took to recover from her physical and emotional wounds. After that, she would get back to work and put this relationship behind her. She'd moved on from other painful disappointments, and she'd survive this one, too.

Somehow.

OVER THE NEXT FEW WEEKS, IZZY THREW HERSELF INTO HER recovery. Nolan helped her locate a used Jeep Cherokee with fairly low miles, new tires and a better stereo system than her old one had had. He confirmed the engine was sound and that the airbags had been recently inspected. That last item was more important to her than it had ever been before airbags had saved her life.

Vanessa reported that life in the city with Troy was blissful and that she was planning to give up her place in Boston to make a permanent move to New York. Izzy was so happy for her sister. Some people got lucky. Others didn't. She'd always known that, but she ached for the happy ending that had been within her reach before it was snatched away by the past.

She got her cast off in late January and began the arduous and painful physical therapy to get her left arm working again. As soon as she felt up to it, she began walking every day, trying to get back some of the muscle tone and stamina she'd lost during her recovery. Whenever she could, she worked on her computer, processing the photo shoots she'd done right before the accident and getting in touch with clients to reschedule jobs now that she was on her way back to full health.

Izzy celebrated with Vanessa when she packed up her apartment in Boston and officially moved to New York to live with Troy. She helped to plan Emma's upcoming bridal shower and attended a birthday party for her mother and Noah. If her family wondered where Cabot had gone, they kept their questions to themselves, for which she was extremely grateful. She didn't want to talk about the most painful situation in her life.

In mid-February, Mia left a voice mail message, asking Izzy to call her when she got a minute. Izzy didn't want to talk to her about Cabot or what was wrong with him or what ought to be done about it. She'd worried herself sick over him, but what could she do after being summarily dismissed from his life?

Only because Mia was also her cousin's wife did Izzy return the call two days later. Her stomach was in knots as she waited for someone to pick up at Wade and Mia's house.

"Izzy," Mia said. "Thank you so much for calling me back."

"Sorry it took me a minute. Things have been busy."

"You're feeling better?"

"Much. Almost back to full steam, except for my arm, which

is still giving me some trouble. But even that's way better than it was."

"I'm so glad to hear it. I've been meaning to call you to say... Well, I don't know what to say other than I'm sorry for what happened with my dad. Emily told me what she knew about what'd transpired, which wasn't much, just that you came back from Bermuda the day after you went, and Dad sent you home."

"That about sums it up. I assume you've spoken to him."

"Yes, but he doesn't have much to say about anything. He sounds kind of awful, actually. I'm really worried about him."

Izzy was perversely glad to hear he might be feeling as dreadful as she did. "I'm sorry to hear that, but I'm not sure what I can do about it. He was pretty clear that he wanted me gone, so I'm gone."

"I don't believe for a second that's what he really wants, Izzy." Mia sounded like she might cry. "He's crazy about you. We all saw that."

Izzy's eyes burned with tears that she refused to allow to fall. She'd cried enough tears over him. "I wish I could tell you something that would help, but I'm at a loss. He was obviously undone by seeing your mother."

"As was I."

Izzy had wondered if Deb had gone to see Mia, but asking would've meant contacting Mia and having this painful conversation sooner. "She came to your house?"

"She did. Wade talked to her and asked her to leave."

Izzy had so many questions she didn't ask. It was no longer her concern, and it wasn't in her best interest to become more involved.

"Look," Mia said, "I know it's a lot to ask, but if I could get my dad to come up here, would you see him?"

Izzy ached like she hadn't since that awful day when she last saw him. "I can't, Mia. I'm so, so sorry. I care for him so very much, but I can't see him. He made it very clear that we were done."

"I understand." Mia sounded as sad as Izzy had ever heard her. "I don't know him as well as I should, but I know happy when I see it, and he was happy with you. I want so much for him to be happy and to find some peace. He deserves it more than anyone."

"Yes, he does, and I'm sorry he couldn't find it with me."

"But he *did*, though. I saw that. What happened between you guys wasn't your fault or his. It was *hers*. She did this."

"As much as I want to agree with you, I can't." How could she say this diplomatically? "What was done to him was incredibly cruel and horrible. Anyone with a heart would agree. But how he reacts to it now, all these years later? That's on *him*. Do you understand what I'm saying?"

"I do, and I agree. He's letting her ruin his life all over again, but I don't know how to make him see that. I've tried. Believe me, I have, but he doesn't want to talk about it. Emily says he doesn't want to burden me with the trauma he suffered because of me."

"Which is probably true."

"How can I make him see that I *want* him to burden me? We were both harmed by what she did. Who else can understand better than I can?"

"If you feel that strongly about it, maybe you should go there and tell him that."

"Wade said the same thing. I've felt weird about invading my dad's privacy, but I can't bear to see him working himself into a frenzy rather than deal with the rest of his life."

It pained Izzy to hear that's what he'd been doing, but she wasn't surprised. "If anyone would be welcome in the midst of whatever he's dealing with, I'd imagine it would be you."

"Wade said that, too. I'm going to ask for some time off and go there. I'll coordinate with Emily to make sure he'll be in town. I've heard he's been traveling a lot."

That detail told her a lot because she knew he preferred to be at home.

"I wish you—and him—all the best, Mia."

"Don't give up on him, Izzy. Please don't."

Izzy wanted to weep, but if she started, she might never stop. "Take care of yourself, Mia, and give Wade my best."

"I will. Thanks again for calling me back."

"No problem."

God, if only it hadn't hurt so much to talk about him, Izzy thought as she sat in the dark in front of the fire, aching for Cabot and missing him so much, it made her sick. Talking to Mia reopened wounds that had only recently begun to scab over. But that wasn't Mia's fault. Naturally, she'd be concerned about her father, as she'd probably never seen him like this either.

Cabot had spent just enough time in her home that Izzy saw him everywhere she looked, sitting behind her desk on the phone in the office, in her bed, in the kitchen and on the sofa where they'd spent so many lovely hours in front of the fire talking and watching TV and dreaming about a future that wasn't going to happen now.

After realizing she might not get around to having children, she'd desperately wanted the babies she would've had with him.

A sob caught in her throat at how unfair life could be. She finally found *him*, the *one*, and he was so deeply mired in the trauma of his past that he wasn't available to her. Even as she understood and empathized with the horrific ordeal he'd endured—and was continuing to endure—she ached for herself. She ached for them both, for what could've been and would never be now.

She hadn't been this sad since her dad left, and that was a time she hardly wished to revisit.

"Okay, girl, time to snap out of it and get back on track." She got up from the sofa and went to take a shower, relieved she didn't need to worry about protecting her cast anymore. But her healing arm ached like a bitch this time of day, so after her shower, she took two Advil to ensure the pain wouldn't keep her awake.

If only there was something she could take to ease the pain in her heart.

CHAPTER TWENTY-SIX

"Love yourself first, and everything else falls into line. You really have to love yourself to get anything done in this world." —Lucille Ball

*C*abot worked like a fiend, closing eighteen new deals in the weeks after the Bermuda trip and the inglorious end of the most glorious relationship he'd ever had with a woman. He returned to his previously frantic schedule and hired twelve additional people to help manage the new accounts. Business was booming, just the way he liked it.

If the rest of his life was somewhat of a mess, well, so be it. He ought to be accustomed to that by now. The intense schedule kept him too busy to think about the bad things, and a new prescription helped him sleep. Desperation had led him to seek out the medication after lying awake night after night, aching for the woman he loved and despising himself for how he'd pushed her away.

She must hate him. He wouldn't blame her if she did. One minute, they were talking about having babies together, and the next, he was sending her home to Vermont in a hired car, like she meant nothing to him.

She meant *everything* to him. Everything was her. And he'd fucked it up in every way possible.

He hated himself more than he ever had before. How could

he have done that to her when she'd given him a third chance he hadn't deserved?

The guilt and remorse threatened to eat him alive if he let it, thus the busy schedule and the sleeping pills.

Out of sheer desperation, he reached out to the therapist who'd once upon a time helped him survive his daughter's abduction. Martha was retired now and living year-round in a beach cottage on Cape Cod, but she took his call anyway.

"This is a nice surprise," she said.

"How are you, Martha?"

"I'm wonderful. Retirement is better than advertised. I highly recommend it."

Cabot couldn't conceive of a world without his work to keep him from going insane. "I'm so glad you're happy. You worked hard."

"Yes, I did. I assume this isn't a social call."

"No, but you're retired."

"I told you I'd always be here for you if you needed me, and I meant that. I'm happy to talk about whatever's on your mind, free of charge."

"You're too kind. You always have been."

"If anyone deserves kindness in his life, Cabot, you do."

He sat on the leather sofa in his office that looked out over the Boston skyline, every landmark as familiar to him as his own face, but all he saw was the reflection of a man brought low by his own demons. "I saw Deb."

"Oh Lord. Where?"

"At Logan. She was arriving as I was departing for Bermuda with my new girlfriend."

"You have someone new! That's wonderful."

"*Had.* Past tense."

"Oh dear."

"Seeing Deb fucked me up. It fucked up everything. Like Alice dropping into the rabbit hole, I was right back to day one. And it happened just when everything was better than it had been, well, ever. I've been a complete fucking mess ever since."

"Aw, shit. I'm so sorry."

"I hate that she can still do this to me, Martha. How is it possible after all this time that the sight of her face can do *this* to me?"

"The brain is a complex organ, as you well know. It holds on to things we'd rather let go of and isn't afraid to lacerate us with painful memories that come back to us like they happened five minutes ago rather than decades ago."

"That's exactly what happened. It was all right there, those first frantic days of realizing she'd left and taken Mia and intended to stay gone, of fearing I might never see my daughter again."

"I read about Mia coming back into your life and wept with joy for you. I was going to reach out, but I worried that hearing from the therapist who helped you through that time might take something away from your joy."

"I'd love to hear from you any time. You saved my life."

"I'm glad you think so. I've thought of you so often over the years. Of all the patients I saw in my practice, your story is one that's stayed close to my heart. I was so, so glad to hear Mia had found you. That must've been an incredible day."

"Oh, it was. She's... She's delightful, beautiful, sweet, smart, madly in love with her husband, Wade. Having her back in my life has been a dream come true."

"But?"

"No buts."

"None at all?"

Resting his elbows on his knees, Cabot ran his fingers through hair that had turned gray in his twenties while he desperately searched for his little girl. "She's all grown up. Soon to be twenty-eight."

"Did she know what her mother had done?"

"No. God, no. She was shocked to find out I even existed. Her mother had told her she didn't know who her father was."

"I hope her mother is in jail."

"That would've been nice, but Mia made it a stipulation of our initial reunion that all charges against her mother be dropped."

"Ugh, Cabot."

"I know, but I was so damned happy to hear from her that I agreed to whatever she wanted. And I don't regret that. Putting Mia through an ugly trial wouldn't have been in her best interest."

"What about your best interest?"

"I think that's part of the reason why seeing her triggered me so badly. That she's out walking free and remarried. She can come breezing into Boston, intending to ambush our daughter in Vermont with a visit Mia didn't want, and no one can stop her from continuing to hurt both of us."

"You want vengeance."

"Hell yes, I do. I burn with rage over what she did and what she got away with."

"No one would blame you for that."

"The fire is incinerating everything around me, though. I had a good thing going with Isabella, the woman I was seeing, and I ruined it by letting the rage consume me after we saw Deb at Logan. It was like someone flipped a switch, and I couldn't see or feel or hear anything other than the roar inside my own head. I haven't even seen Mia since then because I don't want her to see me like this."

"Do you think it would harm her to see the hurt her mother's actions caused you?"

"She knows. Those actions hurt her, too."

"But she only just found out about it a year ago. You've lived with it for so much longer while longing for the child who was taken from you. That's a whole different kettle of fish, Cabot."

"I suppose so. I don't want my ugliness to touch her. She's glorious, Martha. I wish you could meet her."

"I'd love to meet her sometime."

"She's been so good about indulging me and my freak-out over finding her."

"I read about the wedding in the *Globe*'s society section. My heart was full to overflowing for you. The picture of you giving her away…"

"I have it framed on my desk here in the office. I look at it any time I need a reminder of what truly matters. She's what matters."

"You matter, too."

His deep sigh was his only response.

"I'd imagine that the lack of consequences for Deb is a thorn that remains firmly implanted in your side, despite the joy of your reunion with Mia."

"It is. I hate that she got away with what she did."

"You said Mia doesn't speak to her."

"She doesn't. Only very sporadically since she found out what Deb had done."

"That has to be a certain kind of punishment for Deb, no?"

"I suppose so. But it's not enough."

"You could pursue civil remedies. Hit her in the pocketbook."

"Then I'd look like a bully to my daughter."

"She'd probably understand."

"I'd never put her through it. While she hates what her mother did, I'm sure Mia still feels love for her after being raised by her."

"So what do we do about this rage inside you that's incinerating all the good around you?"

"I don't know. I wish it wasn't there, that it would go away and leave me alone, and I thought it had, you know? I thought I'd moved on. Mia's back, life is good again, I've met a woman I could truly love and build a life with, and then as quick as all that, it's gone again."

"It's not all gone. Mia is still there."

"Yes, she is, and she's wonderful. I don't want you to get me wrong. She's been a saint to put up with her blathering idiot of a father who can't stop crying and celebrating her miraculous return."

Martha chuckled. "I'm sure it's not that bad."

"I assure you it's worse. But the thing is…" It pained him to say this out loud, but it had been on his mind a lot. "I don't really know her, not the way my sister knows her daughter at the deepest level. Emily knows Caroline's every quirk, every interest, every detail of every day of her life. Caroline even tells her when she sleeps with someone. I'll never have that with Mia, not that I want that last part. But you know what I mean."

"I do," Martha said gently. "And it's outrageous that you were robbed of the things that make a parent-child relationship so deeply special. But that doesn't mean you can't have a different sort of bond with Mia that's intimate in its own way."

"I feel like it might be too late for that."

"It is *never* too late, Cabot. As long as you're both still breathing, there's time to grow that relationship. You said Mia welcomed you into her life."

"She's been great about that."

"Because she wants to know you as badly as you want to know her."

"You think so?"

"I'm sure of it. All her life, she must've had questions about the man who'd fathered her, and to find out what she did at twenty-seven... She must feel as cheated as you do."

"I knew she was upset about what her mother did, but it didn't really occur to me that she'd feel as cheated as I do."

"Of course she does, Cabot. How could she not? It probably took her all of five minutes to see that you would've been the father of any little girl's dreams. I have no doubt she's mourning what she missed with you as much as you are over what you missed with her. We can't rewrite the past, but we sure as hell can determine the future. Perhaps if you focus your considerable energy on building the best possible relationship with her that you can, that might help to mitigate the rage, huh?"

"It might. I've thought about moving to Vermont, for at least part of the year, so I can live closer to her."

"What's stopping you?"

"My business is booming."

"And I assume you have employees you trust who could shoulder more of the load if you wanted to make some changes in your life."

"You make it sound so easy."

"It *is* easy, Cabot, if you want something badly enough.

You've had a very successful professional life. I assume you have the resources to set up the life you want."

"Yeah," he said.

"As my dear husband likes to remind me, we can't take it with us, and life is for the living. You were the victim of a horrible, unconscionable crime. That'll always be a fact of your life. But it doesn't have to define your life."

"Why does it all make such perfect sense coming from you, but in my mind, it's a jumbled-up mess?"

Martha's deep, throaty laugh made him smile for the first time since the night before Bermuda.

"Talk to me about this woman you mentioned. Isabella."

"Isabella Coleman."

"The photographer? I love her stuff. I heard she was in a bad accident a while back. Is she all right?"

"I'm sure she's almost fully healed by now. She's my son-in-law's cousin. We met at the wedding, and it was just instantaneous attraction."

"How lovely for you."

"Naturally, I had to mess it up by not acting on it then or after the next time I saw her."

"Why?"

"I hesitated to bring her into my life because I was afraid of exactly what happened. The rage incinerated what was a very good thing up to then."

"I assume she didn't actually see the rage, only it's ancillary effects?"

"Yes. Fortunately, the rage makes me silent, not violent."

"That's a good thing, indeed. And it makes me wonder if your Isabella might be willing to give you another chance if you're able to explain to her what happened and why. You could share with her what you're doing to put the past where it belongs while celebrating a future with the people you love the most. You have so much to look forward to, Cabot. I'm sure you'll have grandchildren before too much longer, for one thing. They're the best thing since ice cream."

"So I've heard," he said, smiling at her description. "Izzy is… She's quite a bit younger than me and wants kids."

"That's *marvelous*," Martha said, laughing. "You could have a do-over. Not with Mia, of course, but you could do fatherhood and grandfatherhood simultaneously and be happy as a pig in shit in Vermont with your people. In this scenario I picture for you, days, weeks, *months* will pass in which you'll hardly think of Deb or what she did or the desperate years of searching for your daughter. Your daughter will be front and center in your life, right where you've always wanted her to be."

"I want that life," he said softly. "I want it so badly."

"Then *go get it*, Cabot. Go get it. Make it happen the same way you would a business deal. Give it everything you have until you get what you want."

He took a deep breath and blew it out, fortified as always by a good talk with her. "I can't thank you enough for this."

"You can thank me by being happy. And I want to hear from you again next week. Let's do this for a while until you get your ship righted, okay?"

"You're the best."

"Feels good to stretch the old muscles again. Call me next week? Around the same time? Gary plays golf on Tuesdays, rain, snow or shine, so that's a good time for me."

"I will. Thank you again, Martha. Once again, you've saved my life."

"Nah, you did it on your own by realizing you needed help and asking for it. I can't wait to hear what happens next for you. Talk to you next week or before if needed?"

"Absolutely. You're the best. Thank you again."

"You're very welcome, my friend."

Cabot ended the call filled with a pervasive sense of relief that he'd aired out the darkness and found a kernel of light to focus on. Martha was right. He'd worked his ass off and could do whatever the fuck he wanted. And what he wanted, more than anything, was to see his daughter much more often than he did now and to try to maybe put things back together with Izzy.

The extension on his desk beeped for the first time since he'd asked his assistant to give him an uninterrupted hour.

He picked up the phone. "Yes, Anna?"

"Your daughter is here and would like to see you."

Cabot was stunned by that news. His heart gave a happy jolt, the way it always did when he was about to see her. Usually, he looked forward to it for days in advance. There'd been no spontaneity in their relationship—until now. "Send her in, please."

CHAPTER TWENTY-SEVEN

"Take chances, make mistakes. That's how you grow. Pain nourishes
your courage. You have to fail in order to practice being brave."
—Mary Tyler Moore

The first thing Mia noticed when she saw her father for
the first time in weeks was that he looked exhausted.
And he'd lost weight. But the smile that lit up his face every time
he saw her was as big as usual.

"This is a nice surprise," he said as he came to hug her and
kiss her cheek.

She'd grown accustomed to his easy affection and returned
his hug, breathing in the now-familiar scent of his cologne, the
scent of her dad. "I hope I'm not interrupting anything
important."

"Nothing that can't wait. Let me take your coat."

She handed over the black wool peacoat she'd bought at the
family store and unwound the red-and-black-plaid cashmere
scarf Wade's mother had given her for Christmas.

"To what do I owe the honor of a visit from my daughter?
And why aren't you working today?"

"I took today off. Tomorrow, too." Odd how she still got shy
around him, even after a year of knowing him. "I wanted to
come see you."

"Is everything all right?" he asked with concern.

"That's what I wanted to ask you."

They sat on the sofa by the windows where he'd once told her he held lots of meetings. The informal setting made people more comfortable, he'd said. He was good at making people feel comfortable. She'd experienced that herself and seen him in action with others. People stopped what they were doing to listen to what he had to say because it was always worth hearing.

"What do you mean?" he asked in response to her statement.

"You haven't been yourself lately," she said, feeling the shyness again. Did she have any right to barge into his life and demand he tell her what was going on with him? "And yes, I know you well enough by now to be able to tell that, even from afar. Things have been off since you saw Mom." On the long drive from Vermont, she'd thought about what she might say to him and decided she'd need to confront the elephant in the room if she was going to get anywhere with him.

"I've been dealing with some stuff."

"Me, too."

"I hate how she showed up at your house like she had some right to be there."

"I wasn't too happy about that either. Thankfully, Wade was there to send her on her way."

"Has she tried to contact you since?"

Mia shook her head. "Hopefully, she's gotten the message that if we're going to be in touch again, it's going to be on my timeline, not hers."

"I hope you know, if you decide to work things out with her, that's completely up to you. I don't expect you to do anything out of loyalty to me."

"Which I appreciate, but it's more about me and the lies she told me my whole life. That's not something I can just 'get over,' as if it didn't matter. It matters a lot. She took something from both of us that we can never get back, no matter how many times we see each other or how hard we try to get to know one another."

"That's something I've been struggling with myself. Emily

has this shorthand with Caroline that's all their own, and you and I... We don't have that. We don't have the inside jokes, the teasing about early boyfriends or your commentary about my awful dancing."

"Your dancing's not *that* bad," she said, smiling. "I've seen much worse from my friends' fathers. But your point is well taken. I suppose that stuff will come. Over time."

"I hope so."

"What about Izzy?"

His expression indicated a direct hit to the heart. "What about her?"

"I thought you two were starting something together."

"We were," he said with a helpless shrug. "I screwed it up by letting the past overtake the present. I handled it badly, but I suppose it's for the best. Someone like her... She could have anyone. What does she need with all my shit?"

"From what I saw, she seemed pretty happy with you. I hadn't known her all that long before you two met, but even Wade said he'd never seen her light up like she did around you."

He put his head back against the sofa, seeming even more exhausted than she'd thought.

"Is it completely hopeless?" she asked.

"Probably. It didn't end well. She saw me at my worst."

"She saw you dealing with old hurts, something she certainly knows a thing or two about."

With a faint smile, he said, "Did she send you to plead her case?"

"Oh no, not at all. I called her last week and tried to talk to her about you, but she wasn't really into it. She said she wishes you all the best, but she couldn't talk about it."

His grimace said it all. "I hate that I hurt her, that I always knew I would, which is why I stayed away from her after the first two times we met. I didn't want to do that to her."

"You hurt her by shutting her out of what you were going through."

"The last thing I want to do is drag her into my problems, Mia. She doesn't need it in her life."

"Maybe not, but it seemed like she needed *you*—the good, the bad, the ugly. It's all part of it, isn't it?"

"Some ugly is uglier than most."

"From what I know of her, Izzy is made of some pretty tough stuff. Maybe you should let her decide what's too much for her."

"I'm not sure she'd even talk to me at this point."

"I'm almost certain she would."

"Really?"

Mia's heart ached for the hope she heard in that single word. "Really. What could be lost by trying?"

"I'll think about it."

"Excellent. Do you have time for lunch? I want that lemongrass ravioli I had the last time I was here. I *dream* about it."

"Then let's go get it."

He grabbed their coats and gestured for her to go ahead of him out of the office. "Anna, will you please ask Darren to take my meetings? I'm taking the afternoon off."

Anna seemed startled to hear that. "Of course. Enjoy the rest of your day."

"Thank you."

"Nice to see you again, Anna," Mia said.

"You as well."

"You said you had time for lunch," Mia said when they were in the elevator to the lobby of the office building she'd learned from others that he owned.

"I do."

"You had a full afternoon planned."

"I got a better offer."

Smiling at him, she said, "You're pretty much slaying this dad thing, in case you were wondering."

His face went slack with shock. "You think so?"

"Hell yes," she said with a laugh. "If you want to make your daughter feel special, tell your assistant to clear your afternoon because you got a better offer."

"That's all it takes, huh?"

"Yep." When they stepped out into the cold, Mia hooked her arm through his. "I had no idea what to expect when I found out my father was a guy named Cabot Lodge in Boston. The name sounded fancy."

His low rumble of laughter made her smile. "Believe me, I've heard that all my life. Cabot was my mother's maiden name."

"I had no idea! I love that."

"I do, too, now, but when I was a kid, it was hell having a fancy name."

"I'm sure," she said, laughing at the face he made. "And P.S., the name suits you."

"I'm glad you think so."

"Anyway, I was wound so tightly when Wade drove me here to see you for the first time—already a year ago. Can you believe it?"

"Some days I still can't believe you're back to stay."

"I'm not going anywhere. Well, except to Vermont, but that's not far."

"It is, though. I want more of this. Impromptu lunch dates and hikes in the woods and skiing. I used to love to ski and haven't done it in years. Do you ski? See? I ought to know that. I should've been the one to teach you that and so many other things. I should've been there, Mia, and I hate so much that I wasn't."

As tears filled her eyes, she stopped walking, released his arm and turned to face him. "I hate that you weren't there, too. I hate it for you as much as I hate it for me. But we have right now and all the years to come to develop our own shorthand and for you to teach me anything you think I need to know."

A muscle in his cheek twitched with tension. "I'd like to move to Vermont to live closer to you."

She wasn't sure she'd heard him right. "But your whole life is here!"

He shook his head. "Not my whole life. The most important part is three hours away, and that's just too far for an impromptu lunch date."

"You'd hate it there. It's so slow and sleepy compared to here."

"I quite loved being there the last time. Slow and sleepy has its advantages."

"Are you serious about this?"

"I think I might be. I assume there could be grandchildren in my future…"

"Hopefully sooner rather than later."

He put his arm around her, directing her toward the restaurant with the lemongrass ravioli. "All the more reason."

"What about your business?"

"When I was staying with Izzy, I proved I can handle most of it from anywhere."

"This is so exciting!"

"I'm glad you think so. I was sort of afraid you might think it would be too much togetherness."

"No such thing, Dad. We've got a lot of time to make up for."

"Then that's what we'll do."

When the host led them to the same table as last time, Mia took a seat across from her dad and leaned in to whisper, "This is our table."

Cabot looked around before he smiled. "So it is. We have a table."

"We're going to have a lot of tables and traditions and inside jokes. You're going to teach me stuff, and I'll teach you a few things, and we'll have all the fun."

He swallowed what might've been a lump in his throat. "When I got the call that you'd been located and were coming here… I didn't know what to expect. The last time I saw you, you were two. The sweetest, cutest, funniest two-year-old ever. Now you were a grown woman with a husband… I just want you to know that the reality of you is so much more than I ever could've hoped for."

"Stop." Mia laughed as she dabbed at tears with a cloth napkin. "You're going to make me bawl in public."

"It's true, though."

She fanned her face. "Right back atcha, Pops. I used to have this huge blank space where my father should've been, and when I'd think about who he might be and what he might be like, suffice to say I never came close to doing justice to who and what you are."

"Now *you* need to stop."

They shared a laugh and ordered their lunch as well as cocktails in honor of an afternoon off.

"How soon are you moving to Vermont?"

"As soon as I can find a place to rent or buy."

"Stay with us while you look. We've got plenty of room."

"You don't need your old man underfoot in the love shack."

"Oh, please. We've been married a year! We're not doing it on the kitchen floor anymore—well, not every day, anyway."

He scowled in the way of fathers everywhere. "Clearly, this friendship of ours needs some boundaries."

Mia laughed so hard, she nearly cried. "It's decided," she said when she could talk again. "You're staying with us for as long as you need to figure out what you want to do."

"Only if you'll kick me out when you've had enough of me."

"I'll never kick you out, and I'll never have enough of you."

"Likewise, my love." He touched his glass to hers. "Likewise."

IN THE END, IT WAS RIDICULOUSLY EASY FOR CABOT TO PACK UP his life and his office and head north to live with his daughter and son-in-law for a time—hopefully a short time, as they were still newlyweds who needed their privacy.

Emily had hugged him tightly the day before, wishing him all the best in his new home and promising to visit as soon as he was settled. "You're doing the right thing for you, even if I'll miss you terribly."

"I want you to visit all the time, and I'll be back here, too."

His niece Caroline was going to move into his place to act as the caretaker and live rent-free while she saved up to buy a place of her own.

"Are you going to try to put things back together with Izzy?"

"I'm not sure yet. We'll see."

"I really hope you can. She's lovely."

"Yes, she certainly is."

Now as he took Interstate 93 North to Vermont, he had only brought the personal and business things he'd need most. When he found a place of his own, Emily would supervise the movers to bring the possessions he'd packed up for his new home.

Thanks to modern technology, he could continue to run his business from Vermont—and Mia's house was one of the few places in Butler with reliable cell service. He planned to start delegating more responsibility to his very capable team so he'd have time for all the things he wanted to do with his daughter and her family.

What good was it to make this huge life change if he wasn't going to also make some other changes, too?

As rolling highway gave way to the mountains, his thoughts turned to Izzy, as they so often did. What was she doing today? Was she fully healed and back to work? Did she think of him anywhere near as often as he thought of her?

His heart and every other part of him ached for her. He wouldn't blame her one bit if she refused to see him. That was a very real possibility he needed to prepare himself for. But as he rolled toward Vermont's Northeast Kingdom, he was filled with an unreasonable feeling of hope.

CHAPTER TWENTY-EIGHT

"We are most alive when we're in love." —John Updike

Over the last weekend in February, Izzy had shot two elaborate weddings—one in Burlington and the other in Stowe. She had her work cut out for her on the computer, editing and retouching. Other than some residual aches and pains, she was more or less fully recovered from her accident and back to work full-time. Many of her customers had put their needs on hold to wait for her, giving her a backlog that would take a year to work through.

She told herself it was a "good" problem to have.

In a small town like Butler, news traveled fast. It hadn't taken long for her to hear Cabot had moved to Vermont and was staying with Mia while he house hunted. She was so happy for him and for Mia, to have this time together after what they'd both been through. However, she was a little sad for herself that he hadn't even called to tell her he was in town.

At the very least, she'd thought they were friends anyway.

Now she had to dread running into him at the grocery store or the post office or a hundred other places they might cross paths and have to hide that her broken heart was the one part of her that hadn't healed since she last saw him.

He'd made himself clear the day they returned from

Bermuda when he sent her home in a hired car and hadn't reached out to her since.

She needed to move on, to start dating again, to stop wallowing in dreams that weren't going to happen now.

Time and again, she reminded herself how lucky she was to be alive, to have a thriving business and a wonderful family nearby to keep her from spending too much time alone. Life was good, and there was no way she was going to let any man, even one of the best men she'd ever known, ruin that for her.

Two days later, she had just returned from a photo shoot for the family store's catalog and was waiting for the kettle to heat when a knock sounded at her door.

Expecting to see her mom, aunt, grandfather or one of her siblings, Izzy opened the door and nearly died of shock to see Cabot standing there, hands in his coat pockets and an uncertain expression on his face. She noticed right away he'd lost weight and had dark circles under his eyes that hadn't been there the last time she saw him.

She wasn't sure what to say to him. "Um. Hi?"

"Hi."

Since it was still freezing, she stepped back from the door-way. "Do you want to come in?"

"I wasn't sure I'd still be welcome."

"You are."

"Thank you." He stepped inside and unzipped his coat, but left it on. "You're looking well."

"I feel good. A few twinges here and there, and lefty isn't as flexible as she used to be." She grimaced as she straightened her left arm. "But it's much better than it was when the cast first came off."

You're yammering, Izzy. Take a breath.

"That's great to hear."

The kettle picked that moment to let out a piercing whistle.

"Would you like some hot chocolate or tea?"

"Hot chocolate sounds good if it's no trouble."

She wanted to tell him to quit being so damned polite. "It's no trouble."

When they were seated at her kitchen table, with whipped-cream-topped mugs of hot chocolate, she had so many things she wanted to ask him, to tell him. But more than anything, she wanted to hear what *he* had to say, so she silently gave him the floor.

After a painfully long silence, he said, "I want to apologize to you for what happened in Bermuda—and afterward. You deserved much better than what you got from me, and I'm truly sorry."

"Apology accepted."

"Just like that?" he asked with the first hint of a smile.

"Just like that. Seeing Deb the way you did, with no warning, screwed you up. I get it."

"It did, but I shouldn't have let it screw us up, too. That was on me." He looked down at the table and then at her with his heart in his eyes. "I hope you know that screwing this up was the very last thing I ever would've wanted to do."

"I do know that."

"I've been talking to my former therapist, the one who saved me when everything first happened. She came out of retirement for me."

Izzy was so glad to hear he'd reached out to someone who'd been there for him before. "Is it helping?"

Nodding, he said, "A lot. I probably never should've stop seeing her. Maybe I wouldn't be such a mess if I'd stuck with therapy."

"You're *not* a mess, Cabot. You're the complete opposite of a mess. You're the only one who sees yourself that way."

"You're too kind. Much kinder than I deserve after the many ways I've screwed this up."

"You deserve all the kindness after what you've survived. Mostly from yourself."

He took a deep breath and let it out slowly, seeming to wrestle with his emotions. "I have no right whatsoever to ask you for a fourth chance, but I'm asking anyway. I can't promise that what happened in Bermuda won't happen again, but I'm working on trying to control how I react to the triggers."

Izzy took a minute to think about what she wanted to say and how she wanted to say it. "I completely understand that you can't necessarily control what triggers you. I would never blame you for being upset or angry or any of the things you must feel every day on the subject of your ex-wife and daughter. But what I can't handle is being shut out of it, ignored, summarily dismissed. That's not okay."

He winced. "No, it isn't. I've wished for a do-over of those two days every minute since I last saw you."

"That matters."

"I wanted to call you, to come here, to apologize, to try to fix what was broken. But I had work to do on myself before I could be ready to say those things and truly mean them."

"I'm proud of you for reaching out to the therapist who's helped you in the past."

"I want you to be proud of me and not disappointed by me."

"I'm not disappointed, Cabot. Well, I was, but more than anything, I've been sad about what happened with us."

"I hate that I did that to you."

"That's one small piece of the overall pie when it comes to you."

"What do you mean?"

"You were such a rock to me after the accident and so sweet with the way you insisted on being the one to care for me at home. You took such incredible care of me, and at some point, during those weeks we spent together, I fell in love with you. Wait. That's not entirely true."

"Ouch," he said with a laugh.

Smiling, she said, "I think maybe I fell for you the day we met, and I've been hoping ever since that something might come of it. We almost got there."

"Yes, we did, and I hear what you're saying about not shutting you out of whatever is going on. I got very used to keeping all that shit buried deep inside. After a while, I started to feel like even my siblings and closest friends had heard enough about my missing daughter, even though they'd say that wasn't the case. Still, after the first couple of years, it became a habit to suffer through it on my own. It might take me a while to break that habit, but I'll try my hardest to do better with that, even if my first inclination would be to protect you from it."

"I don't need you to protect me from you. If we're going to do this, we have to be all in. No secrets, no private struggles. I want all or nothing."

"I was afraid you might've moved on to find that with someone else."

"I've spent my entire adult life trying to find a fraction of what I feel for you." She put her hand on top of his. "There is no one else, Cabot."

He turned his hand up and linked their fingers. "That makes me feel like the luckiest man who ever lived."

"That said, I'm not sure I can respect myself if we just pick up where we left off like nothing ever happened."

"We'll do it however you want."

"I think we should try a date and see how that goes."

"A date sounds good to me." He covered their joined hands with his other one. "I want to tell you two other things before I go. First, I love you, too."

Her heart beat wildly. Every part of her wanted to hold him and kiss him and love him. "What's the second thing?"

"I want you to know that I've never felt more at home anywhere in this world than I did in this house with you."

To hell with restraint and self-respect. She stood and gestured for him to push his chair back from the table so she could sit on his lap and kiss him.

His arms encircled her as his mouth opened to her tongue. This kiss was unlike any of their previous ones. Whereas the others had been sweet and tender, this one was all fire and desire. He pulled her in so tight against him, she could barely breathe, but who needed to breathe when the man she loved was kissing her and holding her and telling her he loved her?

He withdrew from the kiss. "We're taking it slowly, remember?"

Izzy's eyes were closed, and with her lips—and every other important part of her—tingling, the last thing in the world she wanted was to take anything slowly. "If I welcome you back into my life, my home, my bed, do you promise I won't regret it?"

His lips skimmed over her neck. "I promise I'll give you everything I have and everything I am for the rest of my life."

What more could she ask from him than that? Izzy stood and held out her hand to him.

Seeming surprised, he reached for her hand.

She gave a gentle tug that brought him to his feet and pushed the coat off his shoulders, letting it drop to the floor.

His arms encircled her before he kissed her again.

"Wait! I forgot. I brought you a gift."

"Can you give it to me later?"

"Nope. Now." He kissed her nose. "Be right back." He fetched his car keys out of the coat on the floor and ran outside, returning a second later with a gift bag that he handed to her.

Izzy couldn't believe her eyes when she saw what was in the bag—a red sweater with a big, white snowflake on the front. "Oh, my God, Cabot! Where did you find this?"

"It took quite a lot of searching until I found an Etsy vendor who made it for me."

"I can't believe you got me my favorite sweater that my sister lost years ago. You must've done this weeks ago if someone made it for you."

"I did. I figured maybe I'd send it to you if you wouldn't see me."

She put the sweater and bag on the table and threw her arms around him. "I love it so much. Thank you for going to all that trouble for me."

"I'm so glad you like it."

"I *love* it." Izzy walked them toward her room. "I can't wait to wear it."

He glanced into the living room. "You never finished the stupid puzzle."

"It was no fun without you to talk about how stupid it is."

He brought his gaze back to her. "Are you sure this is what you want, sweet Isabella?"

"I've never been more certain of anything in my life." The

sweater had completely sealed the deal. He paid attention to the details, and she loved that—and so many other things —about him.

"I'm right there with you, sweetheart, and there's nowhere else I'd rather be than with you."

With that statement and the knowledge that he loved her, she was all but certain she'd still respect herself if she made love with him. Standing next to her bed, she unbuttoned his shirt and slid it down his arms while he lifted her sweater up and over her head. Then he brought her into his warm embrace.

His lips found her neck while his hands slid up her back to unhook her bra. When it fell to the floor, they finally stood chest to chest, skin to skin, which made her legs quiver. She'd wanted this so badly for such a long time that she almost couldn't believe it was actually going to happen as she released his belt and the button on his jeans while he pushed her leggings down over her backside.

She shivered.

"Are you cold?"

Laughing, she said, "Not even kinda."

"So these are good shivers, then?"

"The best kind."

"Mmm, the very best kind."

"Does anything still hurt?"

"All my injuries have healed, but I have aches in a few other important places."

"Let's see what we can do about that." His hands and lips were everywhere, setting her aflame with desire as he smoothed his palms over her back and around to cup her breasts. "Do we need protection? I didn't come here planning for this. Not that I'm complaining."

Izzy laughed. "We're good. I'm on long-term birth control. I haven't done this in quite a while, so I'm clean."

"Same."

He reached behind her to pull back the down comforter and flannel top sheet. "How about we get comfortable?"

She kicked off her leggings and went ahead of him into the

bed, reaching for him after he shed his boots and jeans, leaving only silk panties and boxers between them.

"God, this is every bit as amazing as I knew it would be," Cabot said on a long exhale. "It's such a relief to have you back in my arms after fearing I might never again get to hold you this way."

She looked up at him and smiled as she caressed his face. "It feels so good to be with you again. I missed you so much."

"I missed you, too. I started to call you so many times, but I made myself wait until I was ready while hoping I wasn't letting you get away."

"I'm still right here, and I want this. I want you and us and all the plans we made. I want it all."

"I do, too. Anything you want. I'm here for it."

"Including babies?"

"*Anything* you want."

For the first time in weeks, Izzy felt herself relax as she let go of the heartache that had plagued her every day since the last time she saw him.

After that, there was only frantic kisses and desperate need.

She breathed in the fresh, clean scent of his cologne and wallowed in the magic they created together.

"I want to kiss you everywhere," he whispered against her lips.

She turned onto her back and brought him with her, pushing at the waistband of his boxers. "We can do that next time."

"Is my baby feeling needy?"

"Extremely."

"We can't have that."

He moved quickly to give her what they both wanted more than anything, and when they were finally joined, she was moved to tears by the tsunami of emotions that accompanied this life-changing moment.

"Aw, love, don't cry," he said, kissing away her tears.

"Can't help it. It's overwhelming."

"In the best possible way, right?"

Looking up at him, she nodded as she framed his face with

her hands and drew him into another kiss. This was what she'd waited for, *he* was what she'd waited for during years of dating and relationships that never panned out. She'd been waiting for him.

"So good," he whispered. "I knew it would be."

"Mmm, so good. Don't stop."

He laughed. "I'll never stop loving you."

CONTENTMENT, CABOT THOUGHT, WAS SOMETHING HE'D SO rarely experienced. Not like this, anyway, with Izzy asleep in his arms after the best sex of his life, and his daughter just a few miles down the road, safe and happy in her life with Wade. The struggles were mostly behind him now, and the future stretched before him like a ribbon of endless possibility.

When he'd finally worked up the courage to come to Izzy's, he hadn't expected to end up in her bed. He'd prepared himself for every possibility, up to and including her refusal to even see him. He wouldn't have blamed her for that. Thankfully, his Izzy was the forgiving sort, although he understood he'd used up a lifetime's worth of forgiveness at the beginning of their relationship.

That was okay. He would devote himself to making her happy every day. Hopefully, that would earn him more forgiveness for any future missteps. Although he was confident that none of them would ever again be as big as the last one.

At some point in the last few weeks, he'd begun to let go of the debilitating rage. It had been replaced by much more productive emotions, especially love. Changing up his life, moving to Vermont to live near Mia—and Izzy, too, of course, even if he hadn't been sure of how that would work out when he'd made the move—had been good for him. It had given him something positive to focus on, which left little time for dwelling on a past he couldn't change.

He would always be bitter about what Deb had done to him, and to Mia, and would never "forgive" her for any of it. That was just too big of an ask. But he could let go of the rage as much as possible to focus on a very promising future with the people he loved the most in his daily life going forward.

Martha had assured him that the more positivity he welcomed into his life, the less room would be left for the negativity and the things that had hurt him for so long. Joy would replace sorrow. Love would overwhelm the hatred. After only a few days living with Mia in Vermont, he was already seeing that happen. He'd helped her with projects around her house, spent countless hours with her at Lowe's choosing fixtures, hardware and paint and had even helped to put together the office furniture she'd ordered from Ikea.

When they'd finished that job, she'd awarded him an "Official Dad" certificate that had touched his heart. They were years late in developing their own shorthand and inside jokes, but that was happening now, and he couldn't be happier about it. They had even chosen a regular table at the diner in town, and she was making him a maple syrup snob by showing him what he'd been missing with the store-bought "crap," as she called it.

He loved her madly. Every minute they spent together was a priceless gift to him, and he knew she felt the same way. They were like two little kids who'd been separated for years, finding their way back to each other one hour and one day at a time, gleeful for every part of their second chance.

And now he had Izzy. Against all odds, and despite himself, she loved him for who and what he was, and that, too, was a priceless gift.

Darkness had fallen during the hours they'd spent in her bed, making up for all the time they'd lost since the day they met. At least that's how it had seemed to him. He ought to call Mia to tell her he wouldn't be home for dinner, but he didn't want to disturb Izzy.

Another half hour passed in peaceful contemplation before she took a deep breath and stirred. "Jeez, what time is it?"

"Almost seven."

"I totally crashed."

"I wore you out."

"You did!"

"You feel okay?"

She stretched and then snuggled up to him again. "I feel *divine*. You?"

"Likewise. Can't recall a time I felt better than this… Well, except for the day I got Mia back. This is right up there with that."

"I'm honored."

"As you should be."

"Are you hungry? I'm starving."

"I could eat, but I should probably let Mia know I'm not going to make my curfew."

"Did she know where you were going?"

"Yes, I told her. She's been trying to get me to come here since the day after I arrived in town."

"It's good that you had some time with her before you came here."

"We've been having a lot of fun doing stuff around the house. It's all very… normal… and anything but at the same time."

"That's wonderful, Cabot."

"Everything is all of a sudden. I'm preconditioned to be afraid it won't last."

"I can't know what's coming, but I think it's probably safe to relax and enjoy yourself. You can't enjoy the present if you're worrying about the past or the future."

"I'm trying to put that very philosophy to work in my daily life. Enjoy the moment, the right now."

"It's all there is."

"My right now is pretty damned great," he said, kissing her.

"And it's only going to get better from here. We'll need to add on to give you an office and to make room for babies and all the stuff that goes with them."

"How soon can we get to work on having babies?"

"I'm due for a shot next month."

"How about you skip that?"

"You're sure?"

"A thousand percent positive." He twirled a length of her hair around his finger. "One of the things I've spent a lot of time talking to Martha about was the possibility of a second chance at fatherhood."

"What does she think?"

"She's all for it. She said I'll be so busy raising my kids and helping to raise my grandkids that I won't have any time to stew about past hurts."

"She's right about that. From what I've seen with my cousins and friends, kids are all-consuming."

"I wouldn't have it any other way. I want to be consumed by them. Working from home will allow me to be present in a way I never could've been for Mia. That's something I've also thought a lot about."

"I'm glad you have, because my work will take me away from home a lot, so knowing you're here will allow me to do what I need to."

He gave her a tight squeeze. "I've got you covered, sweetheart. We'll make it work. We'll make it all work."

"I can't wait for all of it," she said, smiling as brightly as he'd ever seen her do.

"Me, too."

EPILOGUE

*J*zzy had never known this kind of happiness was possible. Every day, she expected something to happen to mess up the best thing that'd ever happened to her. But if anything, it only got better all the time.

She awakened, as she did almost every day, to Cabot pressing sweet kisses down her back and taking a bite out of her bottom that fired her desire for him. That desire was endless, she had discovered, as he slid into her from behind while cupping her breasts.

He had her on the verge of orgasm in no time at all, which she'd learned was one of his many superpowers. They'd spent entire days in bed, as he said, making up for all the time he'd been a fool where she was concerned.

Cabot continued to speak weekly with Martha and shared his progress—and the occasional setback—with Izzy. They talked about everything. They shared dinners and outings with Mia and Wade, with Izzy's family and with her Vermont friends, who accepted Cabot into their group as if he'd always been one of them.

After he'd coaxed her somewhat effortlessly to a shattering climax, he brought her down easy, kissing her back, the side of her neck and stroking his thumbs gently over her nipples.

"Now, that's how you start a day," he said, as he did most days.

Izzy smiled as she thought about going back to sleep, blanketed in his love and the happiness he'd brought to her life. She'd skipped her latest birth control shot, and they were taking no precautions. Every time they made love, she wondered if they'd made a baby.

Eventually, he withdrew from her and shifted to his side, facing her so he could play with her hair, the way he did almost any time he was near her.

"What're you looking at?" she asked without opening her eyes.

"The woman I love with all my heart."

She kept her eyes closed as she smiled. "Do you ever wonder how it's possible to be this happy and still function in the real world?"

"Every day."

She drew in a deep breath and released it before opening her eyes to look at him. "I'm so glad you came back."

"Best thing I ever did. Thank you for giving me another chance."

"Best thing I ever did."

He leaned over to kiss her. "Now get your butt out of bed. We've got stuff to do."

"What stuff do we have to do?"

"Work, for one thing."

"It's Town Meeting Day. A holiday in Vermont."

"Alas, my company is headquartered in Massachusetts, so no holiday for us."

"Why do you have to be such a killjoy?"

Laughing, he gave her a gentle spank on the rump as he got out of bed. "Work now. Play later."

"Hey, Cabot?"

"Yes, dear?"

"Just in case you were wondering, I love you, too. With all my heart."

He came back to kiss her again. "I wasn't wondering, but thanks for letting me know."

OVER AT MEGAN'S DINER, LINCOLN ABBOTT SLID INTO THE BOOTH across from his father-in-law, Elmer Stillman. "Happy Town Meeting Day."

"Same to you, my friend. A harbinger of spring if ever there was one, even if we're getting another foot of snow tonight."

Later that day, the town's eligible voters would come together to vote on issues of pressing concern to their little corner of Vermont.

"Colton says the sap is starting to run on the mountain," Linc added. "We'll be boiling any time now."

"How's my newest great-grandbaby doing?"

"Young Christian is growing like a weed and prefers to be naked all the time, just like his feral father."

Elmer let out a hoot of laughter. "God help us all with that boy reproducing. They'll have their own little feral community up on that mountain."

"Indeed. He's a wonderful father, though. Completely besotted with his little boy."

"Sunday dinner is quite a scene these days with five babies in residence."

"And more on the way."

"What're you hearing?"

"Well, there's Hannah's second, of course, and a rumor that Lucas and Dani might have some news to share before long. I expect to hear something from Mia and Wade on the baby front any day now as well. Will and Cameron are talking about a second one."

"The baby boom is going to overtake us for a while."

"Seems like it."

"Is Charley still determined to skip the baby thing?"

"I think so. She says she wants to be the funnest aunt around."

"And she will be, for sure."

"I hear Izzy and Cabot are 'trying,' which is more information than I needed."

"Good for them," Elmer said, smiling. "It's wonderful they figured things out, but tell me, what's up with these kids trying for babies before they say their vows?"

"You know how this generation is, Elmer. They do things their way."

"Yes, they do. I think about what my parents would've had to say if Sarah and I told them we were having a baby before we got married."

"Different times, my friend."

"They sure were," Elmer said. "I kind of like it better this way."

"I have to admit I do as well. If they live together for a time before they say, 'I do,' at least they know what they're getting."

"That's a fact. Now how about our Vanessa, officially moving to New York to live with Troy?"

"I'm so happy for her and Troy, and Colton told me she's taking on the selling of the syrup to the gourmet stores in the city. He's needed someone to follow up on what he started there, and he's thrilled to have her on the job. You heard she got that big payout from her former company, right?"

"I did hear something about that from her mother, but Hannah was on the run, so I didn't get the details."

"Apparently, they made her a big offer in exchange for her agreeing not to sue, but they were unwilling to fire the guy who harassed her. She said no deal unless he got the ax. They gave him the ax, and she got her money."

"Good for her," Elmer said, glowing with pride. "I suppose Grayson had something to do with that."

"He did, and he's also settled Hannah and Mike's divorce, at long last."

"Thank goodness for that," Elmer said with a scowl.

Neither of them could think of Mike Coleman without a scowl.

"Do you think she'll marry Ray?" Linc asked.

"She always said she'd never get married again, but I think our friend Ray might be the exception to her rule."

"I tend to agree." Lincoln withdrew a piece of paper from his shirt pocket and unfolded it on the table. "Now, with Vanessa and Troy falling into my column—"

"How in the hell do you figure that?"

Lincoln looked up at him. "I brought Cameron here. He's her best friend, thus…"

Elmer rolled his eyes to high heaven. "That's a mighty big leap, my friend."

"I see it as a straight line from one to the other."

Elmer furrowed bushy white brows and glared at his son-in-law. "If you have to cheat to win, I hope you enjoy your hollow victory."

"Are you boys fighting again?" Megan asked when she came around with coffee refills.

Everyone was relieved to have her back to work and Butch back behind the grill, where he belonged. Her son, Carson, was in a portable playpen in the corner and was often passed around among family members when he wasn't napping.

Elmer glowered at Linc. "Your father-in-law is a huckster."

"You're just finding that out now?" Megan asked with amusement.

"Hey," Linc said. "You need to be on my side."

"He's my boss," Megan said with a grin.

"I see how it is," Linc said.

Elmer guffawed. "She knows which side her bread is buttered on."

"As much as I'd like to continue to discuss my bread and butter, I need to get back to work. Try not to stab each other with a fork while I leave you two unattended."

"We'll behave," Elmer said with a smile. After she'd walked away to wait on other customers, he leaned in and said to Linc, "But you *are* a huckster."

"And you're a poor loser."

"Loser, my ass. What about our young Max?" Elmer asked of the youngest of the ten Abbotts, who'd been the first to make them grandparents when his son, Caden, was born. "What've you got on tap for him?"

"Funny you should ask. I ran into Lexi Johnston's mother in the store the other day. Do you remember her?"

"Duh, yes, I remember the girl Max dated for most of high school. I'm not senile yet. What about her?"

"Mrs. Johnston told me Lexi is coming home for their class reunion this summer and is excited to see everyone. Especially Max."

"Did she say that? 'Especially Max'?"

"She did."

"Well, that is interesting. Where's she been all this time?"

"Her mom didn't say. I know she went to UMass, but I don't think she finished, and I lost track of her after she left town."

"I wonder how Max will feel about seeing her again," Elmer said. "As I recall, it ended because they were spending so much time apart while she was at UMass and he was at UVM, not because they didn't like each other anymore."

"You recall correctly."

"If something comes of this, it's got nothing to do with you, you hear me?" Elmer asked.

"I was the one who saw Mrs. Johnston."

"Oh, for Pete's sake. That's got nothin' to do with nothin'. I'm gonna quit this stupid game of ours if you're gonna keep cheating."

"How am I cheating?"

"You're taking credit for stuff that has nothing to do with you."

"But if the end result is all our kids happily settled, are there really any losers?"

"You think you're so clever," Elmer muttered.

"I am clever, or you never would've put me in charge of your parents' business."

"That can change at any time."

"Hahaha, whatever," Linc said. "I think that ship has sailed."

"I can always bring that ship back to port and boot your ass out of the C-suite."

"I might just surprise you and let you give me the boot one of these days."

Elmer had his coffee mug halfway to his mouth when he froze. "What're you saying?"

"That in the next year or two, I might be ready to turn the show over to the kids."

"Anyone in particular?"

"Probably Hunter, as he's the only one who'd want it. And he'd be excellent."

"He sure would." Elmer returned his mug to the table. "Wow, well... This is some big news. I thought we'd be carrying you out of that office in a pine box."

"Very funny—as if *you'd* be carrying *me* anywhere."

"Don't make old-age jokes. They're beneath you."

"No, they aren't," Linc said with a bark of laughter.

"Seriously, what's brought this on?"

"Since my siblings have come back in my life, I find I have other things I want to do besides work all the time. Molly wants to travel, and my brothers and sister are all approaching retirement, too. We talk about doing some traveling together."

"That'd be wonderful, Linc. You should do it, even if you're not retired yet. The kids can hold down the fort while you're away."

"We're talking about Paris and Rome next year."

"That sounds lovely. I couldn't be happier for you to have them back in your life."

"Thank you. I am, too, but you know, they can't replace the people who've been there for me all along. Those people..." He met Elmer's gaze across the table. "They're irreplaceable."

"Love you, too, son. Love you, too."

THANK YOU FOR READING CABOT AND IZZY'S STORY—AND Vanessa and Troy's story! I had no idea that was going to happen when I started *Here, There and Everywhere*, but I love that it happened! I had so much fun writing this book about two people who've been through life's fires and find each other thanks to a series of events that neither could've ever imagined. My heart went out to Cabot SO MANY TIMES during this book, and even when things got dicey for him and Izzy, I was still rooting for him. I hope you love him as much as I do. I like thinking of him living in Vermont and starting a whole new life there with Izzy and Mia. Join the *Here, There and Everywhere* Reader Group to discuss Izzy and Cabot's story (and Vanessa and Troy's) at *www.facebook.com/everywherereaders/*.

And then there was one more book to come (for now) in the Butler, VT series, featuring our lovely Max Abbott... You'll be glad to know that my German publisher has me contracted for that book, so it will be coming sooner rather than later. More to come on that soon!

A big thank you to the team that supports me behind the scenes: Julie Cupp, Lisa Cafferty, Jean Mello, Nikki Haley, Ashley Lopez and my wonderful cover designer, Kristina Brinton. Thank you to my editors, Linda Ingmanson and Joyce Lamb, who always make time for me when I need them.

Special thank you to my reader friend Gwen Neff, who recently agreed to be my editorial assistant to help with series continuity and other such things. She's been a huge help to me so far, and I appreciate her so much!

A huge thank-you to my primary beta readers Anne Woodall, Kara Conrad, Tracey Suppo and Gwen Neff as well as my Vermont series beta readers Marchia, Alice, Jennifer, Deb, Betty, Katy and Doreen.

It truly takes a village to produce books, and I couldn't be more fortunate to have all these amazing women helping me.

All my appreciation goes to you, my lovely readers, who have made all my dreams come true. I know you're sad to be seeing this series come to an end, but I promise I will revisit the Abbotts and Colemans again in the future. Thank you so much for your support of my books.

xoxo

Marie

ALSO BY MARIE FORCE

Contemporary Romances Available from Marie Force

The Green Mountain Series
Book 1: All You Need Is Love *(Will & Cameron)*
Book 2: I Want to Hold Your Hand *(Nolan & Hannah)*
Book 3: I Saw Her Standing There *(Colton & Lucy)*
Book 4: And I Love Her *(Hunter & Megan)*
Novella: You'll Be Mine *(Will & Cam's Wedding)*
Book 5: It's Only Love *(Gavin & Ella)*
Book 6: Ain't She Sweet *(Tyler & Charlotte)*

The Butler, Vermont Series
(Continuation of Green Mountain)
Book 1: Every Little Thing *(Grayson & Emma)*
Book 2: Can't Buy Me Love *(Mary & Patrick)*
Book 3: Here Comes the Sun *(Wade & Mia)*
Book 4: Till There Was You *(Lucas & Dani)*
Book 5: All My Loving *(Landon & Amanda)*
Book 6: Let It Be *(Lincoln & Molly)*
Book 7: Come Together *(Noah & Brianna)*
Book 8: Here, There & Everywhere *(Izzy & Cabot)*

The Gansett Island Series
Book 1: Maid for Love *(Mac & Maddie)*
Book 2: Fool for Love *(Joe & Janey)*
Book 3: Ready for Love *(Luke & Sydney)*
Book 4: Falling for Love *(Grant & Stephanie)*
Book 5: Hoping for Love *(Evan & Grace)*

Book 6: Season for Love (*Owen & Laura*)

Book 7: Longing for Love (*Blaine & Tiffany*)

Book 8: Waiting for Love (*Adam & Abby*)

Book 9: Time for Love (*David & Daisy*)

Book 10: Meant for Love (*Jenny & Alex*)

Book 10.5: Chance for Love, *A Gansett Island Novella (Jared & Lizzie)*

Book 11: Gansett After Dark (*Owen & Laura*)

Book 12: Kisses After Dark (*Shane & Katie*)

Book 13: Love After Dark (*Paul & Hope*)

Book 14: Celebration After Dark (*Big Mac & Linda*)

Book 15: Desire After Dark (*Slim & Erin*)

Book 16: Light After Dark (*Mallory & Quinn*)

Book 17: Victoria & Shannon (Episode 1)

Book 18: Kevin & Chelsea (Episode 2)

A Gansett Island Christmas Novella

Book 19: Mine After Dark (*Riley & Nikki*)

Book 20: Yours After Dark (*Finn & Chloe*)

Book 21: Trouble After Dark (*Deacon & Julia*)

Book 22: Rescue After Dark (*Mason & Jordan*)

Book 23: Blackout After Dark (*Full Cast*)

Book 24: Temptation After Dark (*Gigi & Cooper*)

Book 25: Resilience After Dark (*Jace & Cindy*)

The Quantum Series

Book 1: Virtuous (*Flynn & Natalie*)

Book 2: Valorous (*Flynn & Natalie*)

Book 3: Victorious (*Flynn & Natalie*)

Book 4: Rapturous (*Addie & Hayden*)

Book 5: Ravenous (*Jasper & Ellie*)

Book 6: Delirious (*Kristian & Aileen*)

Book 7: Outrageous (*Emmett & Leah*)

Book 8: Famous *(Marlowe & Sebastian)*

The Treading Water Series
Book 1: Treading Water
Book 2: Marking Time
Book 3: Starting Over
Book 4: Coming Home
Book 5: Finding Forever

The Wild Widows Series—a Fatal Series Spin-Off
Book 1: Someone Like You
Book 2: Someone to Hold

The Miami Nights Series
Book 1: How Much I Feel *(Carmen & Jason)*
Book 2: How Much I Care *(Maria & Austin)*
Book 3: How Much I Love *(Dee's story)*
Book 4: How Much I Want *(Nico & Sofia)*

Single Titles
Five Years Gone
One Year Home
Sex Machine
Sex God
Georgia on My Mind
True North
The Fall
The Wreck
Love at First Flight
Everyone Loves a Hero
Line of Scrimmage

Romantic Suspense Novels Available from Marie Force

The Fatal Series

One Night With You, *A Fatal Series Prequel Novella*

Book 1: Fatal Affair

Book 2: Fatal Justice

Book 3: Fatal Consequences

Book 3.5: Fatal Destiny, *the Wedding Novella*

Book 4: Fatal Flaw

Book 5: Fatal Deception

Book 6: Fatal Mistake

Book 7: Fatal Jeopardy

Book 8: Fatal Scandal

Book 9: Fatal Frenzy

Book 10: Fatal Identity

Book 11: Fatal Threat

Book 12: Fatal Chaos

Book 13: Fatal Invasion

Book 14: Fatal Reckoning

Book 15: Fatal Accusation

Book 16: Fatal Fraud

Sam and Nick's Story Continues....

Book 1: State of Affairs

Book 2: State of Grace

Book 3: State of the Union

Historical Romance Available from Marie Force

The Gilded Series

Book 1: Duchess by Deception

Book 2: Deceived by Desire

ABOUT THE AUTHOR

Marie Force is the *New York Times* best-selling author of contemporary romance, romantic suspense and erotic romance. Her series include Fatal, First Family, Gansett Island, Butler Vermont, Quantum, Treading Water, Miami Nights and Wild Widows.

Her books have sold more than 10 million copies worldwide, have been translated into more than a dozen languages and have appeared on the *New York Times* bestseller more than 30 times. She is also a *USA Today* and #1 *Wall Street Journal* bestseller, as well as a Spiegel bestseller in Germany.

Her goals in life are simple—to finish raising two happy, healthy, productive young adults, to keep writing books for as long as she possibly can and to never be on a flight that makes the news.

Join Marie's mailing list on her website at marieforce.com for news about new books and upcoming appearances in your area. Follow her on Facebook at www.Faccbook.com/Marie-ForceAuthor and on Instagram at *www.instagram.-com/marieforceauthor/*. Contact Marie at *marie@marieforce.com*.

CPSIA information can be obtained
at www.ICGtesting.com
Printed in the USA
LVHW020156040322
712446LV00003B/6

9 781952 793578